CONCEPCIÓN AND THE BABY BROKERS

AND OTHER STORIES OUT OF GUATEMALA

DEBORAH CLEARMAN

RAIN MOUNTAIN PRESS
NEW YORK CITY

First Printing March 2017

Concepción and the Baby Brokers
Copyright 2017 © by Deborah Clearman

ISBN 978-0-9968384-5-0

Rain Mountain Press
www.rainmountainpress.com
New York City

Printed in the USA

Cover art by Faustino Pablo Bautista
Author photograph by Douglas Chadwick

Some of these stories originally appeared in slightly different form in the following: "Baby Snatcher" in *The Adirondack Review;* "The Race" in *Beloit Fiction Journal;* "The Flor" in *Green Hills Literary Lantern;* "Turista" in *Hamilton Stone Review.*

This one is for Nora

CONCEPCIÓN AND THE BABY BROKERS

AND OTHER STORIES OUT OF GUATEMALA

TABLE OF CONTENTS

A Cup of Tears

BABY SNATCHER

Concepción's idea was to give the jaladores just one baby. Think about it. Is a woman not overblessed with two identical sons? One son is a gift, a joy, a polestar. The second? A redundancy.

The twins had been awful all morning. They both had colds. Globs of snot hung from their pug noses no matter how often she swiped at them. They screamed for the breast. They were too old and toothful to be such nursing fiends, and her nipples were chewed raw. She had finally gotten them to sleep, one swaddled to her back, the other in the playpen on the patio, and she was doing laundry. She bent over the pila, the ponderous outdoor sink that guarded the patio, and raked the twins' little pants and shirts over its cement washboard. She wrung ice water out of their clothes with vengeful vigor. She hated that this job sucked the juices out of her for another woman's children. She felt the sun blasting down on her from a cold sky, lighting up the gloss on her heavy black braid (of which she was so proud), burning into her secret places.

The three strangers arrived stealthily, unheralded by bus-horn blast or truck-gear grind. They must have walked the four dusty kilometers from town, peering into yards. They climbed up the short flight of steps to the pila. Concepción, tall for fifteen, straightened up to her full height, put on a haughty expression and stared at them with eyes like black stones. They were two women and a man, dressed as

Todosanteros. A long silence happened, as if all four people on the patio were the earth's first humans, awaiting the miracle of speech. The strangers took in the sleeping twin, the compound of low buildings that hemmed in the patio, doors opening onto the narrow veranda, the steep rise behind of outbuildings and milpas, the cornfields standing up against the weight of mountain walls.

"Buenas tardes," one of the women said at last. The words jumped out in a clip, instead of the long sing-song the country people gave them. "Is your husband or father-in-law at home?" Concepción could tell she was not really from Todos Santos. The indigo skirts, the hand-woven blouses, the man's red pants were a ruse. The disguise triggered her instinct to be on guard.

"They're not home," she said, not offering information or hospitality. Concepción had so little to give. She had neither of those valuable male assets (husband, father-in-law), but she would never reveal that. What she had was Doña Lala, the twins' mother, and Doña Pancha, their grandmother. In her thoughts she called them la Subcomandante and la Comandante, delegated by the men of the household to rule her.

"We have nice items to sell, baby things. Perhaps you'd like to see. You'll soon be needing more." The saleswoman eyed Concepción's stomach through the thick folds of her clothing. Concepción didn't tell the woman that there was nothing left inside her cavernous bulge except expired dreams. The doctors had taken out her womb along with her dead baby.

The man lowered the bundle he'd been carrying on his back, and they spread out their wares on the patio, next to the playpen: baby slings and plastic bottles and soft, squeezable toys. A suspicion had occurred to Concepción, an idea had burrowed its way into her skull like a bead of glass. She watched and waited for the real reason for the sellers' visit. It didn't take too long.

"So hard when the babies come one after another!" the saleswoman said in a voice like sweet melon. "And so expensive! Yet there are women in other countries who have no children at all—pobrecitas! Rich women who would give anything, *anything,* for a little chuchito like your sons." She looked from the playpen to the bundle on Concepcíon's back with a hungry smile. "So precious. What are their names? These wealthy gringas value girls even more. Perhaps your next one will be a nena. She could grow up in a big white house with a marble kitchen and green lawn, just like on TV. Little Guatemalans every day now grow up to be Americans and go to college and drive big cars with doble tracción. They don't have to live in the dirt like animals, the way we do."

The saleswoman scuffed with the toe of her platform sandal at the dirt of the patio, which, to be fair, had a patch of starved grass in one corner. It was the dry season. A film of grit crusted everything—the cement porch floor, the painted wood bench, the prickled hedge between the patio and the road below, the laundry flung out on the hedge to dry. No matter how many times a day Concepción hosed down the road, every passing vehicle fired up a cloud of dust.

An idea takes time to put together, like stringing the glass beads one by one into a grand chandelier, the kind that hung over the lovers in Concepción's favorite telenovela, *The Body of Desire.* She placed her hands, sun-brown and rain wrinkled, on her big belly, cradling the hypothetical baby, and set a date three months hence for the strangers to return. After they left, she made a slit in the thin mattress in her dark little room off the woodshed, and shoved the wad of dirty quetzales into it. For medical expenses, the woman had said. But they both knew it was a down payment. For of course, the jaladores weren't really sellers; they were buyers.

Concepción, when she was seven, had dropped her baby brother off the balcony of their house. It was an accident. She'd been told to watch him, her job since her sisters had married and moved out. Emptied of older siblings, the house was dull and lonely. Out front her mother washed dishes; her father worked the labyrinthine strings and pedals of his big wooden loom. Concepción could hear the steady thunka thunka of the loom even over the roar of rain pounding the tin roof—the roof that extended in front of the house over the loom and pila, in back over the hanging balcony—heard it even over the TV. Rodrigo, intent on baby things, was learning to pull himself up, first on Concepción's extended fingers, and then, when she got tired of the game, on the table legs. Her mother didn't like Rodrigo to sit on the dirt floor of the house, so Concepción, eager to prove sufficient to her task, plopped a straw mat by the table for him. Rodrigo had just mastered the art when the rain stopped and Concepción, looking through the open door to the balcony, saw a rainbow.

"Look, Rodrigo!" she squealed, hauled him up from the mat, and rocketed out onto the balcony.

The double bow arced the head of the valley, spanning the hoary tops of T'ui Bach and T'ui K'oy, the two sentinels casting off roiling clouds. Under the rainbow the silver-cliffed mountain walls fell into Todos Santos and broke against the ridge, crosswise to the valley, on the crest of which Concepción's house teetered. Below the balcony her father's cornfield dropped like a knife into the part of town called Los Pablos. On the flats of Los Pablos, stretched between the ribs of the mountain town, the red-tiled and thatched roofs of squat adobe houses swam in a sea of corn.

At the balcony railing Concepción stopped short, but somehow Rodrigo did not. In an inexplicable move—a wiggle on his part? a failure of strength on hers?—he shot from her arms, over the rail and out into space. Concepción, horrified, felt herself freeze into something rigid and useless. The baby canonballed out of view, into the green mouths of cornstalks, five meters below. Rodrigo's wail reactivated Concepción, and she screamed.

The baby did not die. In fact, the curandera assured them, after a thorough poking of bones and organs, that he was fine. She did the necessary rituals to ward off his fright. But seven years later, when the thatched roofs of Los Pablos were all gone and new houses had sprouted all over town—many-storied, gabled and arcaded, tiled in dollars from the generous North—when Concepción fell in love with the leader of the Los Pablos gang, Rodrigo had never learned to talk. The Cuban doctor said it was not her fault, that the fall was not the cause, but what did the Cuban doctor know?

<<<< — >>>>

While Concepción went back to her chores, Prudencia—she of the platform sandal—led the other two jaladores down the steps from the patio. No, not jaladores. Prudencia didn't like that rural slang word, smacking as it did of hauling and yanking and dragging. She considered herself a professional, not an ox. She was a baby contractor.

Prudencia had worked hard to get to where she was, on the opposite side of the country from where she'd started out, just as worthless as that girl who had just sold her baby. Prudencia had left eastern Guatemala, where the rainy season never arrives and thirsty eucalyptus trees suck what moisture there is out of the earth and famine comes as

15

regularly as new babies. She'd run away from Chiquimula, the so-called Pearl of the East, and the father who had done unspeakable things, to the capital, where she was taken in and put to work in Doña Merced's household. Doña Merced was a lawyer, an adoption lawyer.

She learned how to clean indoor bathrooms—porcelain and stainless steel, fíjese! Later on how to cook fine dishes. Her new employer recognized her skills, and after they got to know each other, elevated Prudencia from housekeeper to personal assistant. Her rural roots and knowledge of Mayan languages made her perfect as a scout to search the countryside for desperate girls and unhappy families for whom the foreign appetite for black-haired, saucer-eyed babies would be a salvation.

"You're so clever," Prudencia's companion Marta said when they were out of Concepción's earshot. "You talk so beautifully. So convincing."

"I'm not happy," Prudencia replied. "There's something about that girl I don't trust. Something's not right. The house buildings are freshly painted, the flowerbeds well tended. Even a satellite antenna! That household smells of money and lies."

They heard distant honking.

"The bus," Jorge, the man carrying the bundle, said. Prudencia had hired him in Huehue to accompany them. He had claimed knowledge of the local language and customs, claims that had turned out to be exaggerated when they arrived in Todos Santos. His Mam was imperfect and accented by a different region.

"Good," Prudencia said. "Let's get out of here." Having made their deal, they needed to go quickly, before word of their presence could spread to people hostile to baby contractors. Villagers in other regions had been known to

16

attack jaladores, beat them and shave their heads as punishment for their efforts on behalf of poor mothers who didn't want their babies.

The three jaladores flattened themselves against the embankment and waited for the bus, the *Flor de Cuchumatán*, to grumble to a stop. Jorge's bundle, disguised by its cloth cover so that no one could guess their business, went on top. The three blended into the crowd on the bus and wedged themselves into seats. They gripped the metal seatbacks in front of them. The bus bounded over potholes, spewing dust. The dust settled on the town they left behind them as they climbed up out of the valley.

⟪⟪⟪ — ⟫⟫⟫

Two months later, on a Sunday, it was the twins' first birthday, and Doña Lala, their mother, had decided a party was in order. Although it was Concepción who had suckled them these last six months, she knew that Doña Lala would take full credit for their fat bellies and dimpled limbs bulging with health.

Doña Pancha disapproved of the celebration, and said so that morning to her daughter-in-law, in the kitchen, where Concepción, bent over the wood stove, was patting out tortillas. "You'll only tempt God to come after them," Doña Pancha said. Her face was severe and lined with years of suffering; her nose divided it like an escarpment. "When I was a girl we never celebrated birthdays, only funerals. Then at least you know your troubles are over."

Doña Lala only laughed and rolled her eyes. "Nawita!" she said, addressing the matriarch of the house as Little Mother, another thing that annoyed the older woman. Educated and confident, a teacher at the local elementary school, Eulalia shrugged off respect for her elders like a threadbare shawl, lightly and with ease. "Don't be so superstitious! My boys will grow up to be doctors and lawyers and poke fun at those old ideas."

Lala plucked up the chilies and miltomates toasting on the stove's hot iron surface and tossed them into the electric blender with a practiced hand. Doña Pancha measured flour and scowled more deeply. "Watch that the onions don't scorch," she said.

In this dispute, Concepción silently agreed with Doña Pancha. Her Amor would never have a birthday. Better to celebrate death, a fact so much more certain than life. She slapped harder at the tortilla in her hands.

"Concepción! What are you doing?" Lala, as if noticing her taciturn servant for the first time, changed to her subcomandante voice, machete-edged. "The fire's dying. Fetch more wood."

Concepción wiped the dough from her hands on her apron and left the kitchen. She passed the open door to Lala's room, where the twins' father Octavio lounged on the big bed with his two little sons, watching TV, and continued out to the woodshed. Returning to the kitchen with her load of splintered logs, she counted the days. Escape played constantly in her mind like a telenovela, filling her with desire and apprehension. She saw herself running through lush grass toward a many-turreted mansion. She fed a log to the fire. Smoke billowed from the stove and stung her eyes. Doña Lala exploded in a coughing fit. "Híjole!"

"Stand back, girl," Doña Pancha said, and whipped the fan back and forth until the fire caught and drew the smoke. Doña Lala recovered and ran the blender with a grating roar. The scent of burnt squash seeds and cinnamon rose from the stove like bitter memory.

18

The day proceeded as Doña Lala had ordered it, with the guests arriving under a cloudless sky. The guests—all uncles and aunts and cousins, grandparents and great grandparents of the twins—came to honor the new princelings and stuff themselves with the turkey that had been slaughtered that morning at dawn and now swam in golden sauce. Concepción passed plates and bowls and cups of sweetened maize drink, while the twins bounced from knee to knee, and ate her pepián in a corner by herself. Only Octavio's younger brother Wilfredo paid any attention to her. He caught her at the pila where she was stacking piles of plates to wash.

"Poor Cenicienta," he said and put his hand on her waist. "How about a kiss for your handsome prince?"

She pushed his hand away.

<<< — >>>

It was seven years after she dropped her brother, and Jerónimo was back again. That's what the rumors whispered: older, handsomer, and more dangerous from his years in steely Michigan. Always Concepción had kept track of his comings and goings, for she had an instinct that could sense his presence. It was her crime that gave her radar: she was the baby-dropper, self-judged and self-convicted by the weight of her neighbors' pity and fear.

Rodrigo was her punishment. He'd become a strange and secretive child, her special charge, placed on her by her child-worn mother. Concepción and Rodrigo, the last two of six, were on their own, linked by Concepción's crime, and by the fact that only she could understand and interpret the speechless boy. She wore Rodrigo tied by the baby sling to her back until he was nearly as big as she was, because only the tight binding could ease his anxious tremblings, his angry fits.

Jerónimo, ten years older, was already a man and she a grade-school girl when she had first noticed him at the corner below her house, where the dusty track looped down toward Los Pablos. He was with a group of boys drinking beers and breaking bottles against a large grey rock in the shape of an ear that jutted out from the mountainside. His muscled arms flexed with each toss. His thick hair hung to his waist in a luxuriant ponytail. She knew instantly that he was their leader, and that he was bad. She clutched Rodrigo's little hand in her fist and hurried past the gang, keeping her eyes down on the tips of her plastic sandals, to their jeers of "Mudo! Mudo!" Their scorn for her damaged brother burned. Jerónimo's appraisal scorched her.

Then he disappeared to El Norte—to Michigan, the rumors said. Distance didn't lessen his pull. She felt drawn by his criminal magnetism, with its hint of her destruction. If she could have, she would have gone after him, to Michigan. Each time he came back, expelled from the beast of the North, deported or sloughed off, he brought the boys of Los Pablos new knowledge—a secret language of whistles, marijuana smoking, fighting with knives. The boys stayed young while Jerónimo grew older. Concepción grew older as well, until at fourteen she was a quiet beauty at the end of her first year of middle school, tall for her age, twisting magenta ribbons into her long, black braids.

It was October thirty-first. Fiesta frenzy ignited the town of All Saints. Men, boys, and even women were drinking and brawling in the streets. All over town boys and girls walked in furtive pairs, lust hanging over them like a vapor. Tonight there would be a dance in the salón, but Concepción did not intend to wait until nightfall. She knew what to do. She tucked her brilliant blouse into the sash of her dark skirt and cinched it tight.

A bright morning sun shone, boasting that the rains were over. Concepción slipped down the road to the rock in the shape of an ear, where, sure enough, Jerónimo was holding forth to his gang of boys, passing a bottle of aguardiente. Beer was not potent enough for this day. She stopped in front of the group and looked Jerónimo in the eye. "Hombre," she said, "I've lost my brother, the mute, and I need your help." She slid her eyes aside and down, in practiced modesty.

The boys, several from Concepción's class at school, whooped and cawed. "We'll help, mamacita! Whatever you need, Concha."

Concepción tossed her head, flashed her magenta entwined braids. "Not you," she said. "I need a man."

Jerónimo smiled and stretched toward her in a lazy slouch. "OK, chicos. I'll be back."

She led him up the road, past her house, past the humps of buried pyramids, staked by two crosses. Next to them smoke curled up from a ceremonial fire. From the top of a pine tree the clarinero called like a lover. She led Jerónimo on, higher, drawing him after her, casting an occasional glance over her shoulder. They left the road and followed a path through cornfields and into forest. In all this time Concepción hadn't said anything, and if Jerónimo was waiting for explanation, he didn't mention it. She felt him captive.

They crossed a small stream rushing over flat rocks toward a waterfall where, in their season, blackberries ripened. They climbed a steep slope, and before Jerónimo could wonder if she was taking him all the way to the altiplano, she turned off the trail and dove into a copse of black pine. Thick duff on the forest floor deadened the chatter of birds. She stopped, breathed deep, sucking in the silence, quivering like a wire, and said, "I lied to you."

She turned around to face him, look again into his eyes, willing him to be hers. "My brother is with my older sister in Huehue, seeing doctors. I need to talk to you about the mara. I want to join."

"Mara?" Jerónimo said. Gang? "We're just a group of friends." His full lips spread in a dangerous smile. A stud glimmered in one ear, a red bandana knotted around his thick neck, his shirt opened on a sweat-damp tank top. She could see the heat rise off him.

"Is it true, what they say about the maras in the United States, that before a girl can join, the whole gang initiates her?" Concepción picked up his right hand and placed it against her blouse, cupping, through the thick cotton huipil woven with hieroglyphs of sun and rain and corn, her breast. "I only want to be initiated by you."

His other hand came up and tugged the huipil out from her sash. She raised her arms like a child and he lifted the blouse up over her head.

<<<< — >>>>

On the morning of the day appointed for the return of the jaladores, Concepción, jittery with anticipation, took extra care with the twins. She kissed them and tickled them the way they liked, to make them laugh. She dressed them in new clothes: matching blue pants, lighter blue sweaters, like matched pearls. Would even their mother know the difference? She knew the difference. She picked up Cándido and gave him a squeeze. "You're my big boy!"

Felícito tugged at her skirt and raised his arms.

"You too!" She tumbled them both onto their parents' big double bed, with the TV on. Her goal was to keep them perfect until the jaladores came. Anxiety curled in

Concepción's belly like a snake. The house was empty. The twins' parents both worked respectable jobs as schoolteachers. Doña Pancha was at her shop in the market, it being Wednesday, market day. Don Chepe, the head of the household, was safely in his office in the municipal palace, at least for now. If the baby contractors came on time, she would be free. Her bag was packed, ready for escape, ready for a new life with thick carpets and silk negligees, so wonderful it could only be imagined in scenes from a telenovela.

Unable to sit still, she stood in the open doorway room and kept one eye on the peaceful twins, the other scanning the empty sky above the mountain walls. Then, above the sound of the TV, she heard barking dogs and an approaching vehicle.

Now was the moment of decision. Which twin to leave behind for Doña Lala? She hadn't thought about this part of her plan. The magnitude of the choice almost paralyzed her. She picked up Felícito. "Here, my sweet boy," she said. "I have a treat for you."

She plopped him in the playpen, handed him a sippy cup of cherry drink and a cookie. Then she took Cándido in her arms and went out to the edge of the patio to look down the road. A large red pickup arrived in a cloud of dust.

<<< — >>>

The dance was well underway. In the salón a wall of sound blasted from speakers stacked three meters high and six wide at the far end of the crowded room. The basketball hoops had been pushed aside and the cement floor seemed to pulse. Red pants stamped, indigo skirts swirled, heads bobbed, and writhing arms winked in strobe light. Concepción stood at the sidelines in darkness, waiting for her black prince. Before they had parted at the ruins earlier in the day, Jerónimo had promised to dance with her. She felt she must be glowing, giving off blue light like a TV screen. She watched the entry to the salón, where people funneled in through narrow doors past three lurking policía.

Jerónimo reeled through the door, clutching his younger brother Oscar, also back in Todos Santos. It looked like they'd been celebrating and were bien bolos. Jerónimo stopped in the entry and flicked his gaze over the hall, probing for her, Concepción hoped, but not seeing her yet in the shadows. Oscar took a slug from a bottle of Quetzalteca he carried, then held the bottle out to Jerónimo.

"I'll take that. Prohibited inside the salón." An official voice cut through the rockero din. The three policía circled the two brothers. One reached for the bottle. Jerónimo's hand met the bottle first, grasped it, twisted it upward in a defiant gesture just grazing the chin of the policía, and then, in a brazen finale, balanced the bottle on top of his own head. He pirouetted toward Oscar.

"I'm so scared," he piped in a ludicrous falsetto. "I'm so scared of the mean policeman. Hermanito, save me!"

Guffaws erupted from the audience of watching youths, sounding over the Babasónicos' beat. Concepción stiffened. Ever since Jerónimo's return the police had been under pressure from the comité de seguridad, the town elders, to arrest him, get him out. Concepción liked the added luster that the comité's censure gave him. She knew his crimes in town were not so desperate as the comité would have its citizens believe: small larcenies, like the charity fund left on a teacher's desk at the Instituto Urbana Mixta, fist fights with the rival Tiburones gang, occasional blood wounds from a broken bottle or knife slash. But to the elders of Todos Santos his crime was the upending of social order. Jerónimo relished the opportunity to flout their authority.

The cop hit Jerónimo with a hard fist to the gut. Concepción gasped. Oscar swung back and laid the policía out like a petate. The second policía yanked out his stick to flail at Oscar. Jerónimo grabbed the stick and brandished it in the music-dense air, playing to the crowd of revelers. "Coca, too hot in here. Let's take it outside!" he shouted and led Oscar in a charge for the door.

One hand rising in an unseen gesture, Concepión watched them go, watched the police chase after them, like dogs after the fox, watched the crowds at the entry follow out into the night. Caught in the excitement of pressing bodies, Concepión was carried like flotsam out of the hall, into the street, where she raced uphill. She felt her excitement turning to fear, pounding in her ears. She heard feet pounding on the pavement, heard shouts all around and up ahead, heard the firing of a shot, and then another.

She kept running until she reached a wall of people. She shoved her way through the crowd, not hearing shouts, questions, explanations, expletives, exhortations, until she reached the inner circle, found its weak point, and burst through it to the body of Jerónimo, face down on the paving stones. Illuminated in the streetlight, the back of his shirt was bright with blood.

She screamed and collapsed to her knees beside him, not caring if she gave her love away. She knelt beside his head that was turned toward her, his ear pressed against the pavement as if listening for sounds from the earth. She touched his cheek with a tentative hand, wanting to brush aside his knotted hair, to look into his hooded eyes. Blood spread from his nose and open mouth, smashed against the stones.

"He's dead! My brother's dead!" a woman's voice wailed nearby. A hand grabbed Concepción and tossed her aside. More shouts rose in a chorus around her.

"The policía did it! After those bastards!"

"Get the police!"

"Fuck those policía! Kill the sons of whores!"

Concepción, whose life was over at fourteen, slunk home.

Two months later, she discovered that Jerónimo had left her a gift. She named her gift Amor and kept him secret. She kept her secret as long as possible. Her mother was the first to notice, late in the seventh month, the bulge growing under her thick huipil and tightly cinched skirt.

"Ay, hija!" her mother wailed, "Who has done this to you?"

But Concepción wouldn't say. Even when her father struck her a blow across the face that knocked her to the floor, she wouldn't say.

"You can kill me," she said. "I don't care."

Her parents didn't kill her, but they closed their faces and their hearts to her. They kept her out of school, away from the eyes of the world. With Rodrigo gone, in Huehue in the care of her older sister while the doctors tried to make him speak, Concepción was a prisoner in her house. She had no one left to care for, to bundle and feed and protect. She was alone except for Amor. She talked to her unborn baby boy and sang him sad songs while she worked.

Late in the eighth month, despite her parents' efforts, the world's prying eyes saw Amor. Up and down the streets and pathways of town the gossip traveled at the speed of sound. And the leaderless boys who still lolled at the rock shaped like an ear, who had seen her lead Jerónimo away on the morning of his death, dropped his name into the rumor stew.

Her father heard the name and, yanking up her huipil, lashed his leather belt against her back, demanding to know if it was true. "Just kill me," she repeated, her naked and bleeding back to her father.

"Sin vergüenza," he rasped. "I'll sell you instead."

26

Her practical mother defended her by reasoning that no one would buy the services of such an encumbered girl. Her mother took pity and called the midwife when her time came, and wiped her face with a damp cloth when she lay screaming each time pain clamped down on her Amor. The midwife said, "Not long now."

The midwife was wrong. Concepción labored and screamed and labored and screamed until the midwife said, "You must get her to Huehue."

Her father took pity and called for a truck to carry her at bone-shattering speed over the fifty-two rocky kilometers to the hospital, where white-coated nurses delivered her into blackness.

When she woke up, Amor was gone. The doctor told her he had saved her life. Her womb could not be saved. "Where's my baby?" she demanded. "I want my son."

The doctor's voice was like a machine. "Your baby was a girl. She's with the angels."

Concepción wailed and thrashed against the blankets and had to be sedated. When she could leave the hospital, her parents took her home. Their pity and their savings exhausted by the medical ordeal, they sold her to Doña Pancha and Doña Lala, to be a wet nurse to the twins.

««« — »»»

"Stop here," Prudencia told the driver, Doña Merced's nephew. This time there would be no public bus. "Wait for us," she told the nephew. She and Marta got out. This time there was no pretense of the local costume. Prudencia wore her city clothes, a straight black skirt and pink sweater, poised and professional, the kind of outfit Doña Merced herself would wear.

27

The girl met them at the top of the stairs, with a toddler in her arms and a satchel by her side. Prudencia stared at her, trying to put it together. "Where's the baby?" she asked.

"Fix on this, señora! I lost the baby." There followed Concepción's long-prepared tale of medical emergency and woe.

Concepción talked fast and watched the jaladora's face. The woman didn't believe her, she could tell. Her plan was withering in the woman's glare. What would she do if the jaladora wouldn't take the twin and give her the money, money she needed for her journey, for the coyotes to take her North?

"So you see, señora, I lost the baby but you can take my little Cándido instead. He's all I have to give you. Please." She begged, because even the woman could see that her roundness had burst. In the three months since the jaladores' last visit, the bulge Amor had made had collapsed beneath her tender breasts and cinched sash.

The woman's lips drew a tight line. "We want babies, daughter. Newborns. That's what the North Americans want to adopt. Not little boys who run around making messes and speaking their mother tongue."

Concepción felt the panic of her collapsed dream. Escape from Doña Lala, from her hopeless life, from her lost Amor, vanished. It was punishment. Happiness was never intended for Concepción, the girl who had dropped her brother.

From the bedroom came Felícito's cry. He would not be left behind. She shoved Cándido into the second woman's arms, the one who stood like a duck beside the baby-buyer, and ran.

"Hija!" the duck quacked.

Concepción returned with the other twin. "You see, he wants to go too, to El Norte with his brother. The American can have both boys. I want them to be together, to be happy." The wish for both boys' happiness swelled in her with

28

sudden force. "I'm going to America too. My husband wants me to come. He's in America. There's nothing for me here." Concepción spoke faster and faster. "You must believe me. My mother-in-law beats me," she lied. "I can show you scars." With her free hand she tore her huipil out from her skirt, but before she could lift it past the wriggling twin, the baby-buyer grabbed her arm.

Prudencia had done a fast calculation. The risk had doubled. More so. If she had been closer to the capital, she might have turned her back on the lying girl and her goods, and the money she had already spent on the deal. But the boys were healthy and adorable; she knew the foreign hunger for progeny would gobble them up. Would the family come after them? Even if they traveled the seven hours of terrible road, they would never find these two in a city teeming with orphans. They would swallow their sorrow as country people always did, and have more babies. Her decision made, she acted.

"Stop," she said. "Marta, take the child. And you," she poked out her lower jaw at Concepción, "will come with us to sign the papers."

She turned away. Concepción picked up her satchel and followed them down the stairs to the waiting truck.

JALADORA

Don't drown in a cup of tears. That's what my mama told me. My mama cried an oceanful, wouldn't you know, because of what my papi did to me. But I never cried.

I'll never bring a child into this world. Not after what I've seen of family life. When you're a baby, they kiss and fondle and spoil you. Then when you grow and sprout little brown breasts the size of lemons, they kiss and fondle you again. But this time you don't giggle and squeal. This time you carry a knife and threaten to use it. That's what I did to my papi.

I'm capable of anything. But not in a blind fury. Oh no. I calculate and assess the situation. I go from A to B to C. I take my time. I have to. Those foolish girls who get themselves knocked up by their boyfriends, and their fathers are going to kill them, they're all drowning in their own tears. I rescue them. I save their wretched lives and the innocent lives of their unwanted babies. I rescue their babies and send them far away from our poor country that breeds babies like fruit flies. I do this work at my own peril. The campesinos, who call me jaladora—"hauler," as if I'm yanking their babies out of unwilling hands—would rip my hair out if they ever caught up with me.

But they won't catch me. I'll be gone, the contract sealed, the brown baby safe in the arms of his new white mother, the brown mother back in her dirt kitchen with the father who loves and beats her. I know all these things. I've seen it all. Don't trust those men who tell you they love you. I told *this to my own mother, but what good did it do? My mother came to me when she needed help. Figure that one!*

Now it's the surgeon's knife she needs, not mine. There there, Mamita, don't cry, I'll take care of you.

<<<< — >>>>

This was the promise Prudencia carried this day in the cab of the red pickup. A day that had already been long and aggravating. They'd left the city before dawn for the seven-hour drive west, into high godforsaken country fit only for coyotes and narcotraficantes. Then the supposed birth mother had pulled a double-cross, substituting twin toddlers for the newborn that she'd contracted to deliver. Toddlers! Who'd be practically preschoolers by the time the paperwork could be done. Prudencia was no fool, knew better than to believe the caldo of lies the contracted mother fed her, knew better than to accept thirteen-month-olds in a two-for-one deal. But Prudencia was up against the knife. The surgeon needed money. So here she was, with her simpleton assistant Marta, each with a lapful of toddler and their feet on the bag of toddler supplies the girl had packed, crammed into the truck so tight that the driver, Doña Merced's maricón nephew Rosario, could barely wrestle the gearshift from first to second. The twin boys bobbed in unison like matching dolls. The truck climbed, bouncing off rocks and ditches, sucking in dust and spewing it onto Prudencia's pink sweater, her sweater that she favored because Doña Merced had given it to her and it was calidad. Now it was clotted with the toddlers' snot and the yellow grit of Todos Santos, the native town that neither twin would ever see again. They would be better off without it, Prudencia thought.

In the back of the pickup, whipped by the icy wind from the altiplano, the supposed mother of the twins clutched her small satchel of dreams. Unlike the babies, who were mere flotsam in the day's events, this girl, hunched and holding her long black braid in her teeth, had plotted—Prudencia saw it now. This girl aimed to escape Guatemala, the fatherland that had battered her ancestors since the first one was squeezed out of maize. But she couldn't follow the coddled path Prudencia would provide for the babies, cradled in the arms of an adoptive mother. Poor thing. She would slink out like a thief in the night.

Prudencia knew all this. From her command in the cab of the truck she controlled destinies. Across the frigid altiplano and down the neck-snapping switchbacks into Huehuetenango, she thought about it all, while the temperature rose. Suddenly she had an extra child. Doña Merced was expecting only one. An extra child could bring her extra money, money that she needed for her mother's operation. By the time they reached the main square of the department capital, she had her strategy—A, B, C.

"Here," she said, and pointed with her lips and chin at a parking spot on the square. Birds screeched from the tops of tall shade trees. "Wait," she told Rosario.

She left the driver guarding the red truck beside a bougainvillea-strangled gazebo and herded Marta and the girl, carting the twins, into a notary's office. Prudencia calculated that illegal acts done in plain view were the least likely to draw attention. She placed Marta and the girl, each with a twin clamped securely in arms, in plastic chairs against the cracked wall of the airless office, next to a glass case that displayed a dusty assortment of items for sale: typewriters, old radios, clocks and watches, fountain pens, an incomplete set of silver-plated flatware. There was not a peep out of either twin, just saucer eyes surveying the enormous wooden desk in the center of the room, ark-like, piled with yellowed tomes, behind which a small and ancient man drowsed in the noon heat.

"Don Aparicio," Prudencia said.

He blinked awake. "Doña Prudencia," he answered, rising slowly to alertness. "You've come again."

"I'm always here to help the children."

He looked past her at the twins and cocked black eyebrows that bristled. "Sit down. Please."

Prudencia sat herself in front of the desk and tucked a stray hair into her low bun. She would have preferred a stylish bob, like Doña Merced's, but her operations in the countryside necessitated disguise. She waited while the notary rummaged in file drawers and drew out a sheaf of papers. He cleared a space on the desk and arranged a ballpoint pen stand and a tall-necked brass seal like chessmen, then sank back into his chair, lifted prayerful hands to his lips, and stared again at the waiting women, the two babies, his eyes like bullets.

Prudencia had no fears about Marta, who'd been through this baby contracting business many times. She certainly had no fears about the supposed mother, a girl whose anxieties were wrapped in silence. The only thing she had to fear was what the Holy Virgin thought—and the Virgin understood, of that Prudencia was sure. The Holy Virgin had had a mother, too. Prudencia filled out page after page of official forms, filling and signing, filling and signing, her penmanship tight as a noose. Finally she turned to the girl.

"Now, mija," she said in a voice like a bank vault, "it is your turn to sign. For your little boys' future happiness."

The summoned mother stood up and placed her twin next to the other one in Marta's lap. Marta crooned quietly,

34

"Preciosos, tan fuertes, tan bien educados," while the girl sat next to Prudencia and took the pen in her trembling hand. Prudencia never worried about the notary's fierce stare: what mother's hand wouldn't shake, signing her sons away?

"Here, mija," she said, with her finger stabbing the page. "Here. Here. Here. Here." Each time the miserable girl signed, the notary's heavy seal slammed down after her pen with a crash. Then they were done. Prudencia gathered the papers into her case, a hard leather case that gleamed with efficiency, and swept toward the door, creating a movement of inexorable leaving that lifted everyone from their chairs. The girl took a twin, Marta rose with the other, and as Prudencia brushed past her whispered in her ear, "Seño. The DNA test?"

The question caught Prudencia like a snag in the current. With the twin in one arm, Marta attempted to reach into her bag. Prudencia knew what was in there—the cotton swabs, the surgical gloves—and guided her course around the snag.

"Forget that for now, compañera," she said. And she was out the door, crossing the street to the park where a half dozen men, among them Doña Merced's nephew, were luxuriating in a shoeshine under the bougainvillea. Prudencia ushered her group to the red pickup, and Marta slid inside with her twin. Prudencia took the second twin from the supposed mother and handed him to Marta.

She looked at the girl, standing before her, quivering. She wasn't a bad looking girl, tall, with a smooth face that showed no sin, no hint that she'd just sold two babies, nothing in the depths of her black eyes except despair. How old was she— fourteen? Fifteen? Prudencia took a thick envelope out of her case and gave it to the girl. Simple.

But not so simple. The girl didn't know what was in the envelope, only that the envelope would solve her problems, answer her prayers, fulfill her dreams. What the girl didn't know was the amount. She would never know if some of the money had come out of the envelope to go to the doctors who would save Mamita's life. But the Holy Virgin would know. So Prudencia didn't steal, not from Doña Merced, not even from this lying girl. Prudencia was honorable.

"Remember," she told the girl, "you have no further claim on your children."

The girl clutched the envelope like a prayer book. "You'll have no problems from me," she said.

Prudencia got into the truck and slammed the door shut. They pulled away, leaving an after-image of the girl, standing alone, stashing the envelope inside her blouse.

««« — »»»

The red truck picked up speed on the road out of Huehuetenango, where the Interamericana spooled uphill through pine-shrouded slopes, past empty fields waiting in exhaustion for the rainy season. Now the twins had had enough of travel. They squalled in a chorus of infant misery, refusing bottles and sippy cups, bits of tortillas, even sweet snacks. As if they'd consulted with each other and made a pact to avenge themselves on their abductors. Or, as Prudencia preferred to think of it, their rescuers. Rescued from a precarious ledge in cold country, where the best anyone could hope for was relentless physical toil, sporadic bouts of drinking and violence, and sudden death. Not a life Prudencia would wish on a child.

Marta and Prudencia rocked and patted, swaddled and hushed, until their arms ached, past the intersection at Cuatro Caminos, past crowds of people waiting by the highway, waiting in stoicism for buses that would take them,

36

Prudencia thought, to places no better than the places they'd come from, past vendors of chuchitos and peanuts and plastic bags of sliced mango. Finally, before they hit Nahualá, the two boys fell asleep with mango juice dribbling down their chins, diapers beginning to stink.

In the quiet that descended into the cab, Prudencia could turn to the next task in her calculations: buying the silence of her two accomplices, one of whom was her employer's kin. "Compañeros," she said, "we're in big trouble."

Rosario, busy passing a slow-moving bus on a blind curve, kept his eyes fixed ahead but allowed himself a flash of consternation. Could Prudencia, his aunt's formidable majordomo, have some prescient knowledge of what was coming at them from around the shoulder of the mountain? Marta turned toward her, alarmed at her tone, and asked "What trouble?"

"Did you actually believe that little whore was the mother of these two boys?" Prudencia allowed the question to hang like a miasma in the pungent air of the cab, over the heads of the sleeping twins, and sift into the consciousness of her companions.

Marta was confused. "What are you saying, Prudencia mía? We saw the girl with our own eyes not three months ago, and she was pregnant and suckling these two."

"Perhaps. She was big with something three months ago, and greedy for the down payment. Whatever swelled her belly then, I don't believe her story of losing her baby. No more do I believe she is the mother of these twins she was in charge of that day. They'll belong to her sister, her auntie, her mother, or, more likely, her mistress. She stole them."

The driver, having regained his lane, turned to gape past Marta at Prudencia. He was a young man without promise who'd dropped out of university to lead a life of self-indulgence and nightclubs while living in his mother's house. Doña Merced had hired him as a favor to her sister. "Doña Prudencia, why are you telling us this now?"

"Because, Rosario, your aunt must never know. Doña Merced is a fine woman, intelligent, compassionate, honest. She has made me what I am." Not my papi, Prudencia thought. "This could ruin her reputation. We must protect her."

"What about the DNA test?" Marta asked.

"I know a doctor in Guate who will take care of it. You don't need to know any more. Only this. You've committed a crime. Make no mistake. But don't worry. Do what I tell you, and I'll take care of you."

Thus she dispensed with another task and took on another burden. An hour later, she allowed her companions to stop at a roadside restaurant, take the twins inside to change their diapers, and eat a real meal, while she remained in the truck to make cellphone calls in private.

«« — »»

Fighting through rush hour traffic into the dangerous heart of the shabby metropolis of Guatemala City, where the rigid Spanish sensibilities of the Conquistadors had tried and failed to impose their grid on a landscape seething with tectonic faults, earthquakes, and volcanoes, Prudencia jutted out her chin at a peeling wall and crudely lettered sign that read Hotel La Luna and said, "Pull over."

Dusk was descending. A streetlight hissed on. Under its yellow eye Prudencia picked up her black leather case and chose one twin. Which twin? No one in the pickup but the twins themselves knew: it was Felícito, who had already lost his name and would now lose all other connection to his

38

past. He locked gazes with his brother. Prudencia lifted him out of the truck. "Wait," she told the others.

The entrance to the hotel was recessed and barred. Prudencia pressed a buzzer beside the metal gate and waited. She could see down a cinderblock corridor to a dark and empty courtyard. Voices came from somewhere. A girl appeared out of the shadows of the courtyard and shuffled toward the gate. She seemed weighed down by her enormous pregnancy, barely able to ask what Prudencia wanted.

"Mataria is expecting me," Prudencia said. "I called."

The girl retreated into the interior. Prudencia waited. The sound of voices grew momentarily louder, then stopped altogether. The girl returned and fitted a key into a hidden lock. The gate swung open. Prudencia followed the girl down the corridor and into a narrow room lit by a single overhead bulb and a glowing TV. On the screen two close-up faces were locked in a passionate kiss, with the sound off. A short, stout woman in a black dress that was too tight and low-cut for her age and figure waved Prudencia toward a dismal brown couch, the room's only furniture. Prudencia sat with the twin in her lap, no longer a twin, no longer Felícito, and placed her black bag by her side. The broken springs of the couch sagged, and its frayed synthetic fabric scratched through Prudencia's skirt. The room's one window, facing the street, was shuttered with solid steel.

Mataria loomed over the toddler and peered at him in the dim light. "Thirteen months?" she asked.

"I have all his papers," Prudencia said. "He's healthy, well cared for." She spread out Felícito's arms to show him off: chubby legs in new blue pants, lighter blue sweater still reasonably clean over a plump belly, unblemished skin, dimpled brown cheeks, glossy hair in long bangs over his wide-set eyes.

"Let me see." Mataria lifted Felícito into her arms and, grasping his chin, turned his head from side to side, examining ears, eyes, forcing his mouth open and sticking a finger in to probe teeth and gums. Felícito threw back his head and wailed. "Do you have a bottle?" Mararia asked.

Prudencia fished out the bottle from her case. Empty. Mataria took it. "Wait here," she said and left the room with the crying baby. Prudencia waited, her spine stiff, her jaw set. She could hear muffled noises on the street, voices, cars rumbling over broken pavement, and Felícito's fading cries reverberating from the back of the Hotel La Luna, which was, she knew, not a hotel but a fattening house. The pregnant girl lingered in the corner by the door, leaning against the wall, cradling the huge belly under her flowered apron, watching the silent episode of the telenovela. Prudencia knew the series, *The Body of Desire,* in which nothing was as it seemed. The girl in the flowered apron had already sold the contents of her womb. She and the other girls, who Prudencia knew would be hidden in the back rooms of the fattening house, would breed their babies like so many cows.

Prudencia was unperturbed. Beside her, the black bag gleamed.

<<<< — >>>>

A short time later, Prudencia held the remaining twin, the one who until that moment had known himself as Cándido, drooping in her arms. "See, Julian, your new home," she told the sleepy toddler. "Isn't it pretty? See all your new friends? You'll like it here."

In the sparkling dormitory of Nueva Esperanza, uniformed nursemaids were putting the babies to bed. Above the line of cribs, painted ponies and ducks and bunnies adorned the pale blue walls. Its cheer was lost on Cándido, whose only desires after such a day were for his mother and sweet oblivion.

"Delouse him before you put him to bed," Doña Merced told her. Although the toddler looked clean, this was her standard procedure with new arrivals. María de Merced Castillo de Armas prided herself in running the best orphanage in Guatemala, spotless and up-to-date, with beds for 150 and play equipment in its jasmine-scented garden. "Then stop into my office, Prudencia."

"Is there a problem?" Prudencia asked. Doña Merced had accepted the toddler and Prudencia's explanation with equanimity, she thought.

"Your mother is in the hospital," her employer said. "Your sister called."

<<<< — >>>>

Prudencia had been a daddy's girl. Firstborn of four daughters, she'd done her best to be a boy, because that's what her papi had wanted. She was Papi's shadow, following with her child-sized machete in hand, whacking the weeds in cornfields and the tree trunks in the woods where they foraged firewood. He called her his Toyota picop because of what she could carry. She wore pants like a boy, and the kids in her neighborhood—a sweltering village in the parched hills of Chiquimula—taunted her, calling her, as the mood took them, Little Ox, Little Bull, Little Wild Boar.

When she was ten, the fifth child, her brother Fortunato, was born, the long-awaited son and a clear threat to Prudencia's grip on Papi's heart. She caught him showing the baby off to the crowd of men that gathered in front of the cantina on Saturday afternoon, buying them all beers in self-congratulations.

"Mama says come home now," she said, snatching the baby from him and stomping off without looking back to see if he would follow. "Here, *you* take him," she said to her sister Paciencia when she got home, because she couldn't trust herself not to swaddle him with her jealousy until he choked.

She caught Papi singing the baby lullabies at night. It was more than she could bear. She wiggled between her father's legs and tried to make room in his lap, where Fortunato sat like a nesting hen. Papi planted a kiss on Fortunato's baby lips. "Me too," Prudencia demanded.

Fortunato began to cry, and Prudencia's mother took him away to bed. "Me too," Prudencia said again and inserted herself between Papi's outstretched knees in the straight chair next to the woodstove. Papi laughed. "You, too, Toyota picop?"

He took her by the shoulders and put his lips on hers and she felt his moustache prickle and smelled his sweat and chili breath and heard the fire crackle. Then he pushed her gently away and said, "Good night, daughter." He patted her behind, a soft pat.

She liked the kiss. She made him do it again and again, whenever she could, over the next three years. Meanwhile, Fortunato grew and started walking, following his sisters everywhere, demanding their constant attention. "Take care of your brother," Papi would say, "our little man." If Papi thought his love was big enough to go around, Prudencia didn't. She wanted it all.

Still, it was Prudencia who worked beside Papi; she made sure of that, getting up early to go with him for firewood before school. In the dark woods, they would be sweaty with the effort of chopping and would take a rest before hauling the wood down the mountain. Prudencia would ask for her kiss. Under the fading stars, she tasted his lips and tongue and felt his rough hand under her blouse. She let him stroke and pinch her nipples until her breasts began to grow, like lemons. Squeezed out of her by her papi's love, she believed, the love she won through the power of the kiss, something no boy child could do, her secret weapon. The love swelled through her and made those lemons grow, but before they could burst he would get up off her and say, "Time to get home, daughter."

Prudencia didn't know how dangerous her weapon was, but Papi did. He knew their love was powerful and must be guarded, not squandered. He knew how to enjoy the gift of the young body his own loins had made, and when to stop. His hands never went into her pants. He never showed himself. And when the pressure in his loins became too great, he pulled himself up and stepped behind a tree. Most of all, he impressed on her to guard their secret like a loaded gun, which if fired unwisely would blast their lives to pieces.

«« — »»

Her mama came into the kitchen one black morning before dawn (to light the fire? to put the nixtamal on to boil?), switched on the light, and saw them: her papi in the straight chair by the cold wood stove, she straddling Papi's lap, her legs and arms wrapped around him, her lips against his, sucking out his love. Her mama screamed. Her papi jumped up, throwing Prudencia off his lap onto the floor. Her mother's scream went on and on, like a siren. Prudencia got up off the floor and stared at her papi and her mama screaming like the world was splitting apart.

"Shut up!" her papi yelled. "You'll wake up the whole town." Prudencia wanted the screaming to stop. It didn't stop. Her three sisters appeared at the kitchen door. One of them was carrying Fortunato, who was too big to be carried easily now and was squirming and squealing like a pig.

43

"Shut up, woman!" her papi said again. He pulled back his arm, made a fist, and socked her mama in the face. Her mama collapsed to the floor, sobbing and holding her face. Prudencia could see the blood between her fingers and found her voice.

"Mama? What's wrong?" The realization broke on her like an avalanche. She could hear its roar ringing in her ears.

"Shut up, all of you," her papi barked. "Don't make such a ruckus. I'm the man of this family. Prudencia, make a fire. I'll be back later." He picked up his hat and machete and left the room, shoving past the children in the doorway. Prudencia stood by, transfixed, while her sister Paciencia helped their mother up, while Paciencia found a rag for their mother's bleeding mouth. Fortunato was still bawling in Caridad's arms. Prudencia's own tears emptied onto her cheeks. "What, Mama?" she said again. "What did we do?"

"Ay, Dios," her mother wailed, spitting out the rag. "Work of the devil."

Her love for her papi dried up, hardened to packed earth. Her mama took her to the priest, who told her she was dirty and should never again go near a man. Papi wouldn't look at her now. She'd become too dirty even for him. Fortunato walked beside him, swinging his little machete, and Papi smiled on him. Where else he smiled, Prudencia didn't know. From then on, Prudencia carried a knife, not at her papi's side, but in her heart. Against him.

<<< — >>>

"Your sister called this afternoon," Doña Merced told her. Prudencia loved this office, on the ground floor of Nueva Esperanza, with its glass door opening onto the fragrant garden. Now the garden was dark and the draperies drawn, and the lamplight glowed on the leather armchair that encased Prudencia's tired body like a glove, and on the bookcases ranged with legal and historical tomes that proved her employer was an intellectual of the highest caliber, and on the mahogany desk behind which Doña Merced worked late into the night. Compassion shone on Doña Merced's pale face. "But you're not to worry. The doctors have everything under control. Doing the biopsy of the breast, they pierced the lung. These things happen in thin women. The breast is so close to the lung. The lung collapsed. They just have to keep her there until the danger of infection is past."

<<<< — >>>>

Once the priest had helped Prudencia understand how truly awful she was, she made a strenuous attempt at reform. She never wore pants again. She stuck close to her mama's side, trying to win forgiveness in women's work. She went to school with her sisters and avoided the boys. Other girls learned to flirt and smile and duck their heads. Prudencia turned a shoulder. She knew what the boys were up to. She knew about the hand in the blouse, the squeeze of the nipple. She'd hold her sisters' hands, her mami's hand, but never the hand of some nasty boy. She avoided her papi and hoped her mami and sisters did too. He was there in the house because they needed him, because families without fathers were like houses without roofs. They bore him but guarded themselves against him, so Prudencia thought.

Until her mother's stomach began to bulge, to the point where Prudencia had to ask her about it. Outside, when no one else was around and they were setting the wash out to dry, laying it across the ragged thorn bushes that hedged their yard. "But of course, mija. We're having another baby," her mami said.

45

Prudencia had thought that Fortunato would be the last, that having achieved his heart's desire, her father would leave them in peace. "How can you let him touch you?" she said. She felt sick.

Her mami's eyes filled up with tears. They sprang from the ocean her mami kept locked up inside, and they never ran out. "We women have no choice," her mami said.

The next day Prudencia went to the priest and told him that God had called her. She needed the name of a convent in Guatemala City.

"Why Guatemala City, daughter?" the priest asked. "Why not Esquipulas? It's much closer and the holiest place in Guatemala. You could study with the nuns there."

"No, father. God said Guatemala, specifically. I don't know why."

"Who knows the ways of God?" the priest said, and gave her a letter of introduction. She took that letter and a hundred quetzales she'd stolen from her parents' mattress. She hadn't told her mama she was leaving, knowing the tears would drown her if she did. Instead, once her mother knew that she was gone, the tears would be sucked up by the dry dirt of Chiquimula and disappear forever. Prudencia was fourteen.

«««   —   »»»

Zona 10 was a different Guatemala from anything Prudencia had ever known. A place of wide streets, smooth sidewalks of polished stone, wet and slick from morning washing. A place of expensive shops, people dressed to go to work in glass towers, shade trees behind walls topped in razor wire, singing birds, bougainvillea. Prudencia walked between two Carmelite nuns to a solid wooden gate set in

46

one of these walls. The older nun, the one with boxy shoulders and stubble on her chin, rang the bell.

"Doña Merced is expecting you," the woman who opened the door in the gate said. Prudencia, although ignorant of the ways of rich people, knew the woman must be a servant. They followed the servant through the garden, past a splashing fountain, to Doña Merced's study. She was standing in front of her desk and looked down at Prudencia. She was tall, with honey-colored hair that curled around her ears. Prudencia had never seen anyone who looked like her, pure criolla, or had honey hair dark at the roots, or green eyes that pierced.

"She comes recommended by the priest in Chiquimula," the nun with the bristled chin said, handing Doña Merced Prudencia's letter. "We thought of you immediately."

The lady studied the letter. A bird whistled in the courtyard. Prudencia had never been in such a peaceful place. "It commends the girl to your care. It doesn't say anything about work."

"Señora, we can't take her in. We knew you were looking for a maid."

Prudencia was sure that God had led her to the sisters, because they had led her to Doña Merced. In those days there was no Nueva Esperanza, just the sprawling house behind walls in Zona 10, the shady tranquil neighborhood in the heart of the violent capital. In her new life Prudencia didn't have time to miss her mother and sisters. She cleaned toilets that shone like expensive china. She picked up the clothes her employer's three teenage children dropped on the floor, mountains of designer jeans, silky dresses, things that matched and sported logos, things that were only worn once before washing. She scrubbed pots in the kitchen. She saw little of Doña Merced, who was busy with her law practice, finding homes for orphans; it was Trinidad, the cook, who filled her in on the mysterious lives of her employers. Don Antonio spent his days in his office at the bank and his evenings with his lover, according to the cook. It was Trinidad who taught Prudencia which cleaners to use on stainless steel and which to polish mahogany, until Doña Merced caught Trinidad stealing and fired her on the spot.

"You see what happens to liars and thieves in my household?" Doña Merced told Prudencia, boring into her with hard green eyes. Sure that her mistress could see straight into her soul and uncover every bit of rot, terrified of being cast out in Trinidad's wake, Prudencia covered her face with her hands.

"Seño, I have to confess," she said. Trembling, she told Doña Merced that she had a mother and sisters in Chiquimula, who had not heard from her in nine months.

"That's it? No other lies?" Her employer took her chin in her hand and tilted Prudencia's face up to hers.

"No. I promise."

"You must write to your mother, and I'll teach you to be my cook."

So it was Doña Merced herself who taught Prudencia the secrets of the kitchen: jocón and pepián, carne guisado and adobado. Don Antonio left for good, two of the children went away to university, one daughter to Mexico, one son to Pennsylvania, and the big house emptied of people. The one daughter who remained in Guatemala was rarely seen under her mother's roof.

"Prudencia mija," Doña Merced announced, "I have a new project. We're going to bring the orphans here. There's plenty of room, and that way I can assure my clients in the agencies that the children are healthy and well cared for while the Americans adopt them."

So the plan for Nueva Esperanza had been hatched. Prudencia was right there, at the drawing board. While the house filled up with builders, plumbers, electricians, adding rooms and stories until it had grown to three levels of modern dormitories, nurseries, playrooms, and bathrooms, letters had traveled between Guatemala City and Chiquimula, between Prudencia and her sister Paciencia, for of course their mother couldn't read. Paciencia gave her the news—that their mother had wept for the loss of her eldest daughter and the youngest, the baby who had died after Prudencia had left, and had had the operation so she'd not have to bear and lose more children. Prudencia sent money and questions that didn't get answered, but that weighed on her until she confided to Doña Merced. "I'm worried about my sisters. My papi can't be trusted."

"In what way?"

Prudencia told her.

"You should get your sisters away from him."

Prudencia didn't want to go to Chiquimula. She'd escaped once from its sucking dust. She might not be so lucky again. Instead, she sent for Paciencia.

<<< — >>>

Six years later, she did go back to rescue her mother. She got off the bus on the hard road and started up the dirt path to her house. She breathed in the heat and dust and smoke of burning garbage. The strange familiarity made her gag. She looked for signs of change, new block houses rising through the cornfields, sprouting rebar from their rooftop like horns. This was the place of the devil. She avoided the eyes of passersby on the path, filled with shame, afraid she'd be recognized. But how? She'd been fourteen, and a different person, when she left.

Wash was still flung over the thorn bushes around her house. Smoke sifted from the eaves, but no one was in the yard.

"Mama?" she called. She crossed to the door, standing half open, and peered into the dark kitchen. "Mama?" hoping, praying, that would be who was there.

"Ay Dios! Daughter! I didn't think it could be true." Her mother came to her, tears already welling. "Caridad told me you were coming, but I never believed."

"Who else is here, Mamita?"

"No one. The kids are in school. Your papi is . . . out."

Prudencia took her mother in her arms, shocked at how small and stooped she'd become. She felt brittle and fragile in Prudencia's arms. "I've come to take you away with me," she said.

This caused a fresh gush of tears. "You know I can't."

"You can. You will. Caridad will take Dolores and Fortunato. Papi can take care of himself. I won't leave without you. I promised God and Doña Merced."

Caridad had a husband and home of her own; she could take up their mother's burdens and give her a rest. And so Mami moved to the city, living with Paciencia, who had a decent job as a bank teller, where Prudencia could take care of her.

««« — »»»

Oh no, not dead! How can you be dead, Mamita? I said I'd take care of you. After I came back from Huehue, I told you in the hospital, I've saved another innocent child and I'll save you, my mama. We have money for the surgery, I told you. We have money to treat the cancer.

You were hooked up to the ventilator. I touched your burning forehead. I held your hot hand. Don't be scared, I told you. I was scared.

You closed your eyes and whispered to me, "You are a good daughter." Oh, Mama!

"Don't worry," the nurse told me. "She'll be fine as soon as we get the fever down." The nurse was wrong. A week later, my mother was dead. Now I'm the one crying an oceanful of tears.

<<< — >>>

"Look, Julian, here they come. You lucky boy, your new mami and papi." This was the most satisfying part of Prudencia's job. She held the toddler up so he could see the couple coming through the glass doors and crossing the marble lobby of the Marriott, flanked by Doña Merced and followed by a porter wheeling piles of luggage. The American woman was plump, with golden hair rippling to her waist. She moved in waves of flowing beige fabric. The husband beside her was tall and balding, with a pink, boyish face. He carried an enormous black and white teddy bear. They threaded their way through clusters of cooing adults, crying infants, and stroller jams toward Prudencia. The American woman scooped Julian into her heavy arms and held him up toward the chandelier, crying out in excited English. Doña Merced spoke to them in English and steered them to a bank of sofas. They all sat down, Julian on the American woman's lap, casting anxious glances toward Prudencia, who sat beside them. "Say hello to your mami," Prudencia told him.

Julian looked up at the woman with a grave expression and said, "Mami?"

She hugged him with delight, and the husband, who was sitting beside her with the great bear in his lap, reached out to ruffle his long bangs, which had been neatly trimmed to frame his dark eyes. The husband grinned, and Julian smiled back. Then the husband made the bear's arms move up and down and come toward Julian as if to hug him. Julian pulled back with a look of alarm. The bear was almost as big as he was. It had a huge white head with round black ears and black circle eyes that made it look sad.

"Don't worry," Doña Merced told him. "Your papi wants to give you the big bear to be your friend."

Julian reached out and touched the bear's arm and it was soft and squishy, so he let the man hug him with the bear's arms and he put his arms around the bear and squeezed it, and put his face down and pressed his nose against the top of the bear's head and giggled.

That made the woman lean down and kiss the top of Julian's head with an expression of rapture. The man said something in English, and Doña Merced said to Julian, "Your papi wants to know what you're going to name your new friend."

Julian looked at Doña Merced, who was sitting in an armchair across from him. He glanced up at Prudencia and the strangers above him with a thoughtful expression and looked around the glittering room teeming with babies and strangers, as if pondering the miracle of it all. In the five months he'd been at Nuevo Esperanza he'd gotten used to babies and strangers, but the lobby of the Marriott was a new experience for him. He took time to absorb it, then returned to the big bear in his arms with an odd expression. He tipped his head to one side, met the light blue gaze of the tall American, and said, "Felícito."

THE ADOPTION

On the happiest day of her life, the agency in Guatemala called to tell Sunshine Kelly that her little boy was ready. Sooner than expected! It was hard to believe. She held Julian's photo in her hand. If she looked any harder at the toddler's face, his black eyes hiding under wispy black bangs, his wide Buddha cheeks, she was sure it would disappear in a puff of smoke.

Her good husband Tom Kelly was less prone to magical thinking. He said, "Honey, pack your bags. We're going down to Guatemala."

He called the contractor in charge of the Oak Lane renovation and told him the cabinets would be done on time, but he was taking a few days off. They hired the neighbor to look after their menagerie—a pampered golden retriever, four cats, some chickens, two nanny goats (they were hoping to be organic farmers if they ever got out of Bergen County, NJ)—and hopped on a plane. Sunshine had failed for nine years to conceive a child of her own, despite herbal remedies, colon cleansing, charting, homeopathy, acupuncture, Clomid, meditation and yoga, rounds of in vitro fertilization, despite the entire medical profession telling her there was nothing medically wrong.

When Tom had suggested in vitro, Sunshine had objected, "It's so expensive!"

"We'll get another credit card," he had said. And another, and a mortgage on the house his great uncle had left them, and a loan from his folks. With the adoption, the debts had mounted higher and higher. But Tom wasn't a worrier; he was an optimist. Now at last everything was going right.

They flew into Guatemala, passed Customs without a hitch, rode through streets of a city she could barely see through heavy rain, and checked into a hotel the agency had arranged. It was one of those glitzy five-star places Sunshine would normally not be caught dead in even if she could afford it, but upon seeing babies in strollers in the lobby and the elevator and hallways, she knew it was a happy place. Until late that night, when she lay in bed and listened to Tom snore and her worries came loose. What would Julian make of her—his new mom? She would look so big, so white, so strange to him; she would sound so foreign. Trying to calm her nerves, she rehearsed Spanish phrases she had learned for the trip: *good morning; my son; I love you.*

In the morning, she was just dry from her shower and twisting her long hair into a thick yellow braid when the phone rang. Tom picked up and shouted to her, "They're here!" He hugged her until she gasped for breath. They descended the elevator holding hands like a young couple in love. When she saw Julian across the lobby, unmistakable in a nursemaid's arms, Sunshine squeezed Tom's hand to keep from racing toward her baby. *Take it slow,* she told her beating heart, and measured her paces across the marble floor. Julian buried his face in the woman's shoulder. The lady lawyer Merced, who guarded the nursemaid and child like an angel of mercy, introduced herself and said, "He may be a little shy at first." A *leetle* shy.

Then the lady lawyer said something to Julian in Spanish, and Sunshine caught the word *mommy* and Julian turned and looked at her with wise eyes that seemed to hold all the secrets of the universe, and she would swear the first word he said to her was, "Mommy?"

"Yes, baby!" Sunshine said, and Tom reached out, lifted up his cute little polo shirt, and gave him a raspberry right on the belly.

Julian smiled. Julian laughed! The nursemaid held him out to Sunshine, and she lifted him for the first time, feeling his heft. He was a solid thing, plump and healthy- looking, although a little small, she thought, for eighteen months. But all the Guatemalans were small, except for Merced, who was blond and had gone to the University of Pennsylvania and spoke English, although with an accent.

"He'll stay with you here at the hotel while we do the final paperwork. It should take about a week," Merced told them. "I'll leave you now, to get settled. I'll call you tomorrow."

Merced and the nursemaid set sail across the grand lobby and disappeared through the sliding glass doors, leaving the brand new family, an island of stunned happiness in an archipelago of similar islands. All around them in the hotel lobby, couples were lifting and cuddling infants and pushing strollers in a chorus of coos and shrieks and squeals of delight.

««« — »»»

Clouds sat like old dogs over Guatemala City. Rain pelted the garden outside Merced's office. It had been a terrible September. Days of downpour had washed the cardboard hovels of the poor into the ravines, flooded schools and houses in middle-class colonias, and clogged drains even in immaculate Zona 10, where Merced fought against the forces of nature and politics to keep Hogar Nueva Esperanza afloat. Not only was the rain making life miserable for the 79 orphans and dozen staff in her care, but UNICEF, the US State

Department, the Hague Convention, and who knows who else were threatening to end Guatemalan adoptions. Fíjese— just imagine! Throwing 370,000 orphans out onto the sodden streets.

Merced felt besieged. In between filing paperwork and making court appearances for her little ones, she had written letters to watchdog agencies, published columns in *Prensa Libre*, and lobbied members of the Guatemalan Congress for a battle she was about to lose, as soon as the US endorsed the Hague treaty. A country like Guatemala could sign a treaty without it changing how business was actually conducted. The United Transparent States of America was a corncob of a different color. With sadness in her heart and bile on her tongue, Merced was trying to clear the Hogar of orphans before it was too late.

There was a knock at her office door, and her chief of staff came in. It was Prudencia, the dark-skinned Indian girl Merced had rescued as a runaway of fourteen and raised to be her right-hand assistant, now twenty-five. "A man wants to see you, seño. An investigator."

"Investigator?"

"He wouldn't tell me what it's about. He will only talk to you." Prudencia's face could have been a mask lifted from an ancient stele. She had been moody lately, distracted, as if carrying a weight, a two-ton ill-omened owl as the country people believed. Pues, it was to be expected. Poor Prudencia herself was now an orphan.

"Bring him in, then," Merced sighed. She was fed up with investigators, congressmen, human rights attorneys, reporters. All she wanted was to do her job: run a first-class orphanage and find families for her children.

The investigator presented her with his embossed card. "Umberto Tecún Puac, Investigaciones Privadas y Descretas," it read. He was an officious type, the new Indian, educated and proud of his Mayan surname, rather than tattered and poor and deserving of pity. Merced was also weary of being held accountable for the last five hundred years of oppression of the Maya people, now that the tortilla had turned over and former guerrillas were in powerful government posts. The investigator spread papers and photographs across Merced's mahogany desk. While his short fingers poked the photographs, his words formed byzantine arabesques in Merced's head.

She stared at the photos. She could no more hear his words than she could decipher Mayan hieroglyphs. She felt short of breath, and wondered if he'd seen her already light skin blanch. Involuntarily, she raised a hand to her face; then, not knowing what to do with it, tucked a strand of hair behind her ear. She lowered the hand to her lap to clasp it with the other, so he wouldn't see them tremble.

Disaster galloped toward her, faster than she had foreseen. Disaster had singled her out—because of her fame in the small social circle of the capital, no doubt—and now threatened her name, her reputation, her livelihood, and her orphans, those out of the 370,000 who good fortune had chosen to be rescued by her. Disaster, if this investigator were to be believed.

She pulled herself back to his speech as he pointed at the photo on her desk. "The twins boys, Cándido (finger poke) and Felícito (finger poke) Ramírez Calmo, were stolen from their home in Todos Santos on April 11. The serving girl believed to be responsible has never been found."

There were three photos: identical newborns swaddled in identical cloth of an Indian weave, a second too fuzzy to see, and the third showing two serious little men in red-and-white striped pants, pale shirts with wide red collars, and tiny fez

57

hats, standing side by side. "Their first birthday," Tecún Puac explained, "a month before their abduction."

Merced made a quick decision. Tecún Puac would simply not be believed. "We've had no twins at the Hogar in the last year," she said. She fixed her green eyes on him like jade-tipped spears, as her ex-husband had once called them.

"They could have been split up by the broker," he parried.

She made herself into a wall of stone. "I will check our admissions records. Leave your card so I can contact you."

"May I see the children currently in your care?"

She stood up, all tremble gone from her hands. "Of course. I'll cooperate completely with your search. The Hogar is scrupulous in its policies. We are one hundred percent transparent." She glided slowly and smoothly to the office door, which had been closed for the interview, turned the key and pulled the heavy brass lever to unleash the investigator into her world. "Prudencia, please show Don Umberto around the Hogar."

Merced watched the stone-faced Prudencia lead away the investigator in his cheap suit and shiny shoes, with his briefcase and questions and photographs of two toddlers, younger double versions of the orphan she'd delivered just that morning to the Marriott.

««« — »»»

Rain drummed on the plate glass of a high window at the hotel, threatening to break in on the newly constituted Kelly family of Mom, Dad, and Jules—as Sunshine thought of them already. Jules was trying to eat lunch. Perched in the highchair supplied in the family suite of the Marriott, he gagged on the bite of sandwich Sunshine had inserted into his little bow of a mouth.

"Try it, Jules honey. You'll like it," Sunshine pleaded.

Accustomed to the fare of the Hogar—soups of garlic, vegetables, and mashed tortillas—the organic peanut butter on home-baked whole wheat bread that Sunshine had brought from New Jersey revolted him. Jules spit out the bite and howled.

"My poor baby!" Sunshine lifted him from the highchair and cuddled him.

Tom said. "Let's try a bottle of milk."

The lady lawyer had told them Julian liked his bottles warm. Tom filled the bottle with milk from the mini-fridge and heated it in the hotel's bottle warmer. Sunshine sat on the sofa with Jules on her lap, next to them a giant stuffed panda. Dabbing her baby's copper cheeks with Kleenex filled her with tenderness. Jules reached for the bottle Tom brought and leaned back into Sunshine as he sucked, content.

With her nose full of the perfume that seemed to rise off the black hair and brown skin of her boy, like something sweet wafting from the center of the earth, Sunshine looked out the window. She'd never seen so much rain. The city sprawled below like a drowning victim, its edges dissolved into fog. How terrible the weather was here. She'd thought they were coming to a tropical country and had packed sundresses and linen pants. She'd imagined beaches and palm trees. Only Tom had thought to check weather.com, so they were prepared with a rain bubble for the stroller and heavy sweaters for the dank chill that penetrated walls.

The dark day and unending torrents couldn't depress her. Jules was here. After years of delivering other people's babies as a nurse midwife, and nurturing anything alive, including babies, kittens, goats, vegetables, and Tom's doddering great uncle, who had owned three practically rural acres in New Jersey and had needed someone to move in with him and change his diapers—Sunshine finally had a baby of her own. Jules was real, and he was hers and Tom's. They were a family. When he'd finished his bottle, she stretched him out to change his diaper. She tickled his tummy. She kissed his cheek. He was docile under her touch as she wiped him clean and dry. In a few days they would leave this drowning country and go home to sunny days, crisp nights, and apples ripening in their garden in Bergen County.

«« — »»

After the investigator left, Merced called Prudencia into her office. Merced had checked her records. She had needed to know. The date on the Julian García Mendoza admittance was as she'd feared.

"I trust Tecún Puac was satisfied," she said. In the quiet office, removed from the hubbub of the nurseries, the two women sat in matching leather armchairs, their feet on the Persian carpet, facing the glass doors leading out to the garden, transformed by the rain into a jungle of emerald, fuchsia, and orange. "I think this weather is driving everyone crazy," she said with disgust.

"There's a lot of flu going around," Prudencia said. "I've ordered extra hand-washing with disinfectant for everyone."

"You don't seem too well yourself, mija."

"I'm all right, thanks." There was steadfastness, not evasion, in Prudencia's tone.

"Your mother's death hit you hard, dear. I know. I remember my mother's death. You never get over it. You just have to bear up." As Merced had to bear up, under the assaults of political foes, her own complaining adult children, her ex-husband's false charges. And now this. She proceeded carefully. "The investigator claims to be looking for stolen children. Two twin boys from Huehuetenango."

60

As expected, Prudenia's visage retained its Mayan stoicism. Merced could rely on that. "Who knows what's behind it," Merced continued. "An angry father perhaps, who only wants his daughter's illegitimate children in retrospect, because the poor girl did what was best for them. There's so much misery in the world, Prudencia, so much suffering. Fíjese, what will happen to the orphans once the Congress is finished? We have to think of them. Nobody else does. That boy we took to his new family this morning, he was from Huehue, wasn't he?"

"I think so, seño." Prudencia gazed past her employer at the radioactive green garden.

"The notary you use in Huehue. Can he be trusted?"

"Absolutely, seño."

"These are terrible times, Prudencia. I can't feed seventy orphans out of my pocket. Nueva Esperanza isn't the ultimate solution for our children; it's their waystation to a better life. We can't have a scandal now. We're not criminals."

"Of course not, Doña Merced. You can count on me." Prudencia looked with steely confidence into the older woman's eyes. This was the girl, Merced knew, who'd carried a knife in her underclothes to protect herself from her father. Merced reached over and took Prudencia's hand between her two, stroking it with gratitude.

"I know I can, my dear. I know I can."

<<<< — >>>>

Don Chepe Ramirez Gomez was known by the standards of Todos Santos as a rich man, although he would deny it. He'd put away a few quetzales in his thirty years of teaching, bought several small parcels of land in the mountains over Pajón and down past San Martín, planted a little coffee, and retired to devote himself to public life. He had secured a post in the Municipal Palace and had visions of expanding his influence beyond his small town, when calamity came out of nowhere and struck his household. He arrived home at the end of a busy day to find his formidable wife wailing in the kitchen, their three grown sons unable to calm her. His twin grandsons, two precious toddlers he loved even more than his own sons, had disappeared.

His daughter-in-law Eulalia was in bed in her darkened room, sobbing. The nursemaid Concepción, a worthless chit of fifteen, was also missing.

When Chepe got the story from the distraught family, including their suspicions about Concepción, his first reaction was to explode with fury. "I'll find that daughter of the great whore," he vowed. "Her parents will answer to me if they don't get my grandsons back to me tonight."

Action was preferable to anguish. He got on his motorcycle and roared back to town. Yet his threats, his stature among the town elders, and all his efforts proved futile over the next few days. The girl's parents knew nothing. No one had seen anything. The mayor made promises, but what could he do? Every day Chepe returned empty-handed to his house, still strewn with the little boys' toys and deep in mourning. Crazy with frustration, Chepe went to the police chief in Huehuetenango, the department capital, and begged him to put all his forces on the case. He offered a 30,000-quetzal reward for the return of the twins. He didn't have 30,000 quetzales. But he could sell some land. Even if it meant financial ruin, he had to find his nietitos.

Every day he waited for a phone call, an arrest. A week later he returned to Huehue to check progress on the investigation. Carlos Montt Figueroa, the chief, known as el Gordito, spread his fat fingers and sighed. "Nothing, Don Chepe. I'm sorry."

"Who have you interrogated?" Chepe demanded.

"Listen. These cases are difficult. Bands of criminals swarm the countryside like a plague of vipers. If they're not stealing babies and selling their organs, they're trafficking in drugs. They're armed, very dangerous. You must be patient, hombre."

"Patient! My daughter-in-law won't eat. My wife cries all day long. My babies are gone. You want me to be patient!"

El Gordito offered a lead. Some campesinos up by Gracias a Dios had seen a suspicious black van parked at an abandoned farmhouse near the border. Perhaps the kidnappers had taken the babies into Mexico. The chief contacted the authorities in Tuxtla Gutiérrez. They promised to search for the van. Chepe snatched at the clue and clung to it for hope.

Weeks passed. While Chepe roamed the countryside conducting his own desperate investigations, Eulalia remained in bed, cared for by Chepe's eagle-browed wife, Doña Pancha. Only oatmeal mush and the sweet bland squash chilacayote kept Lala alive. She insisted that the chilacayote be dyed black, the custom on Good Friday, before she'd touch it.

"Every day without my sons feels like a crucifixion," she told her mother-in-law.

Lala had always been a proud girl. Daughter of Don Porfirio Calmo, Chepe's rival in the village hierarchy, she had been voted Señorita Instituto her last year in school. She went on to high school in Huehue and wanted to be a doctor, a remarkable aspiration for an Indian girl. These were remarkable times in Todos Santos, which in the course of one generation had gone from hidebound agrarian hamlet cut off from the world by rugged mountains into the age of the Internet.

63

Octavio was Chepe's handsome eldest son. Lala's ambitions had been waylaid on a full moon night when the frisson of Montagues and Capulets (she knew the story from the telenovela) resulted in the twins' conception. Lala insisted on a church wedding, graduated with a teacher's license, and moved into her father-in-law's house, where she tangled with Doña Pancha and sniped at Octavio's younger brothers. She was polite but refused to kowtow to Don Chepe.

The first months of the twins' life brought Lala deep into bliss. From Capulet, she'd gone to madonna. One baby or the other was always attached to her breast. She sang to them "Yo Que No Vivo Sin Ti." She slept little and dreamed constantly.

When the doctor told her the twins were underweight and needed to be put on the bottle, she woke from the dream. She wanted her babies breast-fed and had her father-in-law hire a wet nurse, a disgraced young girl who had lost her own illegitimate baby. In January Lala started teaching and studying at the university in Huehue on the weekend plan, the flame of ambition rekindled. She'd been teaching her third graders in Pajón, only a few hundred meters from her in-laws' house, when her babies disappeared.

<<< — >>>

The rainy season began in May. Out in the campo the milpas sprouted their trinity—corn, beans, and squash rising from Mother Earth in their annual ritual. The campesinos offered thanks with their hoes; the first cleaning of the milpas occurred in June. Chepe had been to every village between Todos Santos and Mexico, searching for informants on the kidnappers. Still the twins had not been found.

He stormed into el Gordito's office for the dozenth time.

"Bad news, Don Chepe," the police chief told him. "Tuxtla located the black van. Nothing but a group of tourists. Your babies never went to Mexico. If I were you, I'd look in Guate."

The capital, with its offices, courts, and embassies, was the control center for all adoptions. If not Mexico, the baby-snatchers must have taken Cándido and Felícito to the capital.

"Two months wasted chasing a false tip!" Chepe pounded his fist on the police chief's desk and cursed his impotence.

"Not to worry. Two months is nothing in an adoption, lawful or not," el Gordito reassured him. "You'll find the boys in Guate."

Chepe set out for the capital, where, due to the nature of all things Guatemalan, nothing happened very quickly. He made the rounds of everyone he knew in government offices. All were solicitous. None was helpful. He pounded on doors in the Public Ministry and haunted the warrens of the secretive PGN, the national attorney general's office, gatekeeper of all adoptions. They sent him in circles. "Just tell me," he wanted to ask, "Who do I bribe?" But they wouldn't tell him. Back and forth he traveled from Guate to Todos Santos. The trips were arduous, too far for his motorcycle. He rode the bus, a seven-hour journey one way, longer when there were landslides and construction delays.

Finally, word of mouth took Chepe to the services of Umberto Tecún Puac, Private Investigator. The private eye was expensive. The sale of his coffee trees in San Martín paid the retainer, but if the investigation went on too long, Chepe would have nothing left but the house he lived in.

<<< — >>>

"Tom, I had such awful nightmares last night," Sunshine whispered, so as not to wake Jules, who was asleep between

65

them in the king-sized bed of the Marriott. Morning light was dimmed by the drawn curtain.

"I don't know how you had time to dream. I barely slept."

Nights with Jules had been long and wakeful. They put him down with his bottle in the bed, rather than the crib, because Sunshine believed it was the best way to bond. "He's used to sleeping with a roomful of people," she said.

However, in the five months he'd been at the Hogar, Julian had gotten out of the habit of the family bed. He woke with a start every time Sunshine or Tom turned over, and then cried inconsolably while one of them paced the halls of the hotel with him over their shoulder.

"I dreamed something went wrong when I delivered Beth Morton's baby; the cord wrapped around her neck, and she was born dead. It was horrible."

"Work anxiety. It's natural. Don't worry. Meredith and Rochelle will hold down the fort." Sunshine's partners had taken over while she went on maternity leave. The women in her care felt more like friends than patients, after the monthly checkups, the hours spent discussing pregnancy and birthing choices. She hated to abandon them even though they were all thrilled for her.

"The dream went on," she said, "and got even worse. The dead baby turned into Jules. I was losing Jules. I woke up, and you and Jules weren't in the bed. I was terrified! Then I realized you were giving him a bottle. I was scared to tell you, like it would make the nightmare come true to talk about it."

"Honey, take it easy." He reached over the sleeping toddler and touched the corner of her lips with one finger. "Smile. You're a mom."

Jules opened his eyes, and she looked at him and smiled. He was there. He was real. Tom got out of bed and pulled

66

back the curtains. Outside the window they saw patches of blue sky and mountains, visible for the first time.

"Hey Jules, look at that!" Tom said. "It stopped raining. Let's get out of this Ark and go for a stroll." They hadn't left the Marriott in three days, taking all their meals in the hotel restaurants. No wonder they were going stir crazy.

Tom loaded Jules into the stroller and attached the rain bubble just in case. Jules reached out his arms and demanded, "Felícito!" Sunshine handed him the big panda bear he'd grown attached to. He kicked his feet with delight and hugged the bear, almost as big as he was. Prepared for anything, they left the hotel. The sun wasn't out, but its presence behind the clouds was welcome. Merced had told them not to wander, so they headed directly for the Lively Zone, across Reforma, where she had said there was plenty to see and do. They found marble sidewalks, sparkling shops, walls topped with exotic flowers, and fancy eateries. People scurried past them on their way to work. They were the only foreigners in sight, and Sunshine felt conspicuous and blond pushing their dark-haired child. In a sidewalk café they ordered coffee and croissants by pointing, since the waitress didn't speak English. She cooed over Jules and he babbled back, in his cheerful morning mood. He chomped happily on pieces of croissant.

"Better than peanut butter, huh Jules?" Tom tweaked Julian's nose, then stuck his thumb through his fist, to teach the toddler his first English joke. "Got your nose!"

Jules laughed.

They had just finished breakfast when a drum roll of thunder announced a new downpour. "Fun time is over," Tom said, and Sunshine lowered the bubble over Julian's stroller. Tom opened the enormous golf umbrella he'd thought to bring, and they splashed back to the hotel. Inside its sliding glass doors they stood dripping among clusters of dampened guests.

"Sunshine! Sunshine!" Gail and Bob Boxer, the Ohio couple they'd met at breakfast the day before, came across the lobby. Gail pushed a stroller that held six-month-old Lily, another Nueva Esperanza baby. "We've just come from the embassy," she trumpeted. "We got our pink slip. We're good to go! Tomorrow!"

"How exciting," Sunshine said. "I'm envious. We're dying to get out of here. I feel like I'll never get dry."

"We've been here two weeks, and it's rained the whole time," Bob said. "Helluva country."

"It stopped for two hours this morning," Tom said.

"As I said, helluva country."

"Oh Bob. You're too negative. When we visited Lily in July there were some very nice days," Gail said.

A short Guatemalan wearing a suit and thin moustache under his Mayan nose stepped up to them, said something in Spanish, and raised a camera. Before they could react, he snapped a picture of Jules in his stroller, and another of Sunshine and Tom. Then he nodded his head and strode off in a determined manner.

"Hey!" Tom exclaimed. "The nerve. What was that about?"

"That guy. He's been around the whole time we've been here, taking pictures," Bob said. "Ignore it. Some kinda journalist I think."

"I've heard rumors he's an undercover cop," Gail said, "looking for a stolen baby."

"The staff lets him hang around here and bother the guests?" Tom said. "I thought this was a first class hotel."

Bob snorted. "This is Guatemala. All he has to do is grease a few palms."

"It's scary," Gail said with a shudder. "We're lucky we don't live here."

<<< — >>>

Merced found Prudencia crying in the locked pantry off the kitchen where they stored the beans and flour and powdered milk and sugar, the cans and jars of all the things needed to provide healthy meals on a large scale, as well as the medicines they kept on hand for the infirmary next to the kitchen. Prudencia was leaning against a wall, her head bowed, her shoulders shaking, holding onto a shelf post. Merced went in and put her arms around the smaller woman and said, "Mija."

Prudencia moved her face to Merced's shoulder and sobbed. They stood a while in grief, then Merced sighed. "It's not that bad."

"Seño," Prudencia said in a voice broken of guile, "I'm afraid that inspector will come back." She paused, and their gazes locked with all that went unspoken between them, with what Prudencia couldn't tell Merced and what Merced didn't want to hear. "My sister Caridad wants me to come home to Chiquimula and help with her children and my brother."

Merced knew that the brother, Fortunato, was fifteen and running wild. Merced knew almost as much about Prudencia's wretched family as she did about her own, had helped Prudencia rescue her sisters and mother, had wept with Prudencia when her mother died. Now, to protect them both, she had to send the girl back to that awful place. She held Prudencia's shoulders in her hands and looked her sadly in the eye.

Prudencia's head dropped. "I've let you down, Doña Merced!"

Merced wanted no confessions. "Don't be foolish," she said. "Be strong. You'd better go now to Chiquimula."

<<< — >>>

In Todos Santos, cornstalks were tumbling down the mountainside and impaling the bank of tall impatiens that bordered Don Chepe's patio. "What in the name of holiness is going on here?" Don Chepe, surveying the flattened milpa from his porch, shouted at his son Octavio. Chepe felt like a force of nature, like the rain that wept buckets and the wind that howled down from the altiplano.

Octavio looked bewildered. "Fíjese, Tat, I'm a schoolteacher with a job and a crying wife, and somebody forgot to do the second cleaning of the milpa."

Somebody? Octavio's brother Wilfredo was lazy from too much high-paying work in El Norte. But surely Efraín, the third brother, could have chopped out the weeds and hoed the earth into the little volcanoes at the feet of the cornstalks that protected them against the autumn winds. Chepe saw his whole family rootless and collapsing under the strain of the prolonged search.

"Do I have to manage every little thing around here?" He raged. He feared that, in fact, he could manage nothing. The phone rang in his bedroom office. He looked across the wall of rain in the patio that separated him from his bedroom. "I'll get it," he said, and ran for the phone.

"Tecún Puac here," said the voice, fading in and out of static. "... information ... you should ... Guatemala ... earliest ..."

"I'll be there," Chepe said, slamming down the phone.

<<<< — >>>>

Tom, Sunshine, and Jules joined Bob, Gail, and Lily for a celebration dinner at the Marriott that night. Jules and Lily sat in side-by-side highchairs. Lily was excited. "Eeeeee!" she shouted, and threw her bottle on the floor. Jules took the pieces of banana and papaya Sunshine handed him and popped them into his mouth. He and his new mom had reached a dietary accord. Everybody laughed with the pleasure that new parents find in every eccentric act of their little ones. Bob picked up the wayward bottle and gave it back to Lily. "Toss away, sweetie," he said. "Plenty more where that came from. Tomorrow you'll be in the land of milk and honey."

His jingoistic attitude annoyed Sunshine. But she raised her wine glass with the others as Bob toasted, "To our children's long and happy lives!"

"You're getting in just under the wire, you know," Bob said over his steak. "Guatemala's about to pull the plug on foreign adoptions."

Tom, who had been following the blogs in New Jersey while Sunshine was baking bread to bring on their trip, said, "There really should be an exemption for families already in the process."

"Don't bet on it. State Department's cracking down. This country's a cesspool of corruption."

"You'll scare them to death!" Gail interjected. "Nueva Esperanza is perfectly above board and takes wonderful care of its children. We haven't had any problems in Guatemala. I don't like seeing so many cripples and beggars on the streets, but you have to expect that in a poor country."

Maybe Gail had never been to New York, Sunshine thought. "You do plan to bring Lily back to visit?" she asked. "When she's older, I mean. To get to know her birth country?"

"Oh yes," Gail assured her.

"Only if it's safe," Bob said.

<<<< — >>>>

Thursday morning Merced picked up the Kellys to take

them to the embassy, loading their stroller into the trunk of her BMW. Sunshine strapped Julian into his baby seat and got in back, next to him. Tom handed Julian his panda. Jules clutched the bear and chortled. Tom slid in front next to Merced, who fired up the BMW.

"He loves his bear buddy," Tom told Merced. "He calls it Felícito. A long name for a little guy. I can barely pronounce it."

"Ah yes." Merced, hearing the name, didn't betray a shiver. "In Guatemala, we learn very young to say words of many syllables. Felicidad means happiness, you know."

"Nice. I guess that makes Jules an optimist," Tom said.

Half a dozen blocks up Reforma the US Embassy was a commanding presence on the wide avenue. They parked in back and Merced whisked them past guards, past a long line of waiting Guatemalans, through a security clearance and an immense bare room where several hundred more Guatemalan sat on folding chairs. "What are they all waiting for?" Sunshine asked.

Merced lifted an eyebrow. "Visas. To visit your country. And tour Niagara Falls, the Grand Canyon, the Lincoln Memorial." Sunshine couldn't tell if she was kidding.

The room for American citizens was smaller but equally spartan. Fifteen rows of folding chairs lined up before a bank of windows where immigration officials stood behind bulletproof glass. It reminded Sunshine of the DMV. They filed through clusters of American couples with their Guatemalan babies and toddlers. Sunshine's excitement grew. Merced led them to a row of chairs where a scruffy Guatemalan teenager wearing a baseball cap rose at their approach. After a brief exchange in Spanish he left and Merced explained. "Rony has been here since the embassy opened at six, holding our place."

They sat down to wait. Sunshine had come prepared. She

entertained Jules while they waited, reading to him from picture books she'd brought. She pointed to pictures and said, "Balloon. Bunny. Cow. Bear." Jules cocked his head to listen. He grinned. He liked the sound of her voice. She tried to get him to repeat the words. Finally they heard their names called, and Merced led them to a window. A grey-faced man behind the bulletproof glass looked at them over his computer screen without speaking. Standing behind Merced, Sunshine held Jules in her arms and sniffed the aroma of his hair, hoping he couldn't feel her nervousness. Even now the Boxers were in the air, heading home to Ohio with Lily. Oh to be with them! The grey face studied the computer screen, then shuffled through a thick ream of papers on the counter in front of him, pulling one out.

"Ms. Castillo de Armas, you're representing the petition for the visa?"

"Yes," Merced replied.

"What I don't understand is this DNA test done by a Doctor Álvarez here in Guate. The birth mother signed off in Huehue. Álvarez doesn't appear on my State Department Approved list." He tapped the computer screen. "And the birth mother's signature isn't on the test."

"That was the second test, Meester Locke." Merced was unruffled. "She signed the first one, in Huehue." Sunshine noticed the name on his badge: James Locke. Merced hadn't needed to look at it. She knew him, Sunshine realized with relief. Merced could manage the embassy hurdles.

Locke shuffled the papers again. "Not here. And she has to sign both tests. If she's illiterate there has to be a notarized thumbprint. I don't know how you got the pre-approval. Look, Miz Castillo de Armas, you run a reputable organization. It's not like you to bring in an adoption with incomplete paperwork."

"There's been a lot of estress. I'm sorry if there's been an oversight. We'll be back Monday with all the papers."

"Right. Make another appointment." He looked for the first time at the stricken family: Sunshine holding Julian, Tom pushing the stroller that held the giant panda. "Hey Julian," he said grinning. "Who's your friend?" He nodded at the stroller.

Merced spoke to Julian in Spanish. He ducked his head against Sunshine's breast, speechless.

"He calls his teddy Felícito," Sunshine said in a rush. "Mr. Locke, is there a problem? We've waited so long. We love him so much."

"Don't worry. You can wait a few more days."

«« — »»

Three months after she had taken to her room, while her father-in-law was still engaged in fruitless search, Lala had come out. She was pale and thin from her diet of oatmeal and black chilacayote. She went back to work, grasping at the hope that work could save her. Her third graders had not done well under the substitute, and she was determined to pull all fifty-five of them into shape for their exams in October. She drilled them on spelling and sums and the rivers and mountains of Guatemala, gave them extra homework and poems to memorize, and permitted no fooling around. When they were absent, she asked them why.

"Because I had to help with the farmwork."

"Because I went with my mother to Xela."

"My mother was sick. I had to take care of my little brothers."

None of these excuses was acceptable in Lala's view. She threatened to visit the parents and chew them out if it happened again. A couple of times she did.

"Do you want your child to grow up to be a blockhead

like you?" she would ask both the father and mother. "Do you want him to scratch his living out of the dirt like a chicken?"

People trembled in her presence because she was fierce and sad. She visited her mother in town, who cried when she saw how thin her daughter had become. "You have to eat meat or you'll die, mija."

"I'll eat meat when my babies come home," Lala said. For now it was only vegetables.

She was convinced that Cándido and Felícito would be back. She thought of them with every breath. In the classroom, with a student in the middle of a column of sums, she would suddenly see herself at home, on the porch, and feel Cándido's arms wrapped around her leg as they watched Felícito totter across the patio toward them, Lala calling, "Come! Come!" and Cándido shouting with laughter. Then she would come to, staring at the blackboard, at the third grader whose chalk had stopped moving, and who now was watching her. It would take a minute for the numbers on the board to make sense to her again, and then she'd say, "You forgot to carry the one."

When Cándido's face or Felícito's laugh would flash into her mind, she would feel like she was standing at the edge of a deep canyon, about to fall in. She tried not to think about where they might be right now, because it caused her too much anguish. She snapped at her husband and brothers-in-law, was impudent to her mother-in-law, and every day she asked Don Chepe at supper, "What did you do today to find them?"

Don Chepe was ready to smack her long before an evening in September when he returned from the phone call in his bedroom to the family gathered around the wood stove in the kitchen. Their conversation broke off. Everyone

75

looked at him. "The investigator says I should come to Guate."

"He's found them?" Lala said.

"Maybe."

"I'll go with you."

««« — »»»

Sunshine—with Julian in her arms and Tom at her side—left the American embassy Thursday morning, stunned. Why the missing DNA test? Who was Julian? He clung to her as she strapped him into the baby seat in the back of Merced's BMW. She popped a reassuring kiss on his lips, plunked the panda into his grasp, and went around to get in the other door. She couldn't stop the unsettling questions. Why the man with the camera in the hotel lobby?

Merced and Tom in the front seat were carrying on as though life was normal. "I know Jeem Locke well," Merced was saying. "He seems harsh, but once we get the papers to him on Monday, no problem! He'll be all smiles and congratulations when he gives you your pink slip."

"He's just doing his job," Tom said.

"Exactly. Everyone is very stressed these days. So many babies! So much pressure! Everything will come out well, you'll see."

Sunshine didn't see. In the back of the car, splashing through the rain, she felt herself drowning. She couldn't see Jules through her tears. She'd had a dream of taking Julian someday (when he was ten? twelve?) to a pretty village in the mountains to introduce him to his birth mother. In her gratitude the birth mother would say, "Thank you for loving my child."

"Our child," Sunshine would say.

And Julian would kiss her (tentatively, in the dream) and

76

look up at Sunshine and say, "We love her, don't we, Mom?"

The dream dissolved in tears. The car stopped. Her door opened. Tom said, "Buttercup! What's this?"

He pulled her to her feet. She swallowed, wiped her eyes with the backs of her hands, and said, "Nothing."

Together they loaded Julian into his stroller and reentered the Marriott to wait for Monday. Waiting. Was there anything worse? Especially in a hotel, in a foreign city, in a country with dysfunctional weather. That night, after Julian was asleep and Tom was watching TV in their room, Sunshine phoned Gail. In spite of her obnoxious husband, Sunshine felt connected to Gail. She'd been on the same infertility roller coaster, the hopes and disappointments. She'd toughed it out and gotten what she wanted, what every woman deserved—her baby. Sunshine needed to talk to someone, and she had Gail's number. "Let us know how it goes," Gail had said.

"How is it? Being home with Lily. Wonderful?" Sunshine asked over the phone, scarcely able to believe they were in the same time zone, on the same planet, Gail at home with her baby seemed so far away.

"It's crazy," Gail said. "People coming over all day long. Our whole church is giving thanks. Everybody has to see the new baby." The connection was so clear that even Gail's breathlessness communicated itself over the line. "Then they're shocked she doesn't look like Bob and me. They didn't realize before what it means to adopt in a foreign country."

"We didn't get our visa."

"Oh honey. I'm so sorry."

Sunshine explained that it was only a temporary setback, a missing paper, that they were going back Monday, that they were *sure* to be on a plane Tuesday heading for New Jersey. "I believe in my feelings, Gail. I just know that Julian is my baby. I've known it since we got the first picture."

"What paper is missing?"

"A DNA test. The first one. And there's something not right about the one we have."

"That Merced Castillo is sharp. She'll get your paperwork right, no matter what it takes."

"But Gail, . . ." Sunshine stopped. She didn't want to know what Gail meant. Not if it meant Julian wasn't her baby. "That man who took Julian's picture. What were the rumors you heard?"

"Terrible things. Babies being stolen. Girls getting paid for their babies, babies sold on the black market for their organs."

"Those things can't be true."

"You don't want to know what goes on there. Just take Julian and get him out as fast as you can. I'll pray for you."

For once, Sunshine found herself hoping for the power of prayer.

«« — »»

Tom could keep in a good mood—debt, delay, disaster, no matter what. It was one reason she loved him. Next morning over waffles he said, "We're getting out and having fun today, guys."

And they did. He found out about a movie theater a few blocks from the hotel in Zona 10, the safe zone. They put Jules in his rain bubble, Tom carried the golf umbrella, and they pushed through the drizzle like survivors. They found a multi-storied shopping mall with a fast food joint in front that looked so American they decided to give it a try out of curiosity. It turned out to be slow food. They had to sit at a table and get waited on by someone who didn't speak English. Tom made valiant attempts with his Spanish phrase book. "Look at this," he

78

said, studying the menu. "What the heck are 'divorced eggs'?"

He couldn't understand the waitress's explanation of huevos divorceados and ordered fried chicken. It came with a pile of black bean paste on the side. Tom laughed. "You don't get that at KFC!"

Jules smacked down the gooey black beans even though Tom and Sunshine didn't like them, and they decided there were advantages to being a Guatemalan baby.

The mall was smaller and crummier than the malls of Jersey, but it was clean and dry. Sunshine took Jules out of the stroller and let him toddle beside her holding her finger, stopping to press his nose and lips against the glass of storefronts. "Look," Sunshine said. "A Gap!"

Tom took Jules on his shoulders while Sunshine went into the store. She came back out disappointed. "They're knockoffs. Jeans for twenty dollars, but not worth even that."

"Just as well," Tom said.

They found the movie theater tucked out of the way in the basement of the mall, an odd place for it, they thought. They watched a Spanish dubbed Disney cartoon that none of them understood but all enjoyed. The day felt like a triumph, a normal family outing in this foreign place, proving in Sunshine's mind that they were a family.

That evening in the hotel their waiter told them the rain was causing mudslides. Houses were being carried down mountainsides, a whole village had been buried, and the Interamericana had been closed in the western part of the country. Scores were feared dead.

"That's the way it is in my country," he told them, putting down plates of soup. "It rains. People die. It is dry. Crops fail. People die. Death is the only thing Guatemala has enough of to go around."

Sunshine shivered.

«« — »»

Monday morning Sunshine opened the drapes on a brilliant blue sky. The city dazzled in every direction within its circle of green mountains. It was a miracle. She and Tom and Jules went downstairs to breakfast, and outside into birdsong and air that smelled like perfume.

Merced beamed from her car. "At last Guate shows you her pretty face."

The change of weather followed them into the embassy. Even the waiting room for Americans looked brighter. Jim Locke greeted them from behind the glass with the smile Merced had predicted. "Congratulations. The DNA tests look fine. All papers in order. You've got your pink slip, Julian Kelly. Go get your doctor's exam and come back this afternoon for your exit visa."

Exploding with joy, Sunshine hugged Merced. Merced hugged Tom. Just like that, by the end of the day, the waiting was over. In the new brilliance they went back to the Marriott like rock stars. Sunshine felt the glow of celebrity follow them through the lobby. They had their baby! They had their visa! They felt world-weary from their week, compared to the new arrivals in the lobby. Don't give up, Sunshine wanted to tell them. All it takes is patience and a good attitude. All it takes is American optimism, she wanted to say.

The good weather held. The sun shone down on them Tuesday on the way to Aurora Airport. The sun lit up the silver wings of the jet, Julian strapped between them, the engines roared and lifted, and Tom said, "Here we go Jules. Up, up, and away."

«« — »»

The sun had dried the puddles in Merced's garden. She opened the French doors of her office to let in the smell of jasmine and the shouts of the children playing, a sound that once had brought her such pleasure. Now she felt only sadness. She missed Prudencia. The loss was just the first of the changes that were coming, but like the first gray hairs that presage all the declines to follow, it hurt. Prudencia had been smarter and less spoiled than Merced's own children, and much more loyal. Whatever Prudencia had done would remain hidden, and so would she. There was no turning back now, after what Merced had had to do. This was a fight to survive. Without Prudencia at her side, she had no one. The future yawned, bleak and fearsome.

"Seño?" The muchacha had opened her office door while she was staring out into the garden. "People to see you." The muchacha gave her a card. She knew without looking at it.

"Send them in." Her voice was resolute. She closed the garden door.

Tecún Puac came in, followed by Don Chepe Ramírez and Doña Eulalia, whom the investigator introduced. Like Tecún Puac, the other two were the new Indians. Unlike him, they were dressed traditionally, Don Chepe in red-and-white striped pants and elegant black chaps, Doña Eulalia in an immaculate dark skirt and splendid magenta huipil.

"Please sit down," Merced told them, all courtesy. Don Chepe and Doña Eulalia sat. Tecún Puac stood at her desk and placed two photographs there, as he had the week before.

"My clients have identified one of the missing twins."

Merced picked up the photos and studied them without speaking. Sunshine and Tom and Julian in the lobby of the Marriott.

"Do you know them?"

"Oh yes," Merced replied. "They just adopted a little boy from my Hogar. Julian García Mendoza. Their names are Kelly."

"Where are they now?"

"They left this morning for the States. Julian got his visa yesterday. All his papers are in order. You can check with the embassy."

"His papers were forged. I can prove it. This is his mother."

Merced looked at Lala, tall for an Indian, erect in her chair, looking back at Merced with a haughty stare.

"I don't know how you're going to prove that," Merced replied matter-of-factly.

<<< — >>>

In his short life Jules had experienced many new things: new faces, new languages, new mothers. He was an expert at change. He liked his new mother. He couldn't understand her words, but he understood her body's warmth when she held him, her lemony smell, and the blue light in her eyes when she crooned his new name. Jules. He understood her name was Mom and his name was Daddy (not Papi). It annoyed him when Daddy tickled him to make him laugh when he wanted to cry because his ears hurt on the airplane (new word). But then Daddy stopped and his ears popped and stopped hurting and Mom let him stand up in the seat next to her (he'd been belted in a lot in the past week) and play with her long yellow (amarillo) hair, which he liked to do. He liked it when Daddy lifted up his shirt (camisa) and blew on his estómago (tummy).

A long time after more ear pain and more new people

and new language, he was belted again in a car (not carro) and arrived at a place that excited Mom and Daddy very much called home (not casa). There were animals (perro, gatos) and a new bed where he slept because he was tired when they got there. When he woke up there were lots of new toys, but his favorite was still the big bear (oso) he called Felícito. Now, like Mom and Daddy, he was starting to call it Felix.

‹‹‹ — ›››

Eulalia, Don Chepe, and Tecún Puac left Hogar Nueva Esperanza in a state. Don Chepe fumed, "That lying woman! She's a criminal. We should go straight to the PGN and denounce her."

"Calm yourself, Don Chepe." Tecún Puac was cool. "We must proceed intelligently. Doña Merced is a lawyer and well connected. The PGN and US authorities will not be easily persuaded. We must have all our ammunition ready. First we talk to Doña Merced's nephew, Rosario Peralta Castillo."

Tecún Puac drove his battered Toyota sedan out of Zona 10, into the sprawling, tangled zones of the city with Chepe beside him. In the back seat, Lala's thoughts were as chaotic as the traffic, veering from right to left, hope to terror. She barely heard the two men talking in the front seat until the detective's voice penetrated her despair.

"Marta was a girl working at the orphanage," she heard him say, "not too bright. She was caught stealing the pharmaceuticals they keep in the infirmary. Kept locked, but the staff, someone named Prudencia who has vanished without a trace, had a key. This Marta was fired and fled back to her village outside the city. I went there last week and found her."

"Is that what led you to the nephew?" Chepe asked.

"A circuitous route, like this one." The detective careened around a traffic circle.

Lala wanted Tecún Puac to drive straight to the point: how would they find her babies?

"Marta was holding a grudge, and willing to inform on the jaladores who stole your grandsons, Don Chepe, no doubt about it. She confirmed that one of the boys was brought to Nueva Esperanza."

"Only one?" Lala burst out, her heart contracting.

"The other was dropped at a fattening house."

"What is that?" The words struck her with dread.

"A place for young girls to go have their illegitimate children. Someone pays them to get knocked up and give the bastards up for adoption. It's a good business. You haven't heard of this?"

"We're from the country!" Lala snapped. "We don't have such places. Why would we?"

"Even in the country you have girls selling babies. Your servant, for example. Marta suspects that Prudencia, who was the head of the operation, sold one twin and brought the other one to her employer."

"Doña Merced," Lala said, feeling sick with fear.

"Exactly."

"Now what?" Chepe asked. They had driven through slums to reach a well-kept green park across from a high wall. Behind the wall they could see a maid hanging out wash on the second-story terrace of a house.

"The park is Kaminal Juyú, last remnants of the Mayan city that was buried by people like Merced Castillo de Armas." He turned left, away from the park and followed the wall to a gatehouse. "Merced's nephew lives in this colonia. Marta, who doesn't know the capital well, couldn't tell me where the

84

fattening house is. Rosario was driving that day. He knows."

A guard came out of the gatehouse. "Police," Tecún Puac said, flashing a phony badge. Under the badge ten banknotes beckoned. The guard stepped aside and pointed his rifle toward one of the houses at the end of a quiet street. Children played on green lawns. A gardener washed a parked car. So peaceful, so protected, Lala thought.

"Wait here," the investigator said when he had parked. Don Chepe moved into the back seat, next to his daughter-in-law. They watched Tecún Puac disappear into the house.

"I'm very afraid, Tat," she said, calling him father, which she didn't usually do.

Chepe patted her knee stiffly. "He's very good, this Tecún Puac. The best, I'm told."

"Maybe," she said. "But, my baby is in a *fattening house?*"

"It sounds terrible, I know." They sank into anxious silence. The minutes passed ominously, while Eulalia imagined a scene inside similar to the one in the lawyer's office, the Indian investigator rebuffed, outclassed. People like this could get away with anything. They built walls around their homes and their crimes and posted sentries to keep their victims out. They were heartless. She remembered the lawyer's green eyes, empty of all remorse. Did she not have children?

"Thank God!" Chepe exclaimed. The door of the house opened, and two men emerged. Tecún Puac was followed by a tall, slender young man, light-haired, wearing pressed jeans and a tailored shirt. Tecún Puac held the passenger door for him.

"Don Rosario has agreed to take us to the establishment where one baby was left," he said, starting up the car.

"I don't know anything about the place," Rosario said. "I just followed Prudencia's directions. Prudencia! My aunt's hatchet lady." He spoke in a high whine. "She's the one you should talk to if there's anything," he paused, as if at a loss for the word, "*illegal* going on."

"Don't worry," Tecún Puac said. "We'll take care of the hatchet lady—I like your language, young man—and your name will be left out of the undertaking. Your reputation will be protected." He spoke as if he had access to all the secret powers and brutality of the police.

They passed the gatehouse, Rosario turning away and shielding his face from the guard. "If our name isn't protected, my aunt will have you taken care of," he said.

Silence descended on the car, punctuated only by Rosario's instructions to the driver. Eulalia, her mouth dry, her hands clutched together in her lap, tried to believe she would soon be holding her little boy. She tried to imagine him, grown taller in the last five months, wrapping his arms around her neck, his lips calling her name, her tears of happiness dropping onto his. Felícito! She was sure it was him, sure that she could still tell her boys apart even after all this time. She had never needed to look for the little mole on the first knuckle of his right hand that the rest of the family used to distinguish him from his brother. The one in the photo, in the stroller with the Norteamericanos, the one Doña Merced had told them was in los Estados now, was Cándido, her dear Cándido. She would get him back too. She vowed.

"Left on Sexta Avenida," Rosario said. Tecún Puac turned.

"The next block, on the corner. Hotel La Luna, it's called."

They all leaned forward in their seats. Eulalia held her breath.

"Where?" Tecún Puac asked. "I don't see any hotel."

"The sign is gone. Stop here." They stopped in front of the crumbling façade. The place emanated abandonment.

Eulalia stayed in the car with Don Chepe. Rosario got out with the investigator and they peered through the barred entrance.

"I don't like this," Chepe said.

Eulalia bit her lips and pressed her cold hands together. She couldn't stop their trembling. She watched Rosario and Tecún Puac go next door, ring a bell, and disappear through a door. Even before they reappeared minutes later, and moved further down the block trying more doors, disappearing, reappearing, crossing the street, repeating the pattern, until finally they came back to the car, Eulalia knew.

"They're gone," Tecún Puac said. "The house is empty. No one has seen the owner in two months."

Eulalia broke into sobs.

⟪⟪⟪ — ⟫⟫⟫

Sunshine stood in her kitchen, looking out the window at Tom swinging Jules in the new swing set. The phone was pressed against her ear.

"This is Hugo Alvarado Escobar. I have important information about the child you recently adopted. Please call me immediately."

The voice, in heavily accented English, left a phone number, twice.

Sunshine's hand hesitated over the phone's keypad. She debated. To hear this message again, press 1. She didn't want to hear it.

To save it, press 2.

To erase it, press 3.

Her finger wavered between the two buttons and settled finally on 2. She put the phone down, feeling the earth spinning.

It was Sunday. They had been home from Guatemala for five crazy, sunny, joyful days. Busy days of running errands, doing laundry, canning tomatoes from the overabundant vegetable garden, mucking the goats' shed, feeding, tending, grooming, all with Jules at her side. Tom had gone back to his shop immediately, way behind on the cabinets for the Oak Lane kitchen, but she was taking a leave for as long as they could afford it. Maternity leave! Every moment of every day they'd been back had been precious, extraordinary, because now Sunshine had her boy. She was a mom.

What could the stranger's voice on the message have to tell her? Maybe some bureaucratic detail. A paper they had forgotten to sign, or a vaccination the lawyer needed to tell them about. Why hadn't the lawyer herself called? Who was this Hugo person? Should she tell Tom about the message? The phone call must have come in the morning, when they were over at his mother's, the whole family meeting Jules. Tom would never hear the stutter dial. She could dial back, delete the message, and pretend they never got it.

Instead, she dumped the bucket of apples into the sink and started washing. She'd go ahead and make pie. Cooking relaxed her. She watched Jules going up and down on the swing; Tom's back was toward her.

The phone message continued to nag at her while she peeled and cored and cut the apples into uneven chunks, darkening the blue autumn sky, eating a hole in her happiness. Hugo Alvarado Escobar intruded while she blended butter and flour, sprinkled it with water. She couldn't forget the name, although she'd only heard it once. She rolled out the crust. It stuck and tore. She patched and pinched and rolled the name away. She put the pie in the oven and let it fill the kitchen with a happy smell. Her kitchen was safe. Nothing could violate that. Tom and Jules came in to watch the game, eat pie, play in the bathtub, look at picture books, go to bed. It was a perfect day. But every time Sunshine passed the phone it seemed to light up with its secret.

Monday morning, another cloudless September day, Tom

went to work early. Sunshine and Jules fed the animals. She let him scoop the kibble for Molly. She laughed when he wrinkled his nose at the cat food.

"Kitty, kitty, kitty," she called. "Come on Jules, say kitty."

"Keedy, keedy," he said, in his funny baby Spanish accent.

They were coming in from the chickens and goats, Sunshine holding Jules by his little hand, toddling through the kitchen, when the phone rang. Sunshine stared at it and stiffened. It could be Tom calling from work, it could be her mother, who had been calling daily from upstate New York where Sunshine had grown up, it could be a robo call, anything. She could wait and let it go to voice mail. Something made her pick up the receiver and say hello.

"Meeses Kelly?"

"What do you want?" It came out fast, as if she were talking to a blackmailer. "I can't talk now." Jules meandered out of the kitchen and into the living room. She didn't want to let him get out of her sight.

"A mother's heart is breaking, Mrs. Kelly. She begs you to return her stolen child."

"My child is *not* stolen! I don't know who you are." She slammed down the phone and felt her happiness drain out of her. It was true. Her worst fear. But it couldn't be true. The man had no authority. If he did, there would be police, State Department officials, agents, Sunshine didn't know who. But not just someone she had never heard of, calling to beg. There would be warrants.

She hurried after Jules, scooped him up, hugged him. "You're Mom's baby boy, aren't you, Jules?"

She looked into his black eyes. They told her nothing new. She blew a puff of air into his face. He chortled. She swung him up into the air. He kicked and laughed and grabbed her hair in his fists. She hugged him again and nestled him against her.

"I know you are."

A horn sounded in the driveway and made Sunshine jump. It was a struggle just to keep herself normal. "They're here!" She lifted Jules and headed for the door.

Outside, the autumn crispness held, under a blue September sky deepening toward October. Sunshine's favorite time of year. Nancy, her best friend from when she'd lived in the city before meeting Tom, stood by her car, having made the journey from Queens. She hoisted Amanda out of her child seat to set her down on the gravel drive. The two-year-old ran toward Sunshine and Molly, barking in a joyful ruckus. Sunshine squatted to receive the girl, with Jules placed between her knees. "Hey, Amanda, meet your new pal."

Nancy came up behind her daughter. "Sunshine! He's gorgeous."

The two women hugged and Amanda tugged at her mother's jeans. "Mommy! I want to feed the goats." She tore around the corner of the house into the backyard.

The women followed at Julian's slower pace. Nancy studied the toddler. "He looks just like a little Mayan god. He's perfect! Girl, after what you've been through, you've got a winner."

Sunshine couldn't tell Nancy about the phone call. Nancy was her rock, through the fertility treatments and failed IVFs. Her cheerleader when the adoption came through. This first play date was just the beginning. Their kids were going to grow up together. She wasn't going to give up on that without a fight. She was determined. She wouldn't give in to the voice on the phone or the voices in her head. If that Hugo Escobar wanted Julian, he'd have to come and get him. He'd have to convince the US embassy and officers of the US law of his

90

evidence. Let's see how far he gets with that, she thought.

The goats jumped down from their perch on the roof of their shed and ran to meet Amanda at the enclosure. She stuck her fingers through the wires, trying to pat them. They poked their noses toward her. "Careful," Sunshine warned. "They nibble."

She opened the gate, shoved the nannies back, and let the people in. She gave each child a can of feed to pour in the trough. Excited children and prancing nannies nuzzling at them, what could be better?

"Goats! Goats!" Jules shrieked.

"His English is mostly nouns," Sunshine said.

"You *are* going to keep up his Spanish?"

"Later on," Sunshine said. She had shared her fantasy with Nancy, all those long months when Jules was just a photo and a dream and endless home visits and paperwork and waiting, of taking her boy back to Guatemala, her gift to him someday in the unimaginable future. Now the birth mother—not the imagined peasant woman who would press Sunshine's hand to her lips with teary eyes and murmur "Gracias, comadre"— now the real birth mother wanted Jules back.

No! Not the real birth mother. Sunshine wouldn't believe it. She made a rule. She had been making rules ever since Monday.

Never pick up the phone when it rings. Let it go to voicemail.

Listen to the message at once. She had listened to and deleted a dozen: from her mother, from Tom, from friends and colleagues she called back with excuses, sales calls she ignored. And two more from Hugo Alvarado Escobar that she deleted as soon as she heard his name, without listening to what he had to say. But for some reason she couldn't delete his first message. "I have important information" remained in her saved messages.

After feeding the goats and chickens and filling a bucket

with vegetables from the garden for Nancy to take home, Amanda wanted to swing. The women stood together at the swing set, each pushing her own, Amanda yelling, "Higher, higher!"

"Amanda's nonstop," Nancy said. "Fortunately, I don't have a farm to take care of. You must be exhausted. When does Tom get home?"

"He's in his shop until ten at night these days. He's got jobs lined up till doomsday, cabinetmaker to the rich and tasteful forever. It's OK though." In fact, it was good. Around Tom she couldn't trust herself. She'd never had a secret from Tom. She didn't know what he would do if she told him about Hugo Alvarado Escobar. Probably he'd tell her to ignore him, a fraud, a lone hustler. Probably Tom would get pissed, outraged at the guy's nerve. Not a shred of truth, Tom would say. What she was afraid of was what she would say to Tom: *A mother's heart is breaking.*

"I wish you could afford to get a little help around here," Nancy said. She also knew about the debts, and Sunshine's anxiety over them.

"My mother's coming next week."

"Your mother, a help? Hoo boy!"

Nancy was right. Sunshine dreaded her mother's arrival. Not that she would have any trouble keeping secrets, she always had from her mother, back when she was a teenager running with a wild crowd in her little upstate town. But the constant tension of waiting for the phone, and how could she screen the calls, with her mother right there watching? The children swung back and forth in dappled sun, a gentle breeze blew, her best friend stood beside her, pushing in sync.

A mother's heart was breaking.

<<<< — >>>>

Thursday morning Sunshine picked up the phone. She stared at it for a while, then switched it on and dialed her voicemail box. She listened to the message twice, writing down the number. She switched off the phone and paced. Jules in his high chair sucked contentedly on a sippy cup. Light glanced off the battered maple kitchen table they had inherited from Tom's uncle, along with the houseful of furniture, a hodgepodge of every decade since the 50s, none of it nice enough to be considered vintage, but serviceable. Homey. She sighed.

"I'm sorry, Jules. I have to do it. Let's just get it over with." He looked at her. She wished she could ask his opinion. Here she was deciding his fate. What did he want?

She dialed and waited until the ringing began and then was answered.

"Hugo Alvarado Escobar?" she said.

"Speaking."

"Who are you? What evidence do you have that Julian is the child you're looking for?"

The man went into an explanation, difficult to understand because of his accent and the faulty phone connection, that his associate was an investigator hired by a certain, Sunshine didn't catch the name, who recognized the photograph of her son, one of two stolen twins.

"Two?" Shock. Had she understood? Did two missing babies double or halve the woman's misery? "Have you found the other boy?"

"No, Meeses Kelly. He is most completely lost. Without a trace. The family's only hope is the boy Cándido, who is with you."

"If I bring Julian to Guatemala, what then?"

"We perform a DNA test on him and on Doña Eulalia. If

93

they don't match, you take him home again."

"And if they do?"

There was a pause. "You will not be prosecuted."

"And if I don't bring Julian to Guatemala?"

"We are working with the police. They will come to you. You could be charged."

"I don't believe you! If you had any authority, any real evidence, Merced would have called me. Or the State Department."

"I have moral authority. Do you want to steal a child?"

Another pause. "I'll think about it." She switched off the phone. "Oh God, Jules!" she wailed. "What are we going to do?" She stared at the phone in her outstretched hand as if it were a weapon. She heard a clatter.

"Mommy?" Jules had dropped his cup to the floor.

"It's OK baby." She put the phone in its cradle, picked up the cup. It was empty. "We'll get through this together." She ruffled his long black hair.

When Tom got home that night, Jules was asleep in his crib, the intercom on, and Sunshine was in bed, the light on, the TV on. She wasn't paying attention to the *Sex and the City* rerun. She listened to Tom pad down the hall to Jules' room; she pictured him taking a quiet peek, then he came into their room. "Hey, babe. How was your day?" He sounded tired and sweet.

She clicked the remote on Carrie and Charlotte. She stared at the blank screen through tears. "Oh Tom. We have to go back to Guatemala."

««« — »»»

Tom argued. It was crazy. They should seek advice from the blogs. They should consult a lawyer. Sunshine was

94

adamant. She had made up her mind. She didn't care what a lawyer might tell them. Tom called Merced, who told him not to worry, the adoption was entirely legal, but advised them not to come back to Guatemala under any circumstances. It didn't matter. Sunshine said she would go, with or without Tom.

"For God's sake, Sunshine! You can't do that. He's my son, too." He wouldn't let her go alone. They left the day after he installed the Oak Lane cabinets, her one concession. They needed the money. Two weeks after leaving Guatemala, they were back again, checking into the Marriott, old hands at its sliding doors and porters. Only Jules seemed unfazed by the somber return. He prattled in a variety of toddler tongues to his giant panda, clutching it in the hand that wasn't holding Sunshine's. "Call us in the morning when Mr. Alvarado Escobar gets here," Sunshine told the front desk.

She had insisted on meeting the alleged birth mother face to face. Sunshine was in charge now.

They'd finished breakfast and were back in the familiar family suite, when the call came.

"Hey, Jules, people to see. Let's go!" Tom said with forced jauntiness. He picked the boy up and hugged him to his chest. His voice broke when he said, "I don't know how you can do this, Sunshine."

In the vast marble lobby with its strollers and excited clusters, Alvarado Escobar, short and plump and not at all what she had expected from the voice on the phone, shook their hands and ushered them onto a bank of sofas. He drew out his cellphone and said, "Excuse me. They are coming. Their bus was delayed on the Interamericana, but has arrived."

Sunshine watched him, sick with misgiving. Why had she put their lives into the hands of this pudgy little guy? She watched families being joined in the lobby of the Marriott, the familiar cooings and cries and tears of joy, with Jules tucked in her lap. All she wanted, she thought, was what was best for him. What could that be? She tickled him under the chin, blew on top of his head. "Hey sweetums. What do you want?" she whispered.

Jules fidgeted, not understanding the meaning of the occasion, only that it was boring and that he was waiting. Across the lobby Sunshine saw the doors glide open and a group come through them—a man in bright red trousers and a shirt with a flapping red collar, a woman in a long dark skirt and top woven in purple hieroglyphs, and the investigator she remembered, the man who had snapped the photo. Alvarado Escobar waved them over.

"Here we go." Tom, sitting next to her on the sofa, took Jules' hand.

The three newcomers made their way to the space formed by the heavy sofas, the concrete urns and lavish orchids. Alvarado Escobar stood up. "Doña Eulalia, Don Chepe. Mr. and Mrs. Kelly," he said.

Sunshine wrapped her arms around Jules in her lap and watched the Indian woman's face looking down at them. The woman's dark eyebrows shot up, tears sprang to her eyes, her mouth opened in a muffled gasp of emotion. Sunshine couldn't tell if it was pleasure or pain. Then, holding herself back and erect, hands clasped over her chest as if in supplication, gazing at Sunshine and Jules with liquid eyes, "Mi hijo!" the woman said, and continued speaking in a rush of guttural sounds and sudden stops. Sunshine, heart racing, tightened her hold on Jules and felt his head cock against her breast. Again she wondered what was going on in his mind, as she had so often in the last two weeks. What did these sounds mean to him? The woman stopped, and Sunshine held her breath. Tom dropped his hand. The men were looking at Jules, even Alvarado Escobar whose only role was interpreter, even the investigator, wielder of the nefarious camera, even the older man in the bright red pants, everyone deferring to this exchange, waiting for Jules to speak, it seemed, as though a toddler of eighteen months possessed the wisdom of Solomon. Jules looked up at Eulalia and said, "Mami?"

The Indian woman strangled a sob and reached for Jules. Sunshine let him go.

STORIES

THE RACE

Fiesta in Todos Santos, and Fausto Mendoza Ramirez sat tensed at the rail, on the back of a bony white steed, his pick from the herd of rent-a-nags driven down from a ranch on the altiplano. High octane sun burned off the last scraps of fog slinking up green mountain walls, but couldn't dry the layer of ooze coating the road, sludge left from a month of cold drizzle and liquid sky—the month that Fausto had been back in Guatemala. His mount pranced and pawed the mud, jostled by more than a dozen horses and riders jammed into the road cut. Fausto yanked at the useless reins and tried to tighten the grip of his butt against the saddle. It was more or less his first time on a horse. The size of it, and his distance from the ground, alarmed him. He stuck his legs out straight, to show off his electric turquoise ostrich skin cowboy boots, the pride of his labors in the North, to the crowds gathered at the rails and on the steep embankment above the road.

"Oye, chico! Where'd you get the boots?" The voice came accompanied by a trill of giggles from a nearby cluster of girls, Todosanteras arrayed in their holiday finest, dark indigo skirts, bright hand-woven blouses, ribbons plaited into their long black hair. Fausto, twenty-three, felt his manliness shine. He flicked his pink satin cape. "Michigan!" he told them. In the city where he'd toiled knee-deep in blood and entrails these past six years. His hands, clutching the reins, had not yet lost their northern pallor. His hands felt like nervous foreigners in his native town. The North had drained his copper hue, but left his wide cheekbones and the curving Mayan nose that stamped his face, the same face carved on ancient stelae.

The white horse spun away from the adoring señoritas, nearly spilling Fausto. His stomach lurched to his throat and for ballast he grabbed at a bottle being passed among the riders, pressed in around him, ricocheting on their own bouncing mounts. The bottle was their only solace against the anxiety of the day. Fausto tipped back and took a pull of aguardiente, the clear fire he'd been drinking all night at the captain's party. The fire soothed the palpitations in his heart, the pulsing in his temples. The captain's party, like the nine days of ritual building up to it, was obligatory for those who rode in the famous race. For the last year, since he had declared his intention, swearing an unretractable oath, Fausto had been putting away money to pay: for the horse he rode, the slaughtered bull, the plumed sombrero and red-striped pants, for the shaman's prayers, the marimba and beer and aguardiente to entertain scores of joyful guests. His mother, in her dirt-floored kitchen, wept at the expense. "For this you came home, mijo? To risk your fool chicken neck?" At least, he told her with bitter humor, Uncle Sam had paid his return flight.

A man wrestled with the heavy rail at the starting gate. Fausto handed the bottle off and raised his reins. Around him horses snorted; men jittered, pressed thigh against flank, and prayed. The gods of their ancestors glared down from cloud cushions on the tops of grey-toothed cerros, the four guardian peaks at the head of the valley. It was November first, the Day of the Dead.

The rail pulled back. Fausto's heartbeat ratcheted up; he touched the lion's claw he wore on a chain for luck and remembered Ofelia's kiss. The horses, bucking, skidding, stumbling, and spewing muck, lunged through the gate and down the road toward Mash.

When he was four he had found a man's head outside the door of his house, resting in a pile of boulders. The head he had last seen atop his father's brother, a guerilla. The head was apparently a message that soldiers were coming to seek and exterminate the Guerilla Army of the Poor. Civil war sucked the inhabitants out of villages all over Central America, spewing them into mass graves and refugee camps. Government against people, neighbor against neighbor, no one could be trusted. Fausto's family fled that same day to the altiplano, and thenceforth lived far from the known world, in a wooden hut slouched against a huge rock, knocked askew by wind. Fausto never saw people, and he never missed them. He and his sister Flor and an emaciated dog they called Chita watched sheep on the empty plain, where tough grasses broke through rock and frost to survive. Their father Desiderio made sporadic treks to the distant market to sell potatoes and buy corn. Their mother Rosalinda ground the corn and made tortillas to fill their bellies. There were never enough tortillas. Even so, Fausto would save some of his for Chita.

By the time Desiderio announced to the family that it was safe to move back to town, Fausto had forgotten what it was like to have neighbors. His mother and Flor, now twelve and bored with sheep, greeted the news with cheer. Desiderio sold all the sheep save one and brought back costly skeins of thread—red and white, magenta, deep violet—and bolts of indigo cloth. While Fausto mourned the loss of his flock, with its sweet stupid ewes and clownish lambs so dependent on his manly protection, his mother and sister wove new clothes for the whole family. Their reappearance on the social scene would be decked in finery.

In the relentless rains of late October they arrived at their new house in the center of town, at the corner of a steep stone street that ran with a river of garbage. The new house was not much more promising than the old, except that in addition to its dirt-floored kitchen it featured a second windowless room in which they all could sleep. They tethered the last remaining sheep in the muddy yard. On November first, in the hour before dawn, Desiderio killed the sheep and hung it from the low limb of a peach tree to let the blood drain out. They all dressed in the new clothes: Fausto a small copy of his father in red-and-white striped pants, Flor a vision of maidenly beauty startling to her brother, and their mother, already big with the next baby who would be born in early January, holding the toddler Magdalena's hand. They paraded through town, through crowds of excited Todosanteros, meeting the parents' old friends and relatives who welcomed them back.

"The bad times are over," people said. "Don't talk about them." They joined the crowd on the high grassy bank to watch the race, Fausto's first. The horses thundered by below them. Fausto, standing as tall beside his father as his stature would allow, his shoulders squared, thought he'd never seen such splendor.

Later, Desiderio grilled the butchered sheep and invited all the neighbors in. The women gossiped among themselves, the men drank, and the children ate until they were stuffed, then ran around and ate some more. The celebration raged all night and into the next day, when it moved to the cemetery.

On the outskirts of town, the city of the dead was a packed place of narrow aisles between cement crypts. Here Fausto, dizzy with lack of sleep, straggled after his family, hemmed in on every side by revelers dancing on the tombs as marimbas played, and by mourners wailing their prayers, lighting candles and firing off rockets. He watched his father disintegrate with drink, become disheveled, dirty, incoherent, leaning into a knot of similarly foul men, whose combined efforts failed to keep them on their feet and so they slid into a pile of reeking bodies and lifted their voices in a chorus of ululations. Fausto, his mother, and sisters left the men in the cemetery and went home to clean up the mess in their new house.

"Will Tata die?" Fausto asked his mother that evening.

"Oh no, mijo," she laughed. "That's just the way men are. He'll sleep it off and be back tomorrow."

In fact, it was a year before Desiderio came back.

<<<< — >>>>

The muddy road out of Todos Santos meanders for seventeen kilometers through rugged uplands, through the hamlet of Mash, past the last ancient remnants of cloud forest being razed for firewood, to the inconsequential village of Chanchimíl, where the road dead ends in a space large enough for a broccoli truck to turn around. Only the first half-mile out of town is used for the race, cordoned off with posts and makeshift rails on the first of every November. Fausto bounded astride his horse, each collision of his buttocks with the saddle—an awkward contraption of leather and wood—sending a jolt up his spine that rattled his teeth and split his head. He saw with a blur the crowds at the rails and below them, on his right, the soccer field. He struggled for purchase, lifted his reins in front of him, and leaned back in the saddle, attempting to find a rhythm in its lurches. Beside him a rider flailed with a leather switch at his horse's rump and passed Fausto, spraying him with muck. Fausto swore, gritting his teeth in determination not to spill, not to fall behind. They galloped past a house perched high on the embankment on the left, the home of Santos, Fausto's grandfather. Its patio, carved out of the mountainside that overhung the narrow road, teemed with onlookers. Somewhere in that boisterous mass would be Fausto's mother, anxious for her son, with Flor and Flor's children at her side. On this day Rosalinda, who normally did not drink, would accept the bottle of aguardiente her daughter would press into her hand saying, "Nawita, this will calm your nerves."

Fausto knew all this was taking place as he clattered beneath his grandfather's house clutching the reins with one hand and a clump of mane with the other, for every year as a child, after that first exhilarating and horrifying fiesta when his father had departed, he had returned to it with his mother and sisters and, later, brothers. His family grew each time Desiderio appeared for a brief visit until there were eight children in all, at which point Desiderio gave up conjugal rights and left the family, broken but in peace, for good. Fausto's shaken brain pictured his mother in the center of the patio, imagined her in glory, since this year, for the first time in their family, Fausto had achieved an honor every boy of Todos Santos dreamed of. He had received the call to race.

<<< — >>>

With Desiderio contributing new mouths but no money, their poverty had deepened. Rosalinda countered the family's fiscal difficulties by rising daily before dawn to steam pots of chuchitos, gooey handfuls of corn dough stuffed with nuggets of spicy meat, which she wrapped in banana leaves and loaded into baskets. She and Flor carried the baskets through the streets from one end of town to the other, selling the chuchitos and gathering gossip. Doña Rosalinda's chuchitos became known as the best in town, and she among the most well informed of its citizens. Through these labors she added doubly to her town's well-being and made just enough money to feed and clothe her children and send her oldest son to school.

A year after their return to Todos Santos, on a crisp day in January, Fausto donned his best clothes, the red-and-white striped pants, the coarse-woven, pinstriped shirt made beautiful by its wide embroidered lapels, and shiny black shoes, for his first day of school. Rosalinda insisted that her son would not go to school barefoot, even though his feet cried out at the unfamiliar constraint. Leaving the little ones at home in Flor's care, his mother escorted Fausto on this important day, joining throngs of children funneling down through town, past the town square, the bakery, the fly-filled shops open on the street, to the great iron gates of the school. There Rosalinda left him, and a tall Ladino shook his hand.

"Good morning," the Ladino said in Spanish. "I am Don Roberto, your principal. What's your name, son?"

Fausto, nine years old and an urban dweller for over a year, had by now picked up enough of the national language to answer back, quaking with fear. His grandfather, and the incident of his uncle's head, had instilled in Fausto a mistrust of people in general, and a particular phobia of mixed breeds, like this tall, slow-speaking principal. Don Roberto's verbal examination revealed that Fausto's Spanish was rudimentary, and the principal directed him across the courtyard to the kindergarten classroom, where he squeezed onto a bench in a room dominated by Mayan children of all ages, identifiable by their copper faces and their similar outfits, the indigenous uniform of Todos Santos. Through the babble of Mam, their mother tongue, Fausto heard a voice in the row behind him hiss in Spanish, "Look at the poor Indian. Dirty scum has no sobrepantalones."

It was true. The black woolen chaps with silver buttons that all the other schoolboys wore were beyond the means of the chuchito seller. Fausto felt he might as well have been naked. He turned around to steal a glance at his tormentor, a younger and plumper boy, also paradoxically an Indian. Their eyes locked. The plump boy grinned and held his nose. "And he stinks!" he said, loud enough for Fausto to hear.

Although humiliated, Fausto cowered in silence, and made it a policy to avoid the bully, Oscar, in the schoolyard. Town life had already taught Fausto the power of wealth. Oscar's family was, by the town's standards, rich.

By the end of his first year of school, Fausto had mastered Spanish and learned to read. Money, it seemed, was not a requirement for academic acumen. Hunger was his motivator.

<<< — >>>

A half-mile out, Fausto, still connected to his white nag, met the end rail, and an oncoming charge. The horses, when they reached the rail, spun around, turned by the flailing arms of the gatekeepers, and headed back from whence they'd come. Fausto hauled on his reins, stood up in his stirrups, defying both horseflesh and gravity, and forced his horse to join the flow in its about-face. Bent to his will the horse ran, dodging those who still raced out. Fausto's confidence blossomed. Jubilant, he relaxed back into the saddle and into the rhythm of hooves. He anticipated the animal's lurches, pressed his legs to its sides, rocked with it, and carried it through its gallop. Now it was simply a matter of lasting out the race, lap after lap, jockeying for position among his teammates, until the time for his team was called and the next team took its turn.

He passed his grandfather's house again, and spotted the wizened man. He'd been carried out of the house and propped on a chair at the edge of the patio, looking down on the road.

"The race is long and hard, like life," his grandfather had told him. "There is no winner. The purpose is to bear up, to survive." Fausto could still hear the old man's voice, before the stroke that robbed him of voice and movement, lecturing to his son's son, his first and favorite grandson, treasured in the absence of the father, who had abandoned or been banished from the house, Fausto never knew which and never asked. The central puzzle in his life had remained an unsolved mystery, while Fausto, eager student of tradition, had listened to his grandfather. "The Spaniard tried to keep his horses away from the Indian. To make the Indian weak. The Indian prayed and made offerings on the mountaintops. The gods of his ancestors gave the Indian strength to ride in the race. When I was young," Santos said, "two ropes stretched across the road, above the men and horses. Live roosters dangled by their feet, within the reach of galloping horsemen. The contest then: to yank the heads from the hanging cocks. Ah, how the blood would spurt!—offerings to the gods."

Leaning forward, placing an arthritic finger on Fausto's chest, fixing him with his fervent eyes, Santos had intoned, "If a horseman falls from his horse and dies, the offering increases a hundredfold. The village will have good luck for a year. Tan fuerte! It is strong, the horserace of Todos Santos." The boy had shivered. It was as though Santos had become a shaman, speaking with the voice of gods. Fear and exhilaration had mingled with Fausto's hunger for his grandfather's favor. Fuerte, powerful were the customs of Todos Santos, even now, his grandfather had continued, his voice deepening, "The idea comes to a man to ride in the race. That thought does not come from here." Santos had placed his finger on his grandson's head. Fausto had stiffened and held his breath. "Not from his own head. The idea comes from the Owners of the peaks." He had pointed. Fausto had breathed and followed the finger, looking to the mountains. "T'ui Bach, T'ui K'oy, T'ui Xolik, Cilbilchax." Santos had named the ancestral gods, their names the same as the mountain peaks, and tapped again on his grandson's chest. "The man who gets the call must obey," he said. It was his fate.

Fausto reached the starting gate once more and slithered to a stop, triumphant, his first lap done. The team was taking a rest. The bottle of aguardiente passed again from hand to hand. Fausto gulped a celebratory swig and beamed at the men around him, his teammates, his townsmen. This day he would take his place among them. Now he wore cock feathers in his hat, a horseman, respected. He gulped again, a long draught, and let the fire enflame his heart and boil his brain. He scanned the crowd for familiar faces, caught sight of the pretty girls, and waved. They waved back. The rest of the day looked easy from here. Liquor-bold, he shook the reins, urging his horse back into action. He kicked his turquoise cowboy-booted heels into the nag's sweaty flank and leaned forward, diving into the tide of his fate.

<<<< — >>>

On graduating from sixth grade, Fausto showed up in a compound on the other side of town where his father lived with a second wife and her parents and brothers and their families. Here the houses were well built of brightly painted cinderblock and tiled floors. Through a doorway opening on the patio Fausto could see his half siblings watching TV. In the house where Fausto lived with his mother, television was impossible since they had no electricity. However, he didn't dwell on inequities, because he came with happy tidings. "Is Tata here?" Fausto called to the half-siblings.

Desiderio came out of the kitchen. "What brings you here?" he asked his son.

"Papá, I came first in my class! The principal wants me to continue studying." The words rang with his pride and he watched his father's face for approval. A new Chita had followed him into the compound and approached the kitchen door. Desiderio picked up a rock and hurled it at the dog. Fausto winced. The dog fled. "I need money for secondary school," he said, looking at the ground near his father's feet.

"More studying! How old are you now?" the father asked.

"Sixteen." Fausto was as tall as his father, but slender and fragile, he knew, compared to the barrel-chested man with muscular arms. His father was a house builder, a profitable trade, made possible by his advantageous second marriage.

"Too old for books," Desiderio said. "You can work for me. I'll pay you. Then, after a while, if you still want to go to school, you'll have the money."

Fausto accepted what for his father was a generous offer.

Desiderio was a harsh and unpredictable boss, who taught his son to be alert on the job by dropping a cinderblock on his foot. He was prone to binges, and sometimes would not show up at work, where Fausto waited for him, containing impatience, hopeful. One day they piled block on block, rebar sprouting from the tops of walls. "The rumor is that you're with Ofelia," Desiderio chortled.

In love, improbably, with Oscar's sister, a shy and blushing girl with buckteeth and eyes that slightly crossed, a little like a sheep, Fausto had felt freed from reality's grip. The romance, with its sighs and glances, its secret meetings on hidden paths about the village, had created in Fausto the delusion that love was possible, that desires could be fulfilled. Wishing to keep his secret sacred, he denied the rumor.

"More cement. Quick, quick, you mule." Desiderio stirred a mix of sand and water in a depression in the dirt. Fausto carried the heavy bag of cement. "Don't tell me lies, I've heard all about it. No beauty that Ofelia, but I suppose she puts out. That's what matters, no?" Desiderio swiveled his hips and laughed.

Fausto shook the upended bag with pent-up fury and let fall a cloud of powdered cement.

"Too much!" Desiderio grabbed the bag from his hands and heaved it aside. He thrust a bucket at his son. "Dios mío! What a dunce. Fetch water. Let's hope you're better at making love than mixing concrete, my son."

"Fetch it yourself!" Fausto said. He threw the bucket down and walked away.

<<< — >>>

A rickety Ferris wheel commanded the square in front of the town's sixteenth-century adobe church, towering in the mist that had redescended at the end of the morning races. The appearance of the mighty wheel in the village, as well as the temporary arcade at its feet, was an event of significance equal to the traditional dance of the Conquistadores taking place throughout the day. The wheel turned, the masked dancers shook rattles and false sabers and stamped belled feet, the incessant marimba beat out tunes, the crowds poured into the square. It was noon.

"Look at him! My son, the horseman. Come over here, boy!"

Fausto heard the call as he crossed the main street from the church on foot. Having left his bony steed corralled in a patch of lush grass below the soccer field, he was on his way to the captain's house for the mid-day meal. In the afternoon all five teams would race again, over and over, back and forth. Horse-sore and mud-spattered, Fausto wavered in his course.

"Come on, don't be stuck up. I'll buy you a drink!"

The slurred voice pushed and pulled at Fausto. Desiderio, desired one, raised a beckoning hand. Fausto had not spoken to his father in six years. Time had banked Fausto's anger to dull coals, but had not eased the emptiness. He made his choice, and detoured to the open window of the cantina, where his father leaned against the counter, flanked by three comrades. Desiderio's outstretched hand lowered onto Fausto's shoulder, patted the pink satin cape, and slid down the red sashes of the horseman's costume, as if savoring their fineness. "My son is a big man, who makes his father happy. Don Candelario, another pint of Quetzalteca!" He dug in his pocket and slapped a grimy bill on the counter.

Fausto accepted the tribute to their blood connection, took the proffered bottle. This would be his meal for the day. He greeted the other men: fat and oily Don Juancho the hotel-keeper, Miguel the pharmacist, and another he didn't know, who had a long face and hooked nose. "Fausto is a rich man from the North now, a norteño," Desiderio boasted.

"Norteño!" The hook-nosed man spat in the mud close to Fausto's turquoise boot. "Sold your soul to the Yankee devil, did you? Whored yourself to the whities for a buck. Like Miguelito here."

The words curdled Fausto's pleasure at his father's pride.

"The North was good to me," the pharmacist demurred. Everyone knew that American dollars had purchased his shop on the main street, its gleaming steel shelves, his shiny red pickup.

Ignoring Miguel, the anti-American continued to hammer Fausto. "What did you do up there, Fausto? Pick the white man's fruit or pick up his shit? Then didn't he lock you up and take your balls?!"

All eyes on him, Fausto tensed and clenched a fist.

"Nothing wrong with Fausto's balls," Desiderio snorted. "He's given me a grandson to prove it." The father encircled Fausto's shoulders with his thick arm, as if this were a familiar gesture. As if they had many years behind them, of planting and harvesting side by side and sharing manly secrets. A marvel, considering no word had passed between them since Fausto had stalked off the worksite, no announcement of the birth of Michael, an American citizen. The news had undoubtedly spread as it always did in Todos Santos, along the gossip artery that was the life of the town. Fausto took another gulp of aguardiente, felt the warmth of his father's embrace, and checked his rage.

"I have good work," he said. "Indoors. Honest. Good pay."

But the hook-nosed man squinted into Fausto's face and exhaled a miasma of unburnt toxins. "That was before you went to jail. Tell us, who was sticking it in your ass in prison, looking out for you while you were toning up those pretty muscles?"

Fausto slammed the bottle down onto the counter of the cantina. His father shouted, "Shut up, Bruno, you pubic hair!" and smashed his fist into Bruno's face. Fausto's rage turned to joy. His father! Springing to his defense, a jaguar defending his young!

Bruno's body, made limber by infusions of Quetzalteca, responded to the blow by bouncing back one of his own, catching Desiderio's ear in a sharp jab. Desiderio staggered against Fausto, who caught him with a howl of anger at Bruno. Desiderio growled, plucked a beer bottle off the counter, and swung it down against the wooden edge. The bottle shattered, leaving Desiderio wielding the splintered neck. Fausto jumped back. Desiderio slashed at Bruno's face. A thin stripe of blood sprayed an arc of red. Bruno lunged at him, grabbing the arm that held the broken bottle in his two hands and raising it above Desiderio's head. The two men stood locked in a delicate balance, inches from Fausto.

"Fight!" Juancho shouted. The crowds by the church looked their way, suddenly alert. People peeled away from the crowd and rushed toward the cantina, a few adolescent boys arriving first to cry encouragements. Fausto, adrenaline-pumped and newly fathered, grabbed Bruno by the shoulders and wrenched him away from Desiderio. The three men broke apart and reeled into the street, surrounded by a ring of onlookers. Bruno swung around to face Fausto. They glared at each other, breathing hard, until Desiderio suddenly dropped his weapon, and turned his back on his adversary to face the bar again. "Fausto, come have a drink!"

He took up the bottle of Quetzalteca and waved it toward his son and the swaying Bruno. "Come here, you asshole. A little more of this will calm your viper tongue." Again the bottle passed from hand to hand. The spectators gravitated back to the church, their bloodlust disappointed. Fausto joined in the chorus of drinkers, not yet sure to which Satan he had sold his soul: the golden dollar of the North, the fire in the bottle, or the man who'd given him his name.

««« — »»»

The week after he had dumped the bag of cement and walked out on his apprenticeship with his father, Fausto had met his sweetheart in one last clandestine embrace. "I'm leaving for the North," he told Ofelia. In the eighteen months he'd served Desiderio, he'd earned real money and saved it toward the dream of his own house. Now it was sufficient to make down payment to the coyotes, the men who for a price would take him across two borders.

Ofelia wept. "You'll die."

He kissed her tears and called her foolish rabbit. "Everyone goes. No one dies. Your own brothers are away there." Oscar and his notorious older brother Jerónimo, leader of one of the town's two gangs, had recently decamped for Michigan, leaving the older citizens of Todos Santos to sleep at night in peace.

"I want to come with you," Ofelia begged, aware that if she didn't, he'd most likely find someone else to share his northern bed.

"Be patient. I'll send you money as soon as I can, and you will come."

It took Fausto two years of working at the meatpacking plant and sleeping on a mattress on the floor of a frame house on the outskirts of Grand Rapids shared by ten Todosanteros—a house that for all its central heat and northern pretensions felt very much like the hut of his childhood when the icy winds from Lake Michigan seeped through its vinyl siding—to pay the debt he owed to the coyote, forward periodic stipends to his mother, and save enough for Ofelia's passage. When she finally joined him they moved into their own bedroom in the shared house. Fausto experienced a honeymoon rush of joy, Ofelia got pregnant, and for the first time their lives brimmed with possibilities. The gradual swelling of her belly matched a swelling inside his breast, which threatened to burst when the enormous womb gave forth its light and Michael was born. Here he was, a man with a son and a job living the American dream. Even his childhood enmity with Oscar had abated. So it was he found himself one night in a Michigan bar at the side of his brother-in-law.

With a group of Todosanteros they were toasting their native town on its most glorious day. It was November first. Michael was six months old, asleep in his mother's arms at home in their bed, while the men washed away the sweat and blood and grit and oil of a week's work. With each beer Todos Santos appeared more vivid, more cherished, more distant—its verdant mountain walls, its steep cornfields and humble houses, its ever toiling, ever lovely women with their long black braids, their faces round as the moon. The men at Dirty Pepe's bar raised a cry of loss and longing, like the wordless ayyayyay's that always linger in the pine-scented air over the town of all saints.

Here was Fausto with his brother-in-law and childhood tormentor sitting side by side on barstools in a place where snow would soon be swirling, and Oscar said, "Drink to my brother, a man on the rise. He'll go home to Todos Santos a rich guy and build a house of many stories."

Fausto, well into his second six-pack, juiced with nostalgia, emboldened by Oscar's accolade and feeling their collective strength, declared, "Next year, I'll ride in the race."

"Bravo!" shouted Oscar. "A rich man, an important man, you'll ride in the race." And he bought a round of American whisky so that every Todosantero at the bar could toast Fausto's ambitions and celebrate the sweetness of familial bonding.

Fausto himself remembered little more of the evening except that he drank twenty beers, for like any Todosantero, even when all else failed he could keep count. But he remembered his pledge to ride and knew that the idea had not come from his own beer-addled brain but from the gods of his ancestors. To go back on the pledge, according to his grandfather, would cost his life. So he began putting money away for the race.

Six months later he and Ofelia were celebrating Michael's first birthday. Michael had said his first word, "Tata." *Daddy* in Mam, the language of the household. Fausto visited the Tack and Trail on 68th and purchased the turquoise ostrich-skin boots with their cream-colored flames of inlaid leather curling up around the toes and wore them to Dirty Pepe's on Friday night. When he walked into the bar his brother-in-law, already well ensconced, shouted out, "Look at you, Fausto, wearing faggot boots!"

That was like Oscar, two-faced, always taunting, playing to the crowd. The Todosanteros at the bar laughed.

"Shut up, Coca," Fausto said, and sat down at the far end of the bar determined to ignore him. Oscar was not to be ignored. Grinning, he came reeling down the length of the bar, slapping hands with each Todosantero as he passed, ticking them off like so many notches in his belt. Arriving at Fausto's grimly turned back, Oscar gave one of the flashy boots a light kick.

"Tan bonito, hombre!" in falsetto. Again the audience laughed.

"Cut it out," Fausto said in a low tone.

"I always knew you were *gay*." He said the word in English with a drawn-out lilt.

Fausto whipped around and socked his brother-in-law with a blow that snapped his head back. Oscar roared, lunged forward, grabbed Fausto by the shoulders, and dragged him off the stool. The little bully had grown to be a large man and outweighed Fausto by thirty pounds. His fists pummeled Fausto's cheeks and ears and ribs. Fausto, never much of a fighter, couldn't land another punch. Oscar slammed him to the floor and kicked him until a rib broke and blood spurted from his nose. Finally the bartender came around and pulled Fausto out of range, gave him a wet rag, and told him to get the hell out of there before he called the cops.

Fausto staggered out into the night, a warm night in May flush with the perfume of the northern spring, and limped the ten blocks home. Ofelia shrieked when she saw him. "Your son of a whore brother," Fausto said, "I'll kill him."

Ofelia bathed his wounds and taped his ribs and tried to soothe him while Michael looked on with serious eyes. "Forget about it," Ofelia implored. "He's a nasty drunk, that's all. He fights with everyone. He didn't mean it."

But Fausto could not forget injuries that went back to the schoolroom and playground. His honor must be defended no matter what the consequences. He was, after all, a man, and any Todosantero knew what that meant. A week later he was waiting outside Dirty Pepe's when Oscar pulled up in his red Chevy pickup. Fausto held a tire iron.

"Hombre, what's up," Oscar greeted him, jovial, as though nothing had happened between them. It was possible he didn't remember.

Fausto, holding the tire iron in two hands, smashed the windshield of the pickup.

"Asshole!" Oscar exclaimed.

Fausto smashed the rear view mirror and went to work on the side panels of the truck, inflicting as much damage as he could before the police arrived. It was his first offense. He had no record. He was sentenced to four months in medium security prison.

American prison was not so bad, certainly nothing compared to prison in Guatemala, where you slept on a cement slab unless you had money to pay the guards for a

119

mattress. In the Michigan prison Fausto shared a clean cell with a large and mild Negro with whom he formed an amicable relationship despite their lack of a common language. The Negro appointed himself Fausto's protector and did not ask for sexual favors in return. Fausto's sojourn with incarceration was peaceful. He devoted himself to working out in the prison's weight room and met interesting people from all over Latin America—educated people, a poet, an artist who sketched remarkable likenesses, intellectuals whose only crime was crossing a line on the map. Ofelia visited him weekly, bringing Michael, whose vocabulary and charm grew exponentially. One day he would go to American school and learn English, like the children of the other immigrants Fausto knew, those teenagers whose accents were indistinguishable from any American.

Ofelia was working; they were saving money. Some of it would have to go to coyotes after he was deported, to pay for his return. Still, the future looked bright.

<<<< — >>>>

"I haven't been a good father to you." Desiderio had arrived at the teary-eyed stage of drunkenness. Fausto could not disagree, so he said nothing. They were alone at the cantina. It was time for Fausto to get back to the race. Desiderio gripped his arm, preventing escape. "It runs in the blood. Santos was not a good father."

"He's a good grandfather," said Fausto, buffeted by distaste. Even now that the old man couldn't speak, Fausto believed he still understood, believed in his grandfather's boundless care.

"Do you remember my brother's head?" Desiderio pressed on, locking his son with a glittering eye. Fausto would never forget. "Who did it? Who told the army when they came to Todos Santos? Who traded the names of the guerilleros for his own life? Who was the ear, the betrayer?"

Fausto shrugged with impatience.

"Santos." Desiderio spat the name. Fausto tried to jerk away. Desiderio's grip tightened on his arm.

"What are you saying?" Fausto said. "That's insanity. You're insane."

"They pointed a rifle at his breast and Santos betrayed his own son. This is why I never went back to my father's house."

Disgust rose like vomit, burning Fausto's throat.

<<< — >>>

The white nag balked and spun at the gate and set Fausto's head to spinning. The indigos and reds of the crowd kaleidoscoped against the green of the embankment, the chocolate mud of the road. Neither the nag nor Fausto was in any shape for the afternoon race; the horse had eaten too much of the rich valley grass and, accustomed as it was to the sparse tundra of the altiplano, was commencing to bloat, its stomach distended from an accumulation of fermentation gas. In addition, its front feet were growing hot and sore, inflamed by overeating. At the signal for the race to start again, a whistle that sent shivers over the mass of flanks and twitching ears, the white horse bucked from the gate and slithered out into the road on tender hooves.

Eagerness to keep up with the herd drove the lame horse forward in a lopsided gallop. The pain in its hooves shot conflicting directional signals into its fraught central nervous system that translated into an erratic lope, a veering from side to side. This was added to its normally superstitious vision of its surroundings, seeing threats and predators in the most benign roadside objects. The waving of a hat or kerchief could be a swooping hawk. A darting child could be a venomous serpent.

Poisons had accumulated in Fausto's bloodstream, the result of so many bottles of Quetzalteca he had lost count, as well as too many insults and revelations. He was no longer able to settle into a rhythm on the unsettled horse. In fact, his rear end had developed a number of points of excruciating soreness, as had his thighs and knees from stretching around the horse's girth. Every jolt, every lurch, every hard connection with the ground sent ripples of the pain afflicting the horse's hooves—pain that Fausto, not a horseman, unfamiliar with horsely disorders like bloat and founder, was unaware of—up into Fausto's own body. As if he and his horse were now united in pain.

United in pain but not in movement. Daylight appeared between Fausto's butt and the saddle at each rise and fall. Horse and man rocketed down the slippery road like a bad cartoon, a caricature of parts out of sync. Thus it went, the afternoon race, Fausto clutching at the mane and sometimes the neck of his horse, a man out of control.

This was not uncommon at this stage of the day.

Fausto made the first lap, and the turn at the rail, and murmured his thanks to God, *chajóntate Dios*. He made his second lap, and returned to the starting gate. There stood his father, beaming in drunken pride, an unwholesome sight. Fausto pulled up on the reins.

"Fausto! Your gift to the gods." Desiderio thrust a live rooster by the neck into his son's hand. Tradition dictated that he accept the gift. Holding the neck, Fausto whipped the body of the rooster hard on the flank of his horse. The suffering animal leapt into action once more.

This was also the rule.

Now Fausto would carry the rooster as a switch, a prod, a sacrifice, a sign of the endurance of the Indian over his Spanish conquerors. Neither he nor anyone else at the race knew the significance of the roosters, but they knew there was some important meaning, buried in the past. At the end of the day, the roosters, beaten to death on the sides of the horses, would be offered to the shamans.

Except that, before Fausto's rooster had a chance to entirely die, the white horse made a sudden stop. It was midway down the course, across from his grandfather's house, where his mother and sisters and brothers were eating and drinking and watching the pageant of the afternoon, again cloudless, gracias a Dios.

What made the horse stop? No one will ever know. The chimera of some ancestral enemy, a saber-toothed tiger perhaps, in the crowd. Fausto however did not have time to ponder unanswerable questions. He could not stop. His forward momentum carried him on, over his horse's shoulder, past the roaring of the crowd, beyond his mother's scream, his sister's gasp, the wordless stare of his grandfather, took him in a forward arc that encompassed all the days of his past, the head on his doorstep, the lonely altiplano, his dog Chita, the tossed bucket, and connected his past with the future, so that he saw his son Michael graduate from elementary school in Michigan, then high school, then make it halfway through community college before he gave it up and joined the army, beyond which Fausto couldn't see because at this point he had finished the arc and returned once more to earth, headfirst, his delicate skull that held in its bony embrace all his hopes and feelings and even his love for Ofelia, crashing against the rock of his ancestors.

TURISTA

"Un descanso, por favor!" Elizabeth gasped. A rest, for God's sake.

An American woman, in midlife and freshly divorced, she had shed the constraints of New Jersey and left the known world for Guatemala. Booted and clad entirely in exploration khaki (even her close-cropped hair was khaki!), she clambered up a steep trail after her native guide, gulping in air woefully deficient in oxygen. At well over ten thousand feet, the atmosphere made up in frigidity for what it lacked in sustenance.

The guide—his name was Álvaro, he'd informed her at the outset, with a jauntiness that implied that the very name was a source of self-satisfaction—was half her age at most. He sprang up the trail like a goat, his long black ponytail swinging behind him. Her words brought him to a halt.

"But of course!" The guide sat down upon a boulder placed serendipitously next to the trail, not far from a brook that gurgled amongst precipitous pines. He patted the rock's flat surface beside him. "You're tired. Sit!"

He flashed her a charming smile. His white teeth blazed in a face as smooth and copper as a Mayan god. He called her *tú*. She called him *usted*, adhering with rigor to the formal *you*.

She declined the invitation to sit next to him, choosing instead a moss-covered embankment by the stream. Fog enveloped them, damping all sound except for the brook dropping into a small, dark pool, and Elizabeth's rasping breath. The guide took two bottles of water out of his knapsack and handed one to her. "Here," he said. "Refresh yourself." Again the overly intimate *tú*. "You must not drink from the mountain."

His voice radiated . . . what? It was a delicate question. Concern, Elizabeth decided. That was it, professional concern for the tourist in his care. He'd come recommended by the hotel. She had confidence in him.

"I never drink ground water," she said, wanting to make the rules clear. Not even in the comparatively safe temperate zones. Certainly not here, where the ground oozed amoebae, giardia, malaria, dengue, and other diseases too gruesome to ponder.

"You don't understand," her guide reproached her, raising knowing brows over his obsidian eyes. A silver stud flashed in the nostril of his regal Indian nose. The piercing, the ponytail, the lion's claw necklace—was he a member of a drug gang? Surely not, so far from civilization, eight hours of rough road from the capital, in this remote sierra tucked in the western edge of the country, climbing La Torre, the region's highest mountain. "Nature here is pure," he said with authority. "The dangers of La Torre come from its evil spirits."

"Ah yes." Elizabeth pegged him: the superstitious native. Harmless enough to a woman like herself, well educated, armed with facts.

"I'll tell you a story about a man from La Ventosa." He removed food supplies from his pack—a bunch of miniature bananas, a plastic bag of crisp orange cheese doodles, fresh baked rolls—and laid them out in a seductive array. He and Elizabeth had left the village before daylight, ascending in the bitter dawn, sunrise breaking over them like a rose-foamed wave, before the obliterating clouds of the rainy season descended. After hours of hiking they were hungry.

Elizabeth took one of the bananas. It was tiny and swelling with promised sweetness, but its tough skin resisted penetration, and she was forced to rip into it with her teeth. He watched her intently.

"This man of La Ventosa, down there," the guide continued, pointing with his lips into the swirling mist below them, toward what, if it had been visible, would have been a cluster of adobe huts in a wide, bleak plain, "was up this way last year, gathering fatwood." Another gesture with the lips—how thick and elastic they were!—toward the scarred trunks of the pines around them, where the dark bark had been slashed by machetes to reveal the red flesh of the tree, dripping with resin. "We use the fatwood to light our hearth fires."

"Yes. I know," Elizabeth said. Although recently arrived on the bus from the capital, she liked to believe that she knew far more about his village than the youth imagined.

He fixed her with the practiced flicker of a smile. "In this cold climate, there's never enough fire. Well. The man came upon a pool—perhaps this one beside us, it's not known—a fresh pool filled to the brim with cold, clean water. The man, a simple campesino, stooped to drink. The sun was out that day, and he was hot from his work." Despite the piercing chill of the fog, Álvaro had cast off his jacket. "Gazing down into the pool, it was deeper than he had at first glance suspected, he saw in its glassy depths a large armadillo. Imagine! Like this!"

He lifted his hands to indicate the size of the creature. His thick arms extended from a black tee shirt. Elizabeth's eyes followed the arms, sliding over muscles that appeared powerful and tensed, and rested on his hands, his long fingers surprisingly refined for someone who worked outdoors. A sudden heat coursed over her, jangling nerve endings throughout her body. She silently cursed her time of life, shook off her fleece, and raised her eyes to his. She could tell that he had seen the flush in her cheeks.

"What?" she said. "Pardon. I didn't understand." She blamed a momentary failure of her Spanish.

He repeated. "The campesino lifted the creature out of the pool. A whole armadillo, a delicacy—enough meat to feed a family. It was still fresh, just drowned, the peasant assumed, and preserved in the icy water. The man took the armadillo home to his wife, who made a soup from it, with potatoes and tomatoes and wild greens from the mountains. So rich! The flavors enhanced by the country air." Álvaro moistened his lips with his tongue, as if he could taste the soup. Elizabeth, watching, felt her own mouth water. "The whole family feasted—the man and his wife and their four little ones, and the man's sister-in-law and her children, and one ancient grandmother. How happy they must have been when their bellies were full!"

He stopped to peel a tiny banana and slip it into his mouth, savoring the taste with eyes half closed. Elizabeth took an orange doodle and bit into it with a crunch. Its salty tang was comfortingly artificial. "Have you ever eaten the armadillo?" the young man asked.

"Heavens no." Elizabeth pictured the gleaming aisles of her supermarket, the meat plastic-wrapped and labeled with assurances of its hormonal purity. Armadillo indeed!

"You should. It's very sweet, very tender. Like so much that grows in the country." He said this with worldliness, as though he'd sampled the cuisine of many cities, or as though he had introduced many a jaded foreigner to earthy pleasures.

"Maybe we should go on," she said, glancing up the formidable trail.

"In a minute. There's no hurry. We're near the summit, and from there it's an easy stroll across the altiplano, and back down to the village before night. It's better to cool off before we climb again." He moved down from his boulder to crouch next to her, to reach behind her and plunge both hands into the waterhole. "See how clean it looks." She twisted around to gaze into the depths of the pool, at his refracted hands disturbing the water. He cupped his hands and raised them to splash the water over his bare arms. The heat had left her, and she shivered. He dried his arms with a bandana, which he proffered to her.

"Do you want to wash up?"

Her fingers were orange from the doodles. She dipped them into the pool. It was achingly cold. She rubbed her hands together and withdrew them, shaking off the water. He dangled the bandana until she took it and dried her hands.

He settled beside her on the mossy hummock, so close that their thighs touched, through the layers of khaki and denim. Elizabeth tensed, but there was no more room on the embankment for her to pull away. The pool was at their backs. They both looked out, across the trail, to where the mountainside dropped into cloud. Álvaro said, "Now you must hear of the danger that lurks in this water."

"Only now?" She tried to make her tone joking. "Isn't it a bit late?"

He chuckled, and rested his hand lightly on her leg, just above the knee. The gesture stunned her, but she didn't push the hand away. It was flattering, in a way, considering that he was scarcely older than her son (a teenager safe with the ex-husband, in distant New Jersey). She pretended to ignore the hand, and the guide continued with his tale. "Only one family member did not partake of the armadillo soup. The man's brother was away, on a journey into town. It was he who found them, on the day following the fateful meal, when he returned home. He found them all, from the old grandmother down to the littlest child, his own baby boy, every one of them stone dead." He stopped speaking and stroked her thigh with one finger, idly.

"What did he do?" Elizabeth asked, as much to distract from the alarmingly pleasant hand on her thigh as to move the story along. He looked at her with the raised eyebrow again. Of equal height, they were shoulder to shoulder, and his face was close.

"He called for the police. He believed they had all been murdered. The authorities came, but they could find no clues of a murderer, and no marks on any of the bodies.

It was the brother who found the shell and entrails from the armadillo, that his sister-in-law had put away for another use. The police opened the intestines of the armadillo, to discover remains of a poisonous snake. The armadillo had not drowned after all, and the deadly venom had spread throughout its flesh and blood."

"You would think," Elizabeth, looking away from him, observed tartly, "that a man of the country (*hombre del campo*, she loved its sound in Spanish, virile, mythic) would have known better than to eat carrion."

"You would." Álvaro's hand moved up her thigh, and she swung around to give him a warning look. Again the obsidian gleam in his eyes. "The spirit of La Torre, its dueño, has the ability to confuse a person. For example, this water that looks so refreshing!" Snatching the bandana from her, twisting around, he dunked it in the pool. He wrung it out with a flourish, then pressed the damp cloth against her face, cupping her cheek. She heard ringing in her ears and thought she might pass out.

"There," he said with evident satisfaction and took the cloth away. "Do you feel better? Rested?"

Rested? She searched among a catalogue of sensations—agitated, stimulated, repelled, attracted, horrified—none of them restful. He stood up, perhaps taking her silence for a yes. "Let's go on. At the summit there's a little hut, a rustic place, but cozy, and an old man who'll sell us hot coffee." He held out his hand to her, to help her to her feet, and she took it.

"The dueño, no doubt," she mocked. She considered this a slippery word, translated as owner, or landlord, or old fashioned lord. "Who poisons the coffee."

"No." Álvaro smiled, pleased by her banter. "Just a paid guardian. The dueño is a spirit lord. He lives in a deep cave and only comes out on a white horse. If you see him he takes your soul."

"I doubt I'll see him," Elizabeth said. After this, the conversation lapsed, as they were climbing again, and Elizabeth, for one, had to conserve her breath.

<<<< — >>>>

Rain pounding on the corrugated tin roof of the hut made a deafening thunder. Álvaro poured boiling (Elizabeth hoped) water into a chipped mug and stirred in instant coffee. How long, at 11,000 feet, does water have to boil to kill microorganisms, she wondered. Forty-five minutes? But, perhaps giardia was the least of her worries, considering what she'd just done. The thought caused her to laugh (secretly) at herself. Of course, she wasn't superstitious. He placed the mug in her hands. "Drink," he said. "It will be good for you."

And what was in his tone? Concern, she decided . . . for the tourist in his care. She was . . . grateful. He put more wood on the fire, which burned on an open hearth on the dirt floor, filling the hut with smoke. He had assured her when they arrived in the pelting rain, ducked into the structure—an ad hoc assemblage of boulders and rough wood and odd scraps leaning against the wind—and found that the old man was not at home, he had assured her that the guard was off gathering firewood, was sheltered somewhere, and would not return until the rain stopped. The fire had been banked, the coffee pot readied; a sign scrawled in English in pencil on cardboard propped against a stone wall read "Coffee—Self Servis, 1 Quetzal."

"I know the guard," Álvaro had said. "He would want us to make ourselves at home." *En nuestra casa.* He had made the words inviting.

He had built up the fire. Chattering with cold she had peeled off her wet clothes, draped them on a bench in front of the fire to dry, and allowed him to warm her under the pile of blankets in the corner. It was all so easy, his skin smooth and soft, and quick. Restorative. And now, wrapped in a blanket, she waited for her clothes to dry, for the rain to stop, for the old man to return, for the spell to break and let the toxins in. Holding the mug in two hands, she took a sip.

The Flor

Felix Pérez Cruz drove the last bus out of Huehuetenango bound for Todos Santos, the bus called the *Flor de Cuchumatán*. The night his mother died, as it would turn out, he was driving too fast, and the *Flor* went off the road on the curve above my house, tumbled ninety meters down the mountainside with a big clatter of metal and rock, and landed upside down on my patio. My husband was in town with his lover, that brazen seductress Hilda Florencia, and I had only the help of my two eldest children, roused by the tumult. I flipped on the outside light and sent my Marta running down the path through the milpa to the neighbor's house—it was July and the corn was already taller than a man's head; the trail was slippery with mud from rain that had just stopped, gracias a Dios—while Moisés and I entered the bedlam of the bus, climbing in through the open door.

Felix Pérez Cruz lay unconscious near the door, wedged in against a sign pronouncing "The Lord will watch over your going and your coming now and forever," that had been above the windshield when the *Flor* was right way up. Blood streamed out of a gash in his forehead. Beyond him Miguel, the bus ayudante, picked through a tangle of wailing people, sprawled in a mess of shawls, hats, and bundles spilling all the usual things people bring back after a day in the department capital—a pair of black patent shoes, lengths of PVC pipes, a stuffed Hello Kitty doll. The people and stuff were piled over baggage racks on the ribbed metal ceiling, now the floor, of the bus. The smell of their fear cut through

133

the damp night air, the smell of vomit and piss. One woman screamed over and over, "My baby, my baby, my baby!"

Miguel helped the people crawl through the bus, under the seats suspended overhead, Miguel carrying children and grandmothers, one by one to the door, where Moisés and I got them out. We spread blankets for them to sit or lie down on. By the time Don Enrique arrived, breathless from hauling his bulk up the path, with his wife, the curandera Emiliana, and my Marta, most of the passengers were out, all alive, gracias a Dios, and the shrieks had quieted to moans. Don Enrique and Miguel together wrestled Felix Pérez Cruz out of the *Flor* and carried him to my bed. Doña Emiliana and Marta set to work washing cuts, rubbing salve on bruises, splinting and binding broken bones, and spitting chewed leaves of ruda in the faces of the survivors, to protect their souls from the dangerous aftereffects of their fright. Doña Emiliana had brought the ruda from her medicinal garden.

Meanwhile, I ministered to Felix Pérez Cruz, a youth not much older than Moisés, who already had a bad reputation in Todos Santos—it was said he stole from the owner of the *Flor*—and would now bear the additional burden of the crash and the destruction of the bus. No doubt the authorities would make him pay. He'd lost enough blood to make his face pale, unless the pallor came from a vision he'd had right before he lost control of the bus, felt it slide sideways across the gravel of the road and plunge over the edge. Unconsciousness would have come as a relief. Nevertheless, I brought him back from it, after stanching his bleeding wound and pulling the flaps of skin together with adhesive tape, by using a rag soaked with aguardiente. After his eyes flickered open, looking huge and black and lost in his gaunt face, I put the bottle to his lips, although the consumption of spirits is against my religion, and told him to drink.

There are some kinds of pain that liquor can't blunt.

I felt a great surge of pity, tenderness, felt my bruised heart break for this failure of a bus driver in my arms, and that was how it began. After all, as my husband is so fond of reminding us every Sunday when the culto gathers in our patio to listen to him preach brimstone and salvation: to err is human, to forgive, divine. In which case, Mundo, who spends all week erring with Hilda Florencia only to be forgiven each Saturday when he returns to us, is over-filled with divinity. Being much in the forgiveness habit, I shushed Felix Pérez Cruz when he struggled to sit up, apologizing for the blood on my blankets, the bus on my patio, the owl of calamity hooting on my rooftop.

"Doña Clara Luz, I must flee," he told me. "I saw my mother's face in the rear-view mirror."

"Mijo," I told him and pushed him back down. "You are in no condition to even stand."

I said this as well to that pubic hair, the police chief, who made his appearance as he always does long past the time he could have been helpful, after the survivors had been bundled off by various conveyances to the hospital in Huehue or their families down the valley in Todos Santos. Our community, from long practice, knows how to deal with emergencies. The chief, despite my protestations, insisted on taking Felix that same night into custody and I insisted on riding with them as far as the altiplano because I had promised Felix I would look in on his mother.

The chief let me off in La Ventosa, as miserable a spot as there ever was on a cold night, and Felix told me how to find his mother's house in that cluster of huts where the wind never ceases to howl and you are more likely than not to find a sheet of ice in your pila in the morning. I picked my way by stars up a path through boulders to the house Felix had described, where light leaked like a bad omen out from chinks in the eaves. I pushed open the door, which was unlatched, and found a single room lit up by a fire blazing on a dirt hearth—if Felix was a thief, he wasn't a very good one, unable to provide even the comfort of a cement floor or cinderblock stove for his mother's shack—and candles everywhere. It seemed all the women of La Ventosa, women I knew from the market at Todos Santos, were in the room, gathered around a mattress on the floor.

In a corner of the room, a clot of children with dazed faces huddled together, clutching one another. Everyone stared at me, as if I were a phantasm.

"Felix, the bus driver, sent me," I said, to assure them that I was of this world.

"Ay ay ay Dios!" one woman moaned. "Is the son dead too?"

Of course, the import of the vision in the rear-view mirror was obvious from the motionless, worn-out rag of a woman on the bed. Her funeral vestments completed, even her best huipil and corte were tattered, the women from the village crossed themselves, knelt back on their haunches on the dirt floor, and commenced the ritual caterwauling that always accompanies these occasions. It was the middle of the night. I had no recourse but to join the mourners and offer my prayers for the sobbing orphans, five of them, the eldest not more than ten, helpless as newly hatched chicks.

<<< — >>>

That Sunday, by divine law a day of rest, the Lord granted permission for the task at hand, and the entire culto, over a hundred people, as well the owner of the bus, Porfirio Ramirez Mendoza, and a hired ox, set to work with ropes to right the *Flor*. Two hours later, the shattered hulk was hauled off the patio to rest on busted tires, a miracle, surely as the ark on Ararat, my husband proclaimed, citing scripture: "On the seventeenth day of the seventh month (the very date, as it happened, of the accident) the ark came to rest on the mountains of Ararat." The ark of the *Flor* had carried the souls of sinners over stormy seas, Mundo proclaimed, and delivered them to the land of repentance. My husband certainly has a golden tongue, to have created an ark out of that heap of metal that, even before the accident, had been a wheezing cast-off norteamericano school bus, bought used, resurrected, and repainted a spangled red and gold for its afterlife as the *Flor*. And would be resurrected a second time, Don Pilo, its owner assured us after the sermon, which he attended although he is not Evangelical. The sight of his ruined bus had reminded him that Death awaits us around every corner, always ready to pounce, and inspired him to prayer.

The engine still worked; the chassis was still strong. Don Pilo intended to fit a new body onto it.

"In that case the bus is not a total loss," I told him.

"Gracias a Dios," he said.

"Perhaps you can show mercy to Felix Pérez Cruz, whose five younger siblings have no one to provide for them while he is in jail."

Don Pilo snorted. "The boy belongs in jail. I was planning to sack him anyway."

"If you will renounce your claim against him—fíjese, you've no more chance of recovering money from him than squeezing honey from a lemon—and give him back his job, I guarantee he'll never steal from you again." I was standing at my husband's side as I spoke, taking full advantage of my righteous station as the preacher's wife. "I plan to save his soul, wretched sinner though he be."

And who was my husband to object to such a plan, busy as he was evangelizing that hija de puta, Hilda Florencia?

My argument, plus the promise of at least a partial restitution over time through garnished wages, persuaded Don Pilo.

««« — »»»

My husband had begun spending nights in town a year before the bus accident, in a small room in the back of his pharmacy on the calle real, the main street of Todos Santos. Occasional nights, at first. He claimed exhaustion after a long day of tending to the bodily aches and illnesses of his customers—poor man!—just as he succored their spiritual pains on Sundays. Also he had to rise early in the morning to open the shop. I'd suggested the whole family should move into the pharmacy. But no, he said, there wasn't room for four children, let alone the little ones he believed were still to come. I didn't tell him there would be no more, that I'd had the operation after baby Ezequiel was born, that for me, four was enough. Mundo wanted to be the father of a tribe: nothing was ever enough.

It was true, the back room of the pharmacy was too small for a family. There was barely enough room for one double bed.

Besides, Mundo didn't want to live in town, he claimed at the time. The noise, the crowds, the drunks, the bus fumes. Only in the peace of the country, in our house high perched in the mountains where you look straight into the eye of God, could he hear messages from our Lord. At the time, I believed that Mundo spoke with the voice of God. Not a large man, my husband, nor overly handsome. His nose was too long and curved, his moustache thin like the hair on top of his head, his chin too pointed. But he gave off sparks. He paced. He gestured. His whole body energized by fervor, by

138

spirit that flashed from his eyes like electricity. No one could escape the excitement of his presence.

I basked in his glow. I was proud to be his wife, I won't deny it, and you know Proverbs 16: "Pride goes before destruction, a haughty spirit before a fall."

My fall came swifter than the *Flor's*.

Mundo's nights in town became more frequent. I went to Emiliana, the curandera, my dear neighbor and comadre, who delivered all my children but the last—Ezequiel came by emergency caesarian in the hospital in Huehue, after forty hours of useless labor, and that was when I asked the doctors for the operation so there would be no more. Emiliana who is godmother to my children, who knows all my secrets, told me the gossip going around the market. No one else dared whisper it to me, the preacher's wife. That Hilda Florencia had got her talons hooked into my tender husband. I wept when she told me.

What can I say about Hilda Florencia? You know the type, who must have other women's husbands. She was little more than a chit, living in her parents' house down by the slaughterhouse, teaching preprimario at the Urbana Mixta—no one would trust her with children older than first grade. In her short career, she had already been through: Baldomero, the math teacher who gave her extra help with fractions when she was still in school; Augustín the carpenter, whose nails have bent on the third whack ever since he lay with Hilda Florencia; Prospero the postmaster, but he's slipped his delivery into practically every pretty girl in town, so I don't fault Hilda Florencia there, although his wife Rosa does; and, it is rumored, the priest. Catholics!

Hilda Florencia had never married, never even shacked up, as they say, and this is unusual, and most unusual of all, never had a child. Some said she was barren, and that it was her hungry suffering womb that caused all her troubles. But it's my opinion that she used a potion, and Emiliana concurs on that. Emiliana, practiced herself in brujería, should know.

After Emiliana told me that Hilda Florencia was meeting my husband evenings in his pharmacy, I confronted Mundo, late at night in bed when the children were asleep, and asked him, I confess I was crying and possibly a little hysterical, why he would bring sin and disgrace on our family with such a one.

He grew blustery and red in the face and told me he was driving out the seven devils from her, just as our Savior did from María Magdalena.

«« — »»

There will be those who say I took up with Felix Pérez Cruz for revenge upon my husband. Not so! Emiliana will tell you that everything that happened resulted from a curse gone wrong. Black magic is difficult to control, she will be the first to admit. But, I am getting ahead of myself. I must stick to the natural order of things, before the *Flor* tumbled onto my patio spilling its driver into my life.

When I saw that Mundo could not be dissuaded from his course—men are ever blockheads in these matters and can no more control their urges when lust comes down upon them than a pack of village dogs—I went to Emiliana. "You must put a curse on Hilda Florencia," I told her. "Not for my sake. I have gotten rid of all bitterness, rage and anger, along with every other form of malice, as the apostle tells us. But that Hilda Florencia is a danger to every Christian woman in Todos Santos."

Emiliana paused at her work—we were in her kitchen and she was patting out tortillas for the noon meal—and looked past my shoulder toward the door. The top half of the door was open to let in sunshine and clear the cooking smoke from the kitchen. I knew what she was thinking. To speak of witchcraft in plain daylight invites trouble.

"Don't worry," I said, "There's no one around to hear us. I passed Don Enrique in your milpa, when I was coming down the hill." It was the time of year the first ears of corn were getting ripe, and Emiliana's plump chuchito of a husband was sweating in his field, harvesting elotes and beans. Her younger children were all in school. As were mine, except for baby Ezequiel. I'd left him at home with the hired girl. Emiliana's kitchen was as quiet and secret as a cave.

She sighed. "You know I must do what you ask, comadre. Not only because we're old friends, but to drive the evil spirit out of Hilda Florencia. However, I warn you, it will be dangerous. You have to bring me a photograph of the girl, and a piece of huipil that she's worn, and a hair from her head. How will you do that?"

How indeed? It was not as though my donkey of a husband carried his lover's picture about with him. "I'll manage," I told Emiliana.

"Remember," I added, "our religion prohibits the taking of a life. I just want her to be unattractive to men."

I believe in rooting out temptation at its source.

<<<< — >>>>

The hair was easy to procure, from the bed in the back of the pharmacy, where it lay, long and black and blatant as a billboard across the pillow. To look for her huipil, I went to the cooperative store, where so many of the women of our town place their woven goods on consignment. I went through stacks of folded blouses, each with a name hand-written on a small paper pinned to the fabric, until I came to Hilda Florencia Pablo Matías. Aha! I unfolded the huipil—magenta and black

141

and turquoise blue with triangles of glittering rickrack stitched around the collar. Gaudy, like the girl.

"Won't that look pretty on your Marta, Doña Clara Luz," Martiria, who ran the shop, said. I saw the envidia in her sly face, that here was I, spending good money on a huipil instead of weaving it myself. These days more and more Todosanteras are buying rather than weaving. Martiria, stuck in the old ways, disapproved, although the cooperative provided her livelihood.

"I dare say it's been worn," I said.

"Oh no. Brand new."

I thought not. Surely after three months on her knees, tied by her loom to her porch post, passing the shuttle back and forth, Hilda Florencia would have worn her blouse to the fiesta before putting it up for sale. I had to hope so, for I paid a hundred quetzales for it. The thought of my money filling her purse was another burden to my broken heart. One more hurt she'd done me.

Never mind. Most of the money I got back, after I'd snipped a small piece from the huipil, sewn in a patch a tourist would hardly notice, and sold it to Tomasa to take to her husband's shop down by the lake in Panajachel, where handicrafts go for twice the price they do up here in Todos Santos. Tomasa died soon after, leaving her poor one-legged husband to mind the store alone, but that's another story.

The photograph caused the most trouble. After turning it over in my mind, I knew there was nothing for it but to approach one of Hilda Florencia's former lovers, since I couldn't very well go to the butcher and ask him for a picture of his daughter. I settled on Baldomero, the math teacher, and had to wait for school to start up again after the new year. Months had passed since Emiliana had agreed to help me, and I was seeing less and less of Mundo. I fretted and shed secret tears, but my comadre told me to bear up; the thing had to be done correctly. She cast the miches, the scarlet beans the shamans use to tell the future, and said the time wasn't right.

In January Moisés left to study high school in Huehue, and we became a house of sad women: Marta, Nohemí, the hired girl Patricia, and only three-year-old Ezequiel with his tiny penis. On weekends Moisés came home and Mundo returned to fill the house with God, but that only made the Mondays emptier and more bottomless. As soon as I dared, I walked into town to visit the Instituto, where Marta was in her second year of básico. There she was, my Marta, in the courtyard playing basketball with a gang of students on their break. Intent on the ball, she didn't notice me go by, up the stairs to the second floor classrooms, where I found the math teacher, alone, gracias a Dios, in a disheveled classroom.

"Doña Clara Luz!" He looked up from the papers he was marking, surprised no doubt to see a parent so early in the term, although Marta had barely passed his course the year before.

"Profe," I greeted him with the respect I give our teachers, whether they deserve it or not.

"You'll be pleased," he said quickly. "Marta passed the first test with high marks." He began to shuffle through the papers on his desk.

"Fine," I said. "Don't worry yourself with finding it. I've come for something else." I drove straight to the point, a tactic that will always startle people accustomed to devious pathways to their destinies. "I require a photograph of Hilda Florencia." I stopped and allowed his mind to fill in the rest. If he guessed my purpose, all the better. Witchcraft can be abetted by awareness of it.

Confusion, shame, fear flickered across his countenance with the speed of television commercials, advertising his guilty soul. "But Doña Clara Luz!" he reiterated at last. "I don't have a picture of her."

"Surely you can find one, somewhere. Wasn't she Señorita Instituto in her second year?" Voted the school beauty and brains, she went on to seduce her teacher in the final year. "Baldomero, I've entrusted my daughter to your classroom. If I should find out anything improper is going on, and let the director know, you wouldn't be forgiven a second time." The director, a practical man hard up for math teachers, had permitted Baldomero to come back once the affair was over.

Baldomero thought it over. "Perhaps I can come up with something."

<<<< — >>>>

On a night of no moon, I left my house of sleeping women, the baby Ezequiel in Marta's bed, and went down the hill to a wooden shed Emiliana keeps on her property for her curing ceremonies. I took the prescribed offerings—candles, turkey eggs, a strong chili, aguardiente—as well as the items pertaining to Hilda Florencia. Emiliana built a sacred fire on the dirt floor of the shed, the same as she would have for a benign ritual. She filled a pichacha with copal and swung the censor back and forth until the rancho was full of smoke and incense, all the while chanting prayers to the Dueños de Cerros.

At midnight, I checked my watch, she said to me, "Clara Luz, you're sure you want to go ahead with this? To drive evil from your household you call on the forces of witchcraft and accept the consequences?"

"You know perfectly well I do."

Then she had me light four candles at the wrong end, no easy feat, and stand them next to the fire. She added some chunks of copal incense to the fire, put a turkey egg into the flames, and commenced again with her invocations. Of course, I won't tell you the words she spoke. She kept it up until the egg exploded with a loud crack.

"Ah! That's good," she said. She put another turkey egg on the fire.

"Now give me the hair and huipil," she said. From her bag she drew out a miniature figure made of pine resin. She stuck Hilda Florencia's hair to the head and wrapped the scrap of huipil around it. The doll caused me to shiver. It had a nasty look.

The second egg exploded with a loud noise.

Emiliana placed a third egg on the fire and put the little Hilda Florencia into a tin can, the kind that beans or chilies come in, but the label was washed off. She added the photograph and the chili I'd brought along with four tiny crosses she'd made of twigs of ruda.

"That's it," she said. I helped her bind a cloth over the opening of the can so that nothing could come out and the third egg exploded.

She set the can on the dirt floor by the fire and put the last egg on the fire. The candles were burning low. She poured some aguardiente on the fire so that it flared up, picked up the pichacha and swung it through the smoke from the fire, all the while intoning in a deep voice like a man's, calling on names I'd never heard, until the fourth egg exploded. The fire went out suddenly, making me jump, leaving us in total darkness.

"It's done," she said, lighting a bit of fatwood so we could see the fire's ashes, the wax puddles from the candles, and the soot blackened can. She brushed some ashes from her skirt and hustled me to the door. "You won't know where I bury the can," she said. "That will be my secret."

I can attest that I know everything else, every word and act of the spell. I am responsible.

««« — »»»

Two weeks after the bus accident I waited until Mundo and Moisés had gone for the week, gave little Ezequiel a hug and told my children that God's work called me. Leaving Nohemí and Ezequiel in the care of Marta and the hired girl, I left the house of sad women. Bible in hand I climbed the mountain road to La Ventosa and the house of orphans. There was Felix Pérez Cruz, now standing tall and willowy on his own two feet in that smoky room, with his little sisters and brothers hanging from him like boughs. The gash in his forehead had been pulled together with large stitches and his eyes were still dark pools. Looking at Felix Pérez Cruz, I wanted to drown.

"Doña Clara Luz, how can I thank you!" he greeted me. "Don Pilo gave me my job back."

"Mijo, after supper we will thank God together for His small mercies." I'd come prepared and pulled eggs and onions, tomatoes and tortillas, and a full jar of instant coffee out from my bag while Felix built up the fire. They had nothing but a pot of beans cooking and the little ones watched me chop and cook with wild faces. There were four, not five as I'd thought on that first visit, and Felix told me their names and ages as I worked. Ten, nine, seven, and four, and the father had disappeared to El Norte before the youngest was born and never been heard from since. Two brothers and a sister between Felix and ten-year-old Josefina had also gone to the North, and sent money when they could. Josefina's eyes were as deep and hungry as her brother's and I could see they were going to need all of my love to fill her up. I would teach her to be a good mamacita for her family.

After supper the four children all burrowed into a bed in one corner of the rancho and I opened my Bible to commence

146

study at the very beginning of the New Testament, the generations of Jesucristo. I made Felix read aloud in a soft voice while my finger pointed out the words. It was slow work. He struggled through Amminadab, Rehoboam, Jehoram, Hezekiah, and Zerubbabel, but when we got to the birth of Immanuel, he was on more familiar ground. The fire died on the hearth, and we sat close together for warmth. His eyes followed my hand like a beacon in the night. By the time Jesus came out of the wilderness, snores were coming from the patojos in their corner and the candle we were reading by was sputtering. I closed the Book.

"Clara Luz, you are my angel," Felix said, "but I'm worried for my hermanitos. Who'll take care of them all week while I'm driving the bus?"

"Dear boy, I'll stay with them. My household is in good hands; God has told me to put yours in order." Thus I orphaned my own children for those of a dead woman. Felix made as if to get up from the bed we were sitting on to read, the only other bed in the hut. I caught his hand and pulled him back. "Felix," I chided, "you're not going to make me sleep alone in this cold bed."

Who but God could have given me such boldness?

Felix was an eager lover, with hands and lips as soft and hungry as his eyes. I'd never been with any man but my husband. Every week on Saturday night POM POM POM for ten minutes POM POM POM Mundo wielded his rod of the prophet POM POM POM until with a gracias a Dios he rolled off and went to sleep. God had told Mundo he must spill his seed before he could preach to the culto on Sunday. Mundo, faithful servant, obeyed. And I was a faithful servant to my husband.

Until these last six months, when Mundo's rod stopped coming to me in the night, and I knew the curse I'd put on

147

Hilda Florencia had failed. I was a woman without a husband, empty as a dry well.

Now here was Felix. "How beautiful on the mountain are the feet of those who bring good news," the Scriptures say. He brought me the good news in his hands and his mouth and he asked me, "Doña Clara Luz, like this?"

I praised God who'd delivered this sinning bus driver to my door and into my care and I gave him my faith and instructed, "A little lower."

I enjoyed his bounty and he mine until the small hours before dawn, when he said, "I have to leave for work."

"So you must," I told him, "and fíjese, no more thieving from Don Pilo."

I slept until morning when the little ones roused me. They'd begun to think of me already as their mother. We made fire on the hearth and in the chuj, and after breakfast I took their dirty rags and blankets and washed them, singing hymns as I worked. Josefina worked beside me at the pila rinsing and wringing, until her little hands turned white.

"Ow, Doña Clara Luz," she wailed, "the water's too cold."

I took her hands between mine and slapped them until they were red and she was laughing. We spread the laundry out to dry on the branches of stunted junipers that separated the yard from the rocky mountainside. By then the chuj was ready, and I took the children inside to sweat and scrub the filth and hurt that had accumulated on their skin and in their hair and ears and all their secret places in the months they'd been neglected by their dying mother. When we were done they were bright and blooming as chilca in springtime.

Later on I bought a chicken from a neighbor and showed Josefina how to twist its neck and pluck it clean. We cooked a recaldo. I don't know when those children had last eaten meat. I had them say their prayers and tucked them in and was about to go to bed myself, satisfied with the labors of the day, when the door opened and in walked Felix.

"Híjole! What are you doing here, mi amor?" I asked. I knew that normally, in the few hours between his evening arrival in Todos Santos and his morning departure, Felix slept on a pallet in the ayudante's house in town.

"I've come for another lesson from the Bible," he said with a hungry smile.

"And who is driving the *Flor?*"

"Miguel. I'm teaching him to drive. He's very grateful, and in his gratitude promises to say nothing about dropping me here tonight on the way into Todos Santos. There are only a few passengers, and they're all asleep."

"You're teaching him by letting him drive alone down the mountains?" The road was steep, narrow, twisted and rutted, the very road he'd tumbled from two weeks before.

"It's all downhill. I told him to stay in first gear."

««« — »»»

I had only intended to spend a night or two in La Ventosa, but I ended up staying the week, scrubbing and sweeping by day and instructing Felix by night. For he came back each night and left again before each dawn to walk down into Todos Santos and resume his piloting of the *Flor.* In all that week Miguel did not wreck the bus and Don Pilo did not find out about the driving lessons, which only proves that God was watching over the situation. By the end of the week we had finished twenty-eight chapters of Matthew and seen our Lord resurrected. Friday morning I said goodbye to the little ones and left Josefina making tortillas. I walked down the mountain road and arrived at my house well before noon. To my astonishment, Mundo was waiting for me by the kitchen stove, where Patricia was preparing the midday meal. On his knee he dandled beaming Ezequiel. I could only stare at the spectacle, startled out of speech, thinking I was witnessing an avenging angel in the form of my husband, come to draw his flaming sword.

"Look, my little king," Mundo said in his mortal voice, so I knew he was not a heavenly visitation. He mussed the baby's hair while he spoke with a solid mortal hand. "Here's your mother! A wife of noble character is worth far more than rubies, my son. Where has she been?"

What devilment was this? Mundo was quoting Proverbs and tickling Ezequiel until he squealed with giggles. A sight that six months ago would have brought me peace of heart, and now confused my senses with suspicions of more witchcraft.

"And didn't Patricia tell you where I've been?" I asked. The hired girl didn't have the brains or backbone of a rabbit. "Tending the orphans of Felix Pérez Cruz, of course. What brings you to this house, Mundo? Why aren't you at the pharmacy?"

"La Marta came to me yesterday with news that you had vanished. Oh, amor! I thought you were dead, or stolen by the Llorona. I came home last night to wring my hands and weep. I am nothing without you at my side. What a lot of anxiety you've caused, mi pródiga!"

"Is that so?" I was not to be sermonized by this man who had given me every Biblical reason for leaving his bed. "I will remind you of Paul's epistle to Timothy: he who sets his heart on the work of pastor must be the husband of but one wife. Perhaps you'll not condemn my ministry to suffering children and wayward bus drivers."

Mundo plopped Ezequiel down onto the floor and spread out his hands in that familiar Sunday gesture of his that I

150

know so well, that gathers his flock into his heart. "Ay, Clara Luz," he said. "I am not a good man. I am unworthy to offer you any sacrifice, yet I beseech you to accept my bounden duty. Redeem me!"

Ezequiel ran toward me with arms outstretched, in unconscious imitation of his father. I scooped up the little clown and with tears stinging my eyes I forgave the bigger one, yet again. I'd set my covenant with Mundo like a rainbow on the clouds long ago. "God have mercy on us all," I said.

Outside I heard the hoot of the omened owl in daylight.

<<<< — >>>>

The redemption of Mundo cleared the sadness from our house like the canícula that brings the fresh-washed sun in the midst of the rainy season, and it kept me busy. I rose early to walk with my husband into town. I tended to the customers at the pharmacy by his side. We returned home each evening in the back of Don Enrique's pickup truck. The prophet's rod made frequent visits in the night.

Calamity made its next appearance without mercy or remorse. Once loosened on the world, a curse can't be called back, and will find some way, any way, to do its work. Sure enough, Emiliana hurried up the path to my house bearing the news and shut the kitchen door behind her, as if she could keep out the blasted owl. "Clara Luz," she said, "the whole town is whispering. Prepare yourself. Hilda Florencia is pregnant."

I let the tortilla in my hand drop into the fire. "Sálvame Dios! Is the child Mundo's?"

"Claro. She hasn't been with anyone else, and she's well along." Seeing my stricken face she added, "He hasn't seen her this last month, of that at least I'm sure."

"Poor solace," I said, and felt the bitterness rise. "She'll do her best to get him back. And I've given him Biblical grounds for divorce." I told her about Felix Pérez Cruz.

"You think Mundo knows?" she asked.

"I think it's what brought him back to me," I said.

"Qué justicia. What an endless trial life is! What will you do?"

I had made up my mind. "Hilda Florencia needs a husband," I said, "but not mine."

The very next Sunday, leaving Mundo safe in the bosom of the culto, I took my Bible in hand and climbed to La Ventosa. I hadn't seen Felix Pérez Cruz in a month, but the memory of his eager kisses and soft hands was strong upon me. I trembled, not knowing what I'd find, anger or tears. The sadness I had banished from my own house might have found its way up the mountain to the windy spot I had adopted only to abandon. Filled with misgivings I wound up the trail to the door and discovered the house swept and Josefina tending the hearth. "Mija!" I greeted her with a kiss.

"Doña Clara Luz!" Felix jumped up from his chair by the fire. His face paled like the night I met him. His eyes blackened into liquid. I felt their pull and my loss. I held my Bible tight.

"Have you remembered what I taught you?" I asked him.

"I need more lessons." There was urgency in the air between us. Desire and betrayal urging themselves upon us.

"Take the Bible, then." I gave him the heavy book. "Let it fall open, and read me the first verse your eye falls upon," I told him.

Josefina and the little ones looked on. Felix stood a moment by the table, where bits of onion and tomato that Josefina had been chopping lay scattered. Maybe he was pondering whether to open the book or throw it into the fire. But he let it drop open. "Any verse?" he asked.

"The one that draws you to it."

He looked down, paused, and read aloud slowly. "For this reason a man will leave his father and mother and be united to his wife, and the two will become one flesh." He stopped, and looked back at me, searching.

"God has spoken. He couldn't be clearer. Your father and mother have left you. It's time you marry. Past time, if you want to know the truth!"

"Who do you want me to marry?" As if he knew my purpose. As if he would live or die for me.

"I know just the girl. She's pretty, and she'll come to you already blessed. You'll raise her child as your own, and have others, no doubt. I'll be the godmother and make sure you're well provided for."

Thus it will come to pass, if God intends of course. I can't blame myself; I'm only a pawn in the immortal plan, with no more power over events than I have over the rising and setting of the sun. Furthermore, if I have any regrets over giving Felix Pérez Cruz to Hilda Florencia, it would be a sin.

Fathers and Sons

I'm a simple man, a man of the country. The things people are saying about me, they're not true. Where do people get these ideas? It's envidia, that's all it is. They call me the fox; they say I'm subtle and calculating. They say I'm rich, because I own a little land, a few coffee trees. Have you checked the price of coffee lately? Pues, you're a North American; you drink coffee, but you don't grow it. Let me just say, the price is very low. The Todosanteros say I'm proud, but how can I be proud? I, Amilcar Ahilón Martín, am the most miserable of men. Let me tell you about Rigoberto, my son, my firstborn, my poor misguided boy.

The townspeople, my fellow citizens, nearly set him on fire. Fíjese, this is what passes for justice in Guatemala. They beat him senseless by the fountain in the plaza, and poured on the gasoline, all ready to light him up. It was only a miracle that the National Guard arrived before they set a match to him, and, to save him from the lynching, carried him off to the hospital in Huehue. That's where I found him, after the mayor called to alert me to the situation. I found Rigoberto, lying abandoned on twisted sheets in a dirty corner of the emergency ward. His head was swaddled in blood-soaked bandages. Black stitches crawled up the side of his battered face. My handsome son! (How did such an ugly man create such a beautiful boy?) I winced at the sight. I could hardly stand to keep my gaze upon him. My heart convulsed in my chest; tears sprang to my eyes. I leapt to the most dire conclusion. Rigoberto was dead, I was sure. That girl cowering at the nurse's station had not dared tell me. Blood spatters on the floor and walls made it look like the hospital staff had continued the thrashing that the National Guard had intercepted. In my country you can trust no one— even those who have sworn oaths to save lives. I stared down at my son, his torso and arms bare, covered in welts and bruises, his broken ribs cinched in grayish tape. I hadn't seen him so helpless since he was a baby, almost thirty years ago. I wanted to weep. With my fingers still numb and vibrating from the motorcycle ride over the altiplano, I reached toward my son with slow dread. I felt for a pulse. Relief flooded over me. Rigoberto was alive.

Drained of adrenaline, my blood pounding in my ears, I bent over to examine him. There, on his shoulder, in a spot he'd never revealed to me, I discovered damning evidence. A gang tattoo. A number—three digits unknown to me. A souvenir, I was sure, of his year in the US prison. Again the fear seized me, the dread. I wanted to spit. I wanted to shake him and shout, "You'll destroy yourself, and me with you!"

His eyes flickered open and he moaned. "Papi?"

I controlled myself. I didn't shout, but spoke with measured calm. "What have you done, Rigoberto?"

"Nothing, Papi, I swear. I wasn't even there when that kid was stabbed."

"The Mendoza boy is dead. And the Cholos are accusing you."

"Lies." He grunted with clenched teeth and tried to shift. I could see he was in pain. "They'll say anything, that bunch. They hate me."

Who am I to believe? The gangs of delinquents who are causing havoc in Todos Santos with the rivalries they've brought back from California? Surely not! Or my poor boy who has grown up in such troubled times? Everything I fought so hard for—an education, equal rights to prosper just a little, a little tranquility for my family—is being lost. Violence is taking over. The young people are all fleeing. Is it any wonder he's confused? I ask you; you have a son. I know how much you miss him. Doesn't a man who is any kind of man stand by his son? My child was born in innocence. I held him in my own two hands when he was just an hour old, born out of a union of pure love.

I had to save him. If I couldn't, who would? "Where are your clothes, Rigoberto? We have to get you out of here before the police arrive."

««« — »»»

Did I spoil Rigoberto? I never wanted my sons to cry over twenty centavos. On his first day of kindergarten, I walked Rigoberto to school myself. I walked slowly so that he could keep up. He was wearing new shoes, and wanted to kick rocks all the way to school. You know what little boys are like! When we arrived, I gave him a shiny quetzal coin. "This is for your snack," I told him. "Put it in your pocket and don't lose it." His face was as shiny as the coin. I left him at the door of the kindergarten classroom, and went upstairs to the room where I taught fifth grade. It was a proud day for me, and I made my son proud.

If he had grown up under the harsh and miserly hand of a man like my father, things might have turned out differently. My father had worked on the construction of the highway from Huehue to the coast, when all the Indians were conscripted, forced to work without pay. Indians were treated like animals then. Every road worker had to carry— on his back, fíjese—a box filled with earth, weighing 150 pounds. If the box wasn't full, the Ladino foreman beat the

157

Indian with his whip. However, my father was an intelligent man and could read and write a little, so he was appointed the foreman's helper. He didn't have to carry boxes of dirt. He didn't get beaten. That was how he came to acquire the job of labor contractor for a plantation owner. The only Indian in town to have such a good job, and people envied him for it. He worked very hard, but he didn't own any land, so we were very poor. My mother sometimes had to feed all eight children with one egg.

When I was only seven (and small for my age!) my father took me with him to Huehuetenango, where the nearest road was in those days. We walked—ten hours on foot over the altiplano. My father was delivering workers to the big cotton plantation on the coast. He walked fast. Everyone had to keep up. "If you love me, slow down," I begged him. He would *not* slow down. Not even for his own son, a tiny boy. That's the kind of man he was.

He would tell you it was for my own good, to make me strong. To think about it still makes my guts twist with anger.

My father wanted me, his firstborn son, to get an education, so that I wouldn't have to work like an animal. He moved the whole family into town when I was eight, so that I could go to school. I was supposed to be grateful. In those days, Indians didn't live in the center of town; we weren't welcome there, among the Ladinos. I arrived for my first day of kindergarten not knowing a word of Spanish. There were sixty kids in my class, and I was the only one without shoes. The kids laughed at me because I was so poor.

The teacher was Ladino. Halfway through the morning he came down the row of tables where I sat on a bench with the other students. He asked each student a question in Spanish, and they answered him back in Spanish. When he came to me, I answered in my own language, "My name is

Amilcar Ahilón Martín and I'm pleased to study with you, Profe." *Prof* was the only word I knew in Spanish.

The teacher struck me across the mouth and moved on. The boy next to me smirked. "He'll hit you every time you speak Mam, stupid," he told me in my language.

When I got home I told my father what had happened. "Tata, please, I don't want to go to school," I said with tears in my eyes.

"Don't be a blockhead. Who do you think you are? After the sacrifices we've made for you, you'll go to school and you'll learn, whether you want to or not." To teach me, he made me drop my pants. He took off his belt and struck me across the behind several times. The lashes stung, but not so much as the humiliation.

I learned early to use my wits, to avoid beatings, to survive. If Rigoberto had grown up poor and mistreated by his father and teachers, would he be better fit for survival?

<<< — >>>

"Rigoberto must not come back to Todos Santos," the mayor told me. I was in his office. It was a week after the almost-lynching. "It is for his safety that I advise you, Prof." Modesto, the mayor, is my former student. I tried to stay calm, to control my temper. Modesto! He thinks he's a big man because he sits in the mayor's chair! I remember him when he was in my fifth grade class, failing at mathematics.

"I'm an old man, Modesto, practically retired." I was the one who should have been sitting in the mayor's chair, and not Modesto! "I'm only trying to enjoy the peace of the countryside with my little grandchildren playing around my patio."

"Nothing will disturb your tranquility as long as Rigoberto stays away." How I despise being threatened with mild words!

"Until the ruckus dies down," I amended his statement for him.

Modesto removed his hat, which had remained on his head since I entered his office as a subtle sign of disrespect, and placed it on the desk between us. Perhaps he meant it as an offering, but to me it appeared more like a chess piece. "It won't die down, Amilcar," he said. "Juanito Mendoza is dead. His family members won't forget. Rigoberto must stay away."

My hat remained on my head. "My son did not kill anyone. The Security Committee of Todos Santos is engaged in illegal activities," I said. "They've threatened to cut off my power and water. A man can't live without light and water. How can I take care of my family?"

"I'm sorry to hear this."

"They're trying to drive *me* out of Todos Santos. They blame *me* for my son. They say I'm the father of a gang leader and murderer. Untruths!"

"What do you want me to do, Amilcar?"

"As our elected mayor, it's your job to uphold the law. You must stamp out vigilantism."

"You know the Committee. They can't be controlled. But I'll do my best." He picked up his hat again, leaving his desk bare and his back row unguarded. "I'm sorry to leave you," he said, standing up. "I have a meeting."

I remained seated. I had seen mayors come and go through this office many times. "I hope you succeed, Modesto. Because if you don't, I'll have to lodge a complaint with the governor in Huehue." I still command a little respect in this department.

I left the mayor's office after Modesto and went downstairs to the bank, where there was a long line. I waited patiently for my turn at the teller's window. Normally I would pass the time chatting with people in the line. It's a good place to find out what's on people's minds, and many of my community projects, like the sewer line out to Pajon, have grown out of such chats. However, I was not in a communicative mood, and kept to myself until I reached the teller, Jorge Ángelo Mendoza, another former student of mine. Just as my eyes met those of Jorge Ángelo, he slipped a Cerrado sign in front of the grating.

"Good day, Jorge Ángelo," I greeted him. "I need to withdraw money from my account."

"Sorry, Don Amilcar. The bank is closed."

"But it's only 10:30!" I protested.

"Special hours today."

"I'll come back after lunch, then."

"I wouldn't bother. We're looking into some of our accounts to see if there are any problems. Until these problems are cleared up, you won't be able to make your withdrawal."

Incensed, I put on my hat and left the bank.

««« — »»»

The first time I was given the chance to speak in public, I was fifteen years old and soon to graduate from sixth grade. This will surprise you. In America, this would be a very advanced age. You'll think me very stupid. But my education had been arduous, with a late start and gaps when I had to miss school to work. You can imagine that graduation was a momentous occasion for me. Of the sixty students who began kindergarten with me, only seven remained, two of them Indians. My teacher said to me, "Amilcar, you will recite a poem for the Independence Day celebration."

"Maestro, I can't," I told him. "I've never spoken in assembly." My teachers had never allowed me to give a speech or sing a song as all the Ladino children did, because my Spanish was still very poor and they thought me inferior.

"Then it's about time, isn't it?" Profe Gerardo told me. The maestro was a great one for twisting the ears and slapping the faces of all the students. Because I was an Indian, I received more blows than most. I could not refuse to recite.

How I struggled to memorize the poem Prof had assigned me. It was a long ode in praise of Huehuetenango, written by a famous national poet as he went into exile. I spent hours repeating all nine stanzas after a tape recording. I practiced sweeping oratorical gestures, thrusting one hand out and to the side, then its opposite to the other side, back and forth, as my teachers did.

On the fifteenth of September five hundred people filled the salón for the annual pageant. Not only was the entire school there—students, teachers, parents—but also the mayor, the school superintendent, and other important officials. And in the third row sat Candelaria, the girl with whom I had recently fallen in love, who is now forty years later still my wife. Candelaria, her long black hair plaited with pink ribbon, looked up at me with eyes shining in expectation. At my side, the master of ceremonies intoned, "Ladies and gentleman, please welcome with forceful applause Amilcar Ahilón Martín, who will recite a poem."

I felt my heart pound. I felt my face turn red, my ears burn. I was sweating and burning. I reached out an oratorical hand. I opened my mouth, but not a sound came out. Nothing but a very small hiccup of fear. I closed my mouth and opened it several times, like a fish gasping, but my mind was empty of the poem, a complete blank, with nothing in it but darkness and Candelaria's eyes like distant, unreachable stars. I felt the stage beginning to spin. Before I could pass out, I turned and fled. It was pathetic.

I vowed that never again would I allow myself such humiliation.

"We gave you everything we had, every advantage." My words were coming out in an angry torrent, a bombardment aimed at my firstborn. He was staying in the house of an Evangelical, some friend of his, in a village outside of Xela, in a place nobody could find him. "Have you done any honest work since you've been back? You hang out with a bunch of drug addicts. You've humiliated the whole family. The town has evicted your mother from her stall in the market. Your mother! Who put the food in your mouth! And now she's shunned by the neighbors and can't even earn a few quetzales selling sweaters and socks."

I hate it when I lose my temper. It reminds me of my father. I saw Rigoberto turn away from me. The stitches on his face were gone, and he looked much better. It had only been three weeks. The young heal quickly.

"Which do you care about, Papi, that my life is in danger, or that your political career is thwarted? I'll go back to the States. Everyone will be better off." His voice dripped bitterness.

"Your mother will not be better off! Your mother cries every night for you! She wants you home." Candelaria was sure that Rigoberto would die in the North. So many Todosanteros are dying there now; so many tombs in Todos Santos are painted with stars and stripes. "Listen, mijo. Clean yourself up and I'll take care of your problems in Todos Santos."

"I'm clean. My friends are helping me." He refused to meet my eyes and looked up at a picture of Jesus on the wall behind me, the only adornment in the room. I have no love for Evangelicals—the preacher who lives next door to me had

163

taken to announcing over his loudspeaker whenever he saw me in the road, "Here comes Amilcar. He thinks he's a teacher, but he's just a sinner whose soul will burn in Hell!"—and the picture irked me. Now my son was studying it in preference to looking at me, as if Jesus could save him where I had failed.

"The Security Committee demanded I leave the town." Imagine! Demanded I leave the town of my birthright, after all I've suffered and accomplished. I, a barefoot boy in rags, became the first Mayan teacher of Todos Santos, and now, Coordinator of Rural Plannification. "They want me out, so that *you* won't come back. They can persecute me, I'm used to that, I've been persecuted before. But a man has to stand up to his accusers. Try to act like a man for once, Rigoberto." The minute I spoke I regretted my words; the minute I saw him flinch from their sting. But I couldn't help myself. I turned away from the picture of Jesus and stomped out of the room, banging the door behind me.

<<<< — >>>>

Rigoberto was always wild. I wanted him to study. *I* studied. I had to beg my father for money to go to high school. My father thought he had been generous enough, to send me through sixth grade; a poor orphan, he never went to school at all, and taught himself how to read and do sums. He couldn't see the value in going beyond the basics. I argued with him for a year. I wanted to be as well educated as a Ladino. I wanted to be important. Finally he agreed to loan me the money, if I would pay it all back. He kept track of every centavo he spent on my school fees, books, clothes, food, and boarding for the six years I was in high school.

I went to high school in Huehue, where all the students were Ladinos and taunted me because I wore Indian clothes.

They called me "Fool!" "Dirty Indian!" "Sandal Wearer!" "Blanket Boy!" "Stripy Pants!" "Ugly Face!" I begged my father for Ladino clothes. He bought me two polyester shirts and two pairs of cheap blue jeans. They fit perfectly until the first time they were washed. The pants shrank. I had to wear them anyway, even though they were far too short, because my father wouldn't buy me more.

I gave Rigoberto money for food and books and pencils, everything he needed for school. I always made sure that he was well dressed. I never asked him to pay me back.

My teachers called me stupid, because my Spanish was so bad. I worked hard in school. I improved my Spanish. I graduated and became a teacher. Once I started working, I paid my father back for every quetzal that he spent on my education.

I made Rigoberto's education a gift, when he went to high school in Huehue. Because he was good-looking, with Candelaria's long, straight nose and full lips instead of my crooked beak, he made friends easily. A beautiful face gives a person power over others. He didn't like studying. He got into fights. I worried that he had inherited my temper but not my ambition. He ran around with a group of boys who were always getting into trouble. Every weekend he came home. Midway through his first term in school, he showed up with a new haircut—long on top, and very short in back. I recognized the style. "Rigoberto!" I shouted, the moment he walked into the house. "What are you doing with a gang haircut?"

I grabbed a razor and shoved him into a chair. Right there, in front of his mother and younger brothers, I shaved off the rest of his hair. I lectured him. "Rigoberto, you are the great hope of this family. You will go to University. You'll be a doctor or a lawyer. You'll set an example for your brothers." My second son, Sebastián, was born a little simple, and would not be following Rigoberto. But Vicente—intelligent and a hard worker—was at the head of his class all through primary. He and the baby, Xtilán, all looked up to Rigoberto. He was their leader!

He hung his head and promised to improve his grades. He wore a stocking cap to cover his humiliation, until his hair grew out again. By a miracle he finished high school and began studying law. He was still in Huehue, where his friends were still wild. He didn't come home for four months, and when he came, he slouched into a chair in the kitchen.

"It's no use, Tata. I failed the first term," he said.

Candelaria hurried to give him a plate of food and tortillas, as though he must be starving from four months without her cooking. "Then you'll just try again," I told him. "I too failed courses. You must apply yourself and persevere." I didn't even chide him for the waste of tuition money. I could see his dejection. He put the food aside, untouched.

"No. There's no life here for a man any more. Even if I finish University, then what? There are no jobs, no money. A man in Michigan makes in a day what it takes a month to earn here."

All the youths were going to El Norte: to make dollars, for the adventure, to prove themselves. He would not be left out. We begged him not to go. His mother cried. I threatened to beat him, although I've never laid a hand on him. He went anyway, promising to come back soon. He was just eighteen.

<<<< — >>>>

Things went well for Rigoberto in Michigan. He found indoor work in a car parts factory, and lived in a house with other Todosanteros. He called home regularly and sent us money when he could. He was honorable in his obligations. Candelaria was as happy as she could be, with Rigoberto so far away. She had our three other boys at home, and Sebastián's wife to help with the house. These were good years, after the peace accords ended the civil war that had devastated the Mayan community. It was a time of optimism for Indians. The Ladinos had left Todos Santos. The Mayans had moved into town from the countryside and bought businesses, even won political office. I was teaching in Urbana Mixta and making friends throughout the department and the nation. Suddenly, there were no limits to what an intelligent, educated Mayan could achieve. Many looked to me as a community leader.

But trouble followed Rigoberto like a hungry dog, as it always had. The US is very strict, not like Guatemala, where there is always someone you can pay to get you out of trouble. When a man gets drunk in the US and drives his car (Rigoberto had a driver's license!), they put him in jail. When Todosanteros fight (the Cholos and Rockeros were there in Michigan too), someone calls the cops and they come and arrest a man on charges of assault and battery. The first time, Rigoberto was in prison for two months and deported. I met him at the airport, where migra dropped him off without a cent. I hadn't seen him in four years. How I had missed my firstborn. Even with three sons at home, the heart always yearns for the one who is gone.

"Papi!" he said, and grabbed me in a strong hug. His hair was short and he looked good, with a big smile on his youthful lips.

"Welcome home, mijo. It's time you settle down in Todos Santos. I can get you good work." He didn't say anything to that, but on the bus going home he showed me pictures of his novia, Wendy, a beautiful girl.

"She's a Todosantera," he assured me.

"Really? Who are her parents?"

"You don't know them. They're from, I forget which aldea. But they live in Michigan, too. The whole family is norteño."

For weeks, he lazed at home while Candelaria pampered him with tamales and pepián and sweets, as if every day were Christmas. He disappeared into town with his group of friends, and the rumors started that he was up to no good. I didn't like what I was hearing. "I'll get you a job in the municipal office," I told him. "On a development project. I have connections."

"Don't worry yourself, Tata," he laughed. "I have better ways to make money. I have connections, too."

"How? You've been away four years. Connections here in Todos Santos?"

"Not here. In Huehue. Nobody you know."

"Don't let me catch you with the wrong people, Rigoberto. I'll be retiring from teaching soon, and going on to bigger things."

"I've heard you're going to run for mayor."

"Maybe. But my political enemies will use anything you do against me."

Candelaria was patting out tortillas, and threw one on the griddle with an accusatory slap. "Amilcar," she said, "you'll make your son feel unwelcome in his own house. You'll drive him back to the North."

But it wasn't I who drove him away. It was Wendy who lured him back. She was pregnant. Bring her here, I told him. She won't leave her parents in Michigan, he said. Three months later, Rigoberto left again, to be back there in time for the birth of his son. This time he took with him his brother, Vicente, who had just finished high school with his teacher's diploma. Nothing Candelaria or I could do would stop them from going. The North was taking all our sons, one by one.

We wouldn't see Rigoberto again for another four years, when he returned again. He wouldn't tell us what happened. There was a fight. Wendy called to tell us he was in prison. This time he was a year in prison before they deported him. This time he came back with muscles, from working out in prison. A month after he got home, I found him lifting a barbell in his room. I was incredulous. "Where did you get that thing?"

"Huehue," he grunted.

"Where did you get the money to buy it?"

He let the barbell drop with a heavy clang on the cement floor. "I have a friend in Huehue I did some work for."

"What kind of work? You need to pay money to lift weights?! What kind of a man does that? Are you a homosexual? I can get you plenty of work that will that will pay you to lift weight!"

But Rigoberto rejected my offers. He stayed on in Todos Santos, and I was grateful for that. Candelaria wanted him to send for Wendy and the boy, our first grandchild. But he would just look away and slink out of the room when she suggested it.

I invited a group of friends to my house to ask for their support. The mayoral elections were coming. I served each man a small glass of Scotch whiskey that I bought especially for the meeting (needless to say I didn't invite my Evangelical neighbor), and I told them about my plans for improvement of Todos Santos.

They drank my whiskey and nodded and agreed—we needed a sewage treatment plant, and an incinerator to burn the garbage that was contaminating the River Limón. "So you'll vote for me," I said.

No one spoke. Lico cleared his throat. "Amilcar, there's a problem. Your son is trafficking drugs. Your son is a gang leader. These gangs are destroying our youth."

I protested. I denied his accusations. But I couldn't change their minds. This was what it had come to, all that I had strived for. I didn't run for mayor.

Then came the fight with the Cholos, and a youth was dead.

<<< — >>>

"I have not always been a good man," I said to Candelaria. "But I've always loved you."

We were alone in the kitchen, Candelaria and I, sitting by the stove. It was evening. Her head was bowed, her face in shadow. We hadn't heard from Rigoberto in two months, not since I'd seen him in the Evangelical's house outside of Xela, where he was hiding out. He didn't even call. Candelaria blamed me, because I had told her of the harsh words I'd spoken to Rigoberto the last time I saw him. I tell Candelaria everything these days. "Do you remember that night when we were courting and you made the tortilla?"

"Oh Amilcar," she sighed. "How many times have we heard this story?"

"I have to tell you again. I was so in love with you, Candelaria. But I didn't know if you would be a good wife. So I took you outside and asked you to make me a tortilla. With your eyes fixed on the full moon, not once looking down at your hands, you rolled and pinched and patted out a perfect tortilla, as round as the moon."

"You are always testing people, to see if they measure up. That's why our sons won't stay with us." Her words cut like a machete. Sebastián and his wife had recently left to join Vicente in the States.

"Wasn't I always patient with Sebastián, even though he was slow?"

"You corrected his furrows when they were crooked. You told him how to dig a hole for every tree he planted. Who can't dig a hole, Amilcar?"

He didn't have the capacity to be an educated man, so I taught him to be a man of the country. I gave him work in my milpa and on my land planting coffee. I ask you, you whose North American children are brilliant, what more can a parent do? You've been here long enough to know me. I trust you not to judge me the way the Todosanteros do.

With our youngest Xtilán away at school, it was quiet and lonely in our house that night. You too know the loneliness of an empty house when the children are gone. It's like no other emptiness.

We were roused by the sound of a motor stopping in the road, and a moment later, Rigoberto came bounding through the kitchen door. Candelaria rose and greeted him with a small shriek of pleasure. "Hijo! At last! We've been so worried about you."

He looked around, as if to check who else was present. "I can't stay. No one can know that I'm here."

"No!" I said. "I won't be intimidated by the Committee. Sit. You don't look good." He seemed unsteady on his feet, and his eyes unfocused. His beautiful nose had an ugly hump, where it looked like it had been broken.

"It's not the Committee. There's been bad business in Huehue. I have to go North."

"Not again!" Candelaria said, putting her hands on him, trying to steer him to a chair. "They'll kill you there."

"They'll kill me here. I need money, Papi." He finally slumped into a chair. He looked spent, hollowed out, ruined. I was furious.

"You're using drugs again. You've crossed the narcos. After I warned you. You're a fool, Rigoberto. How can you ask me for money?" I paced the kitchen, while Candelaria poured out a cup of tea and gave it to him, our firstborn. I could see that he was nothing but an addict.

"To save my life."

"To ruin our lives. To shame us." *To break our hearts*, was what I thought. "I regret the day you came back to Todos Santos. Leave! Get out and don't come back this time."

"Amilcar!" Candelaria exclaimed. "Don't say that."

"How can I not tell him the truth?" I slammed out of the kitchen to cool off. A man doesn't weep. Outside, the stars were sharp and clear. In the road below our house I could see the dark shape of the pickup truck that had brought Rigoberto, engine off. My head was throbbing. I wondered what sort of criminal waited for him, what sort of miserable death. I crossed the patio to my office, where I keep my computer, my files, the old landline that we rarely use now, and, hidden away, my cash box. I was spent, exhausted. Rigoberto had exhausted my love. What else could I do.

ENGLISH LESSONS

I hate English. The sounds when I try to make them twist my tongue. To tell *sheep* from *ship?* It hurts my ears when I listen that hard. I work hard enough as a landscape gardener. In my neighborhood in Washington, DC, I don't need English. Everyone speaks Spanish. I watch all Spanish programming on my fifty-inch plasma TV. In my supermarket I can buy every Latin American product I want, including Guatemalan-style tortillas and Picamás Verde.

My wife wants me to learn English. My wife and I speak Spanish together, although she is American, because we met and fell in love when she was a Peace Corps volunteer in Todos Santos. I came back with her to the US so that she could finish her PhD degree in comparative literature. My life in Washington is good. We bought a yellow brick row house after the market collapsed in '08. It has a small backyard where I've planted tomatoes and chilies and roses and lilies. I have a green card and a boss who gives me plenty of work and lets me use his pickup truck until I have money to buy my own. I cook Guatemalan dinners for my wife when she comes home from teaching her undergraduates. Except on the three evenings a week when, after a day's work, I take myself to the public library for my English class. This is where all my troubles begin. This is where I *blow it,* as the Americans say.

"Juanito, qué onda?" I say, sliding into the desk next to my Mexican friend.

"Good evening, George," the English teacher says, looking at me with a stern face carved from pale stone. "Remember,

English only in the classroom!" I roll my eyes. My name in English is made up of painful sounds I can't pronounce. Fortunately, I don't have to say my own name.

"Good evening, Becky Sue," I tell her. It's my good luck that her name is easy to say. "Nice to see you." She gives me a tight nod: my reward for good behavior.

This is what I do for love of my wife.

Roxie's friends from the university all speak Spanish when they come over on Saturday afternoons to drink beer with us while I make carne asada on the backyard grill, so our social life isn't the point of the English lessons.

"You won't be a gardener forever, mi amor," Roxie says. "You're a teacher."

This I believe is the heart of the matter. I *like* being a gardener. Plants don't ask stupid questions and throw spitballs and flunk the same test three times. But that's not what I tell Roxie. "Look at me, Roxie," I say. "I'm an Indian. A redskin!" I punch my finger against my cheek. Actually, my skin is brown, but I like the expression piel rojo. I wear my hair in a ponytail that hangs all the way to my waist (Roxie loves to run her fingers through my long hair and whisper "mi indito" in my ear). I have the hooked nose, wide cheeks, and Asiatic eyes of a Mayan, and the big round belly that comes from eating lots of Big Macs. "Even if I speak like William Shakespeare no one is going to hire me to be a professor. To the gringos, I'll always be a *wetback*." I say mojado in English, to show off my skills.

The one place where they don't speak Spanish is the doctor's office. If it were a regular doctor where you go when you need a shot of antibiotics, or the emergency room where Latins usually end up, of course there would be Spanish. But we are in the office of a fertility specialist, because we've been trying to have a baby for three years,

174

and every time I go home to Todos Santos everyone asks, what, no hijito yet? I shrug them off and tell them, in America these things take more time. Roxie won't go back to Todos Santos now because the last time she was there they made her feel so bad. "Poor Jorge Vitalino," they kept telling her right to her face. "So much time and still no baby. How he must be suffering."

The fertility specialist is a woman and now she has to ask all sorts of personal questions that Roxie translates.

"Have you ever had a child, Jorge?"

"He *thinks* he had a son fourteen years ago, but he's not sure because the mother went back to Japan before the birth, and he's only seen photos."

I know this son is mine, but it is a subject that Roxie and I avoid. It was before I met her, and I had adventures with quite a few tourists passing through Todos Santos. Roxie has green eyes, and she tells me I must be careful not to make her jealous. So I am careful.

"Have you told her how long you were on the Pastilla?" I ask Roxie.

Roxie has red hair and she tells me this gives her a hot temper. I see her face flush with anger, and I expect her freckles to come shooting off her cheeks like sparks. She speaks to the lady doctor with the tendons standing out on her neck.

"She says the same thing I've told you over and over: the Pill does not cause infertility. This is a myth promoted by the churches and all the macho assholes in Guatemala who hate women."

Roxie can get a little worked up. The doctor says something that even I with my library English lessons can understand. "How old are you, Roxanna?"

"Thirty-eight." She sighs.

"And Jorge Vitalino?"

I let her answer, since the number is almost impossible for me to pronounce. "Thirty-three."

They talk some more, then the doctor gives me a cup and a pornographic magazine and shows me where to go. Roxie has already explained about the sperm sample, and because I love her, I agreed to it, although it's clear enough who has the problem here. Guatemalans have many problems, but we're good at having babies.

I don't point this out. It would upset her, and she's already upset enough. To keep her on an even keel, I keep taking English lessons.

"Good evening, George."

"Good evening, Becky Sue."

"How was your day?"

"Good. And yours, Becky Sue?" I give her a wide smile. I show her the white teeth in my brown face. She frowns. She wants more from me.

"Fine, George. I went to work in my office. I proofread documents all day. What did you do?"

"I went to work in a garden. I trim. I clean with a blower."

"I trimmeD. I cleaneD. And blower doesn't rhyme with flower, George."

It does if you're a Latin gardener. It's a word we use all the time on the job, along with trim, which we've turned into Spanglish. Trimmear. We're supposed to be learning past tense. Becky Sue moves to the next student, an older Chinese guy who can read and write perfect English but can't speak a word. There are usually about ten of us in the class—half Latin Americans, but of them Juanito is the only guy, which is why we hang out together. There are several Asians, a Russian, and two sisters from some African country even more fucked than Guatemala. Once Becky Sue has moved

176

out of range, Juanito says to me in a low voice, "What do you think Becky Sue did last night?"

Even if she heard him it wouldn't matter because she doesn't understand Spanish.

"I think she had hot sex with a handsome Guatemalan," I say.

"No," says Juanito. "She had hot sex with an ugly Mexican." It's an ongoing question we have about Becky Sue. We don't know much about her personal life, even though we've had to tell her—in English—all about our wives, husbands, girlfriends, children, mothers, fathers, brothers, sisters, cousins—their ages and where they live and their favorite colors and foods and movie stars. All we know about Becky Sue is that she works as a paralegal and is 25 years old. I suspect she's lying and is really younger.

"OK everybody," Becky Sue says. "Form pairs. Tell your partner everything you did today, from the time you got up. George, you're with Wang. Juan, you're with Dmitri." She goes around the big table, moving people to make pairs.

I smile at old Mr .Wang. "Today, I cleaneD my teefe. Today, I drinkeD coffee." He has no idea what I'm talking about.

At eight o'clock the class ends. Everyone is tired from a day's work plus two hours of English. Everyone leaves quickly, Juanito giving me a warning, "Don't forget your homework, hombre."

I hang back for a word with the teacher. "Becky Sue, excuse me, I need extra help."

She looks at me, suspicious because I managed to say a whole sentence in English without being prompted.

"You don't need extra help, George. You just need to try harder."

"You don't understand. My wife . . . makes much pressure that I learn English."

"Then your wife should help you practice. She's American." She has all her papers packed in her briefcase. She's very legal-looking, in her black pantsuit with her mud-colored curly hair pulled back in a knot, trying to look older.

"Too much stress on the marriage," I say. The last thing I want is for Roxie to start correcting how I speak. "She wants you help." I'm trying to get myself motivated, and a private conversation with a young girl is great motivation, even if she's not so pretty. Also, there are things about Becky Sue that make me curious.

"George, I don't have time. I work forty hours or more a week and volunteer six hours on top of that to teach English."

"Why?" I ask. This is one of the things I'm curious about. Doesn't she have friends, something better to do with her evenings? "You're tired. I just buy you a coffee, one time. To be friends."

She doesn't answer for a moment, and I think maybe she's going to say yes. Then, "I don't think so, George. See you Thursday."

"OK. See you Thursday. You change you mind, any time is OK!" I smile to show no hard feelings. She nods, but doesn't smile back. This is another thing that makes me curious. She never smiles. She seems sad, and anxious.

The doctor calls and Roxie says, "Good news! Your sperm count is fine."

This doesn't surprise me, but I tell her great.

"Only thing is, their shape is a little bit off. Blunt at the tip or something. This could be making it harder for them to get to the egg."

Something wrong with the shape of my sperm? My sperm were good enough in Guatemala.

"But the bigger problem is that one of my fallopian tubes is blocked." You would think they could ream it out, like

178

Roto-Rooter it, but no, Roxie says it can't be fixed. "I can still ovulate, but it's more hit or miss. We have to meet with the doctor again to discuss our options."

We're in bed, with Roxie's head tucked against my shoulder while she plays with my hand. She turns it back and forth, then spreads it out like a palm reader. "Look at these calluses, mi amor. You're a regular campesino now."

Yes, and I make more as a gardener in DC than I could ever have made as a teacher in Guatemala, even with some farming on the side. However, we're not rich people. "What options, Roxie," I say.

"Don't worry. We're not candidates for IVF yet. There are things we can do first." She snuggles into me. "You *do* want a baby, don't you love? A little Jorge Vitalino?"

I'm thinking about ten thousand dollars every time they put my blunt sperm into a little dish with her eggs. No one ever had to spend so much money to make a baby in Guatemala. I'm thinking about the truck I want to buy so that I can go into business for myself. I pick her up and roll her on top of my big belly, like a bird on its nest. "Of course, mi gringuita. I want a baby." Really, I'm not so sure. Maybe I want the truck more, but it's too hard to think about it.

I start making progress in the English lessons. Becky Sue was right: I needed to work harder. I'm finding my motivation. I want to make her smile. She has told us that English is easy because there are only two verb tenses: present and past. It turns out she was lying, which comes as no surprise because life is more complicated than that. One evening she tells us that simple present isn't good enough. She has an old cassette player with her and she puts on a sad song sung by a lone woman with no accompanying instruments or voices or anything to take away from her loneliness. She sings that she is sitting in a diner—and Becky

Sue has brought in a picture of a diner with only one man behind the counter wiping up in case anyone doesn't know that diner means comedor—and in the song the woman is waiting for the man behind the counter to pour the coffee but he is looking out the window at someone coming in who is shaking her umbrella—Becky Sue has brought in an umbrella and is acting out the song—and they are kissing their helloes and the singer is trying not to notice and she is listening to the bells of a cathedral and thinking of her lover's voice. We spend the whole English lesson on this song which it turns out is teaching us the present progressive, a much more popular tense than simple present. But I think the song is about something else, so after the class I ask Becky Sue again to have a coffee with me and this time she says yes.

There's no diner near the library so we go to a MacDonald's. I buy a Big Mac and coffee and for Becky Sue I buy a hamburger and Coke. There aren't many people in this MacDonald's, so even though it's brightly lit, it's kind of lonely. We're eating our burgers and I say to Becky Sue, "I am thinking about the song and I am thinking you are singing about missing someone."

For the first time I see her smile a small sad smile. "Good use of the present progressive, George."

"Who you are missing, Becky Sue?"

"Who *are you* missing. I'm missing my baby, I guess." She looks away from me, out the window at the streetlights and I see there are almost tears swimming in her eyes. Her eyes are blue and I always thought them cold but now with the tears they look like the eyes of a young child who has lost its mother.

"You lost a baby?"

"I had an abortion. My boyfriend didn't want the baby, and I had the abortion to please him. Then he left me. I don't miss him. He was a piece of shit. I miss the baby." This all comes out pretty fast, and I have to wait for the English words to arrange themselves in my mind and make some sense. She looks startled to have revealed her secret to me, so I reach across the little plastic table to pat her hand.

"I'm sorry," I say. This is one English expression I know well, one of the first I ever learned. "You're young. You have another chance."

"That's what I tell myself. It doesn't make the pain go away."

"My wife is not young. She is trying to have a baby. Big problems. Much stress at home." It feels good to tell her this. I don't know why.

"I'm sorry. I guess I should feel lucky." She doesn't look like she feels lucky.

"How old are you, Becky Sue?" This is from one of our first English lessons.

She smiles again. Two smiles in one evening! "Twenty-two. I dropped out of college when I got pregnant. My boyfriend got me this job that I hate, working in his firm for right-wing lobbyists."

"Lobbyists," I repeat. She's about to explain the word. "I know what it means. My wife and her friends talk about it."

"Your wife is a professor. That makes her a liberal. I bet she hates lobbyists, at least the ones I work for. I hate them too. That's why I work at the library."

"Why you not quit your job?"

"Why *don't* you. I'm twenty-two, with no skills, no degree, and no place to go." She sucks on her straw and it makes a rattling noise. Her hamburger is gone. Mine too. "It's late. I should go," she says.

I hold her hand to keep her from picking up her trash. "Becky Sue, is good to talk. You can talk to me." I give her a big smile and let go of her hand. "Extra help!"

The option the fertility doctor gives us: for several months she'll shoot my blunt sperm into Roxie at the time when her hit or miss eggs should be coming down the working fallopian tube. As a campesino I'm familiar with artificial insemination. Only difference is we never gave the bull pornographic magazines to collect his sperm. I guess I should feel lucky.

The doctor also tells Roxie she should avoid stress, which is like telling a hummingbird to slow down. I suggest we take a vacation, a week at the beach. Roxie says, "I can't think of anything less relaxing than lying on the sand like a slab of bacon and getting sunburned."

It's true. Her pale redhead's skin burns in no time. "I just want to keep working," she says. "There's a paper on young Guatemalan poets I want to finish for the conference in Santa Barbara in August."

Poor Roxie! No one gives a flying quetzal for Guatemalan poets. But she can't help her passions. I just hope they don't derail her career, which I hear about in detail every night in bed, where most of our conversations take place. All the politics it takes to climb the academic ladder. I'm glad I'm a gardener. It isn't a good time for me to take off a week of work either. It's the high season for gardening, and I'm saving money for my truck.

"Don't worry," she says, kissing my belly. "The timing of the conference couldn't be better. I'll be back for ovulation." It's all she thinks about. I have to confess, it takes the joy out of making love.

We decide to hold a Fourth of July cookout and potluck, and invite everyone we know: Roxie's friends from the university—associate professors, assistant professors (I'm supposed to remember the difference), and a few graduate students who are stuck in DC for the summer—our favorite neighbors who are all either Latins or African Americans, the guys from my gardening crew, and my English class—Juanito, Lidia, Rosaria, and Estela (whom I think of as the chicas), Dmitri, Mr. Wang, Grace Kim, Yasuko, and the sisters Malia and Akufo. And of course Becky Sue. We've been studying English together in the library for four months now and we're all still hanging in, so it feels like time for a celebration. People are arriving all afternoon bringing homemade sushi, dips and canapés, pasta and bean and grain salads, and six-packs of beer—microbreweries and importeds from the university folks, Budweiser from the gardeners. Roxie makes sure to meet everyone from my English class because she's heard about them. They all practice their English with her. "Thank you for inviting me!" "Happy Independence Day!" "What a lovely home you have!" Mr. Wang still can't say much, but he hands Roxie a tupperware full of dumplings and nods a lot. To Becky Sue Roxie says, "Congratulations! You've worked miracles with Jorge Vitalino. You must be a wonderful teacher. But I had no idea you were so young!"

Becky Sue mutters something, and I can tell she's feeling shy. I've never seen her out of her work clothes. She's wearing a very short skirt and a tight top that shows off her nice little breasts, and she looks prettier than usual.

"Come," Roxie says. "Meet Byron and Sylvie. Byron's in Latin American studies and Sylvie's a grad student in comp lit. Guys, Becky Sue works for the enemy—Wofford, Milton, and Pearl—but go easy on her. No bloodshed, please!" And she drags Becky Sue into the living room discussion about raising the debt limit and the Tea Party assholes. I feel sorry for Becky Sue, but what can I do?

It's hot and humid, a typical DC summer day, and all the doors and windows are open and ceiling fans going and people are all over the house, front porch, and back terrace.

I go out to the backyard, where I have the charcoal ready and the beef has been marinating for hours in my special sauce, and I start grilling. Pretty soon I'm handing out carne asada like candy. With all the food prepared by the people in our little United Nations gathering, I have to say no dish is more popular than my carne asada. The afternoon wears on, with everyone getting pretty alegre. I'm drinking beer. Roxie, who hopes she's pregnant, isn't drinking, but she's keeping the pitchers of margaritas full. The stereo is rocking the house with Latin music. The guys from my crew have homed in on the chicas from the English class, rolled up the rug in the living room, and started in on some serious salsa dancing. Juanito drifts my way in the dining room, where I'm checking the supply of food.

"How's your English working?" I ask him.

"What English? I've just been talking with your wife's friends about Calderón's fucked drug war. They know more about Mexican politics than I do."

"And more Mexican curse words," I add.

"Not possible. But they're good people, if you don't mind a lot of blah, blah, blah. La Becky Sue couldn't take it." We see her come in from the front porch, where the discussion group moved after the music got turned up.

"I think she wants to dance with an ugly Mexican," Juanito says. He threads his way through the dancers in the living room toward her. I head out back to cook more carne asada. Mr. Wang finds me there a little later.

"Good party. Very good. I go now. Many thanks."

"You bet, Wang," I say. "See you Monday at the library." He's old, and I can't blame him for leaving early. The sun is setting at last, taking with it some of the heat. I follow Wang up the stairs to the kitchen, carrying a plate of carne asada. Most of the English classmates have joined the dancing in the living room, and they wave goodbye to Mr. Wang. I fill a plastic cup with margarita and take it to Becky Sue.

"Having fun?" I ask her. She's sweaty and flushed, and her curly hair is escaping from a ponytail.

She takes the margarita. "I'm already drunk. But thirsty, so what the hell!" She drinks it down like lemonade. Oh Becky Sue!

"Dance?" I ask her.

I hold her pretty close, which is the way I like to dance. She's my height, so I'm looking right into her eyes. They're a little glazed from the booze, but shiny. I like seeing her happy. Since she became my motivation in English, I've taken her out for MacDonalds a few times after class. She's told me a little bit more about her piece-of-shit ex-boyfriend, but not much. She's private. No one else except me seems to be trying to make her happy. I give her a chance to get into my rhythm, then I lead her through some turns and spins. She's smiling.

"You're having fun," I tell her.

"You're a good dancer," she says and gives me a flirty look.

"Claro," I say. "I'm Latin. It's in the genes." This of course is a lie. I know plenty of Latin guys who are lousy dancers. But it's good to keep the myth alive. We dance a few numbers, then I give her back to Juanito and ask Akufo to dance. It wouldn't be good to get too hung up on Becky Sue's happiness, I remind myself. I have responsibilities.

Later, I'm out on the front porch, where the political discussion has finally given way to high levels of music and festivity. We're watching the neighbors' display of cherry bombs and sparklers across the street when Lidia comes out to tell me that Becky Sue's in the bathroom throwing up.

"Hombre!" I say. "Somebody's got to take her home."

"I came in Rosaria's car. We'll take her. No te preocupes, amigo."

Rosaria comes out with her arm around Becky Sue, who looks pale and wobbly. "Are you OK?" I ask her.

"Better than I was a half hour ago." She's back to her weak smile.

"You need a good night's sleep." I forget where I learned this English expression, but I hope it will reassure her. I also hope she'll be able to put her head on the pillow without it spinning around all night. To the chicas I say in Spanish, "You can come back if you want."

"Gracias," Lidia says. "But we have another party after this. Ciao!"

Roxie is at my side while all this is going on. "Are you sure you're sober enough to drive?" she asks Rosaria in Spanish. I know that if we had a car she would want to drive Becky Sue home herself. But that would be crazy.

"Don't worry," I tell her. "The chicas will make it. See you Monday, girls!"

I'm glad the chicas are there to help out Becky Sue. Everybody needs a little help. In English, a verb can't do very much on its own. To ask a question or negate itself, it needs a helping verb. This leads to strings of little words. A sentence like *¿Qué hace Jorge?* needs a verb to repeat itself, like a hiccup. What does George do? Notice that the do verb pops up twice. That first *do* has absolutely no meaning whatsoever. It exists only to ask a question.

You can't say *No walk*, as you would in Spanish. It's *Do not walk*. But even that is not what you'll see on signs all around DC, because with all those strings of little words, is it any wonder that people shorten them? *Don't walk.*

The most fucked of all English helping verbs are called the modals. They don't behave like other verbs; they don't

186

take an *s* but they will take *not*; they may have no past or future, they can't act alone, but you can't get far in English without them. We are practicing them on Monday in the library.

"I shouldn't drink twelve margaritas." Becky Sue.

"I could dance all night." Juanito.

"I would like to visit your beautiful home again." Grace Kim, our most advanced student.

"I might invite you." George.

We're having a contest with two teams. We have a stack of cards with modal verbs on them: *can, could, may, might, must, shall, should, ought to, will, would.* When the card comes up, the contestant has to make a sentence using the word. You can negate if you wish. We're all laughing as we make up our sentences.

"I can drink vodka all night." Dmitri.

"I can speak English." Mr. Wang.

"George's friends can really dance." Lidia.

"I could have danced all night." Akufo sings her line.

"I should have stopped at three margaritas." Becky Sue.

"Becky Sue ought to forgive herself. I've been drunker." Rosaria.

"I would like to speak perfect English." Grace Kim.

Coulda, shoulda, woulda, Becky Sue tells us. Not only do we learn correct English, we also find out how the language is actually spoken. These truly fucked modal verbs compress all our longing and regret into a minimum of sounds. Nothing like a party to improve an English lesson.

At home, things are not improving. A week later, Roxie comes out of the bathroom crying. She's gotten her period. I should be used to her monthly despair, after three years, but I'm tired of it. This time we hoped would be different, with my sperm getting injected into her like a round of machine-gun fire, so that even those blunt little guys could achieve their objective. But who knows if the egg ever made the scene? It's not like the fallopian tubes take turns, this month one, next month the other. It's hit or miss. This time it's miss.

I put my arms around her and try to disguise my true feelings "Hey, mi gringuita. We'll try again in August. It'll be our lucky month, I feel it in my Indian blood." I don't like to see her sad. It's my job to keep her happy. It's getting to be a hard job. How bad would it really be, I think sometimes, to not have children? As bad as this?

She throws my arms off and sits down in front of the computer. "I can't take this any more," she says. I look over her shoulder to see her open up our bank account. "I'm ready to start the IVF." She's checking our balance.

I don't like it.

"Come on, mi amor," I say. "Let's take a day off and go to Eastern Market." I hate to shop, so this is a pretty nice offer. Roxie accepts, and we take the bus down into Capitol Hill. Roxie likes to browse for bargains in the flea market, and I buy produce that I can't grow in my postage-stamp backyard—beets, potatoes, fresh corn. We stop to chat with a vendor we know, a woman from Ecuador who imports Panama hats and alpaca sweaters. While we're talking, Roxie looks up and says, "Mira! Tu maestra de inglés con tu amigo!"

It's true. There, in the next aisle over, Becky Sue is strolling along with Juanito.

Híjole! What's going on here? It's ten o'clock on a Saturday morning, and the last I saw the ugly Mexican we were saying good night to Becky Sue after last night's class. I don't remember noting anything that would lead to them andeando together little more than twelve hours later.

Roxie is waving to them, and Juanito is steering Becky Sue our way with a big chili-consuming grin. "Hi guys," he says. "Whaddaya know!" Showing off his deft use of English contractions.

"Hi, George," Becky Sue says, without looking me in the eye, and then Roxie is introducing her to Mercedes, the Ecuadoreana, and they are exclaiming over the artesanía and Mercedes is explaining that Panama hats really come from Ecuador and are the Cadillac of straw hats. The name was a mistake, a fuck job by some gringo importer in the nineteenth century. Becky Sue starts trying on hats.

"Qué haces, chingador?" I ask Juanito.

"Hombre, she likes to dance," he says. "You saw at your party. So I took her to a Brazilian club I know."

"Then you took her home?"

"To her place. I live with a bunch of Mexicans. Was I supposed to ask your permiso?"

"No man," I say in English, but quiet, so the ladies don't hear. "It's a free country." This is an expression that Roxie uses always with irony. Free for some, she adds.

Oh, Becky Sue, I think, what are you doing with this mojado? You know from our unit on family, back in March, that he has a wife and four kids in Oaxaca. She turns to us to show off a hat with a wide floppy brim.

"Bery cute," Juanito says. "Buy it. You need it!"

"What do you think, George?" she asks.

"It's nice. Buy it if it makes you happy." I look into her eyes, but I see no happiness there.

She pays fifty dollars for the hat—a bargain, Roxie tells her. With her job for the lobbyists, Becky Sue can afford it. Roxie doesn't own a Panama hat.

We take the bus home with the vegetables I've bought, the corn I'm going to grill. On the bus I tell Roxie about Juanito's wife and kids.

"How long has it been since he's seen them?" she asks.

"Five years. He missed his oldest daughter's quinceañera."

"Pues," she says. "That's sad. I imagine he can't go home for a visit, with the border crossing so dangerous now."

"We don't talk about it." Maybe she hears my anger.

"You don't expect him to stay celibate forever, surely. He's a Latin man. It would be dangerous to his health!" Roxie likes to make fun of our machismo.

"He could stick to whores and Latinas." I feel uncomfortable, even as this slips out. She detects my racism right away.

"You'd deny him an American wife and a shot at legal papers? Isn't that a little selfish, mi amor?"

I wonder if that's what Juanito is after. It wasn't what I was after when I fell in love with Roxie—I was after the most beautiful, the most intelligent, the most interesting gringa in Todos Santos—but it turned out well for me. Or so I thought at the time. Now I'm not so sure.

Later, I make a salad from the potatoes and beets and grill the corn and chicken breasts I've marinated in lime and achiote. Roxie mixes a pitcher of margaritas. Now that she's not pregnant she can drink, and we sit on our tiny terrace and watch the neighbors' kids splash in a wading pool in their backyard.

"I can wait a few more months for the IVF," Roxie says. "I know that's what you want." I guess she's noticed.

"There's a Toyota pickup on Craigslist, 2006, only 30,000 miles. Want to go with me to Virginia tomorrow, if I can borrow the jefe's truck, to look at it?"

"How much are they asking?" she says.

"Twelve thousand. But they'll come down."

"You go. Try out your English. I need to work." She's stressed out over the paper she's scheduled to deliver in Santa Barbara. She wants this paper to knock the socks off all the over-educated critics who say the great age of Latin American literature is over. She says they don't even read original material in the university any more; they just read work by other critics. She says they've lost touch with the raw power of poetry. Meanwhile, she's crying over her lost eggs. She finishes the last of her margarita and picks up our empty plates to carry them into the kitchen. "Do you want coffee?"

I'm listening to the sounds of the neighborhood—kids yelling, dogs barking, cars swishing by, Latin music—and thinking about money. I'll have to stop sending money to my parents in Todos Santos, to my sister in North Carolina whose husband drinks everything he makes and beats her. Roxie comes back out with the coffee. "We can start looking for a loan," she says. The mortgage, the truck, and the IVF are on her mind, too.

"If it's what you want," I say. So much debt.

"It's not what I want. But what choice do we have?"

"Your friends Byron and Sylvie say, not childless, *child-free*," I say in English. "It's very American."

She looks at me with her green eyes pooling up. I can see another crying fit coming on like a freight train. "Jorge Vitalino! Do you mean that?" she asks in a trembling voice.

I know when to jump off the track. "No." I try for a goofy smile. It takes a big effort. "Es una broma." A joke.

We sip our coffee while the tension unspools. "Why does Becky Sue call you George?" Roxie asks. "No one else has an Anglicized name."

"I told them to call me George," I say. "When I started English lessons, I figured it was time to be an American."

She raises her eyebrows and studies me over her coffee cup. "You're a funny guy, mi amor."

Things are frosty between me and Juanito after Eastern Market, but between him and Becky Sue, nada. From the way they behave in the English classes, you wouldn't know anything was going on between them, and I don't know if she's still seeing him. Roxie pulls several all-nighters, finishes her paper, and leaves for Santa Barbara. I didn't buy the Toyota, so I borrow my jefe's truck to take her to the airport. On the way there she says, "If the gardening business makes you happy, it's fine with me. You don't have to learn English."

I know she's trying to make things OK between us before she leaves. "English isn't so bad," I tell her. "It'll be useful when I have my own customers." I don't want to part in anger either, although, to be honest, I'm looking forward to a week on my own. I walk her to the terminal.

"Be good, Georgie," she says, using my American name in fun, and we kiss a passionate goodbye kiss.

A hurricane moves up the coast from the Gulf right after Roxie leaves, bringing days of hard rain. The gardening crew can't work, so I'm stuck at home all day watching sports on my TV. Roxie calls me every night to tell me about her meetings, to tell me she misses me, to make sure I'm being good. Other than that I don't talk to anyone, so it's a relief to get out in the evening to go to the library. The English class is small. There are high wind warnings for the night. Juanito is among those absent.

The lesson for the evening is the verb "used to." It's pronounced like one word: *useto.*

"I used to live in Guatemala. Now I live in the US of A."

"I used to work in machine shop in Russia. Wife wanted to come to America. Now I'm unemployed."

"I used to live in a mud hut. Now I work in a five-star hotel." Like me, Akufo has a green card.

"I used to be an illiterate girl in Ghana. Now I'm getting my GED."

"I used to teach high school to delinquents and go out with young professionals in Bogotá. Now I wait tables and go to bars."

"I used to be a poet. Now I'm a political refugee." This is a hard sentence for Mr. Wang, but he gets it out.

"I used to be a West Virginia hillbilly. Now I work for coal companies in mountaintop removal," Becky Sue says.

The tropical depression has entered the room, and we can hear the wind beating on the library windows. Becky Sue ends the class early. I linger after the others leave. "Will you have a coffee?" I ask her. We haven't had a word together since before the Fourth of July.

"We'll drown, getting to MacDonald's," she says.

"I have a big umbrella."

She holds my arm and we run through the driving rain. We don't see that the MacDonald's is dark until we've crossed the street. There are big X's of masking tape across its windows, and a sign on the door reads, "Closed for hurricane." My jefe's truck is parked in the library parking lot. I take Becky Sue's hand and we run back across the street. We're drenched from head to feet by the time we get in the truck.

"My house is a few blocks away," I say, although she knows this from the party. "I can make you coffee and then take you home." I don't know where she lives. I don't know what I'm doing, but I need to talk to her. Just talk, I think, to sort things out in my mind. She is shivering. I find a bandana I've stashed in the glove compartment—I use them on the job—and give it to her to dry off as much as she can. She shakes her hair, which has come loose from its knot and is flying wild.

"This is exciting," she says.

I drive through the empty streets, barely able to see through the windshield wipers. No one is out in the storm. Small branches are snapping off trees. Garbage-can lids shoot out of alleys and spin across the street. I park in front of my house and we dash for the front porch. I tied the porch furniture down earlier in the day, but I didn't tape the windows. This house has stood through ninety years of storms. Because I grew up in Todos Santos, I have flashlights and candles ready in case the power goes out.

Inside, I give her my thick terrycloth robe so that she can take off her wet clothes and put them in the dryer. I straighten up the living room a little bit, hide all the dirty plates and glasses in the dishwasher, fluff the pillows on the sofas. Becky Sue comes in just as the coffee is ready. We can hear the wind screeching. "It's scary," she says. She doesn't sound scared. She sits down and tucks her feet under her. I give her a cup of coffee and sit opposite on the other couch. She's let her hair down, and it falls past her shoulders. I look for something to say. I can't think of anything except what's on my mind.

"Are you still seeing Juanito?"

She purses her lips. "You're jealous. I only went out with him once."

"Why should I be jealous?"

"You shouldn't." She blows across cup her coffee and takes a sip. "It's you that I'm attracted to." That's a relief, I have to say. "But your wife is right here, and Juanito's is far away. It seemed . . . cleaner."

"My wife is in Santa Barbara,"

"I know. You told me." She gets up, comes over, and sits next to me, facing me. She leans toward me, looking through the fringe of curls, getting so close that I have to kiss her. I forget about sorting things out and focus on the sensations coming from her lips and body. It's been a long time since I've kissed someone new. The pleasure of it explodes in my heart and pushes out all the worries and anger. After we've kissed for a while, I say, "What about being clean?"

"I'm leaving in September for Oman. To teach English to rich Arabs. This is a parting gift." And so it is.

The storm passes. The sun comes out. I clean house like a crazy man, washing the sheets, vacuuming, scrubbing every dish, removing any traces of Becky Sue, making the house shine. A feeling of reckless power comes over me. If I can make Becky Sue happy with just one night of love, I can do anything. I check Craigslist.

This is how I find myself on my way to Dulles International Airport to pick up Roxie in my brand new, bright red crew-cab pickup. Well, not brand new, but very nice and more expensive than I ever meant to pay. Roxie doesn't know about it yet. One way or another I'm fucked. Either I've blown our chance at IVF or Roxie will find out what else I did while she was away. She has a way of always knowing, and if she doesn't guess, then I might have to confess. And if I don't, then I have to go to the library on Monday night and see the English teacher and pretend that nothing happened.

Something did happen. I'm not mad at Roxie any more.

SAINTS AND SINNERS

Don Roberto hesitated a moment before tapping on the door of the American's house. Perhaps Don Noé would be . . . asleep . . . resting; he hated to disturb the sick man. But there was smoke drifting from the chimney, and Don Roberto needed to talk. Here was the one man who would not judge him harshly. He was relieved when Don Noé, looking wan, his beard a little thinner, but otherwise unchanged—he'd always been a gaunt young man, well, not so young any more, he must be close to fifty now—welcomed him in and offered him a cup of tea.

The room was bedecked in greetings: get well cards, children's drawings, balloons hanging from the low rafters, jars stuffed with wildflowers, unlit votive candles, as if everyone in Todos Santos had been to visit. "I've just come from the faculty luncheon," Don Roberto began. Don Noé poured hot water from a kettle on the open hearth, then suffered a coughing fit that bent him double and finally forced him to sit down. So it was true, what everyone said: his condition was serious. "Can I get you something? Isn't the smoke bad for your lungs?" The room was full of smoke from the cooking fire. Don Roberto had long admired the American's asceticism, but surely the circumstances called for a propane stove. At least the adobe walls were plastered and tight. Roberto liked the house, not so much because it was traditional, but because adobe was a superior building material, in his opinion, with better insulating qualities than the more modern cinderblock. It was warm and dry, for such a rustic house at such an altitude. He carried the two mugs of tea to the table and sat down next to Don Noé, whose coughing subsided, leaving two unhealthy red spots on the pallor of his cheeks.

Don Noé—his American name was Noah—smiled and shook his head. "I'm on a new round of antibiotics. The doctors are cautiously optimistic. Besides, what do I have to fear from death? I'm ready." He patted the pine box beneath the mattress upon which they both sat. He'd had his coffin made when he built his house, and he used it as both bed and sofa, as a reminder. When he'd first stumbled on Todos Santos nineteen years earlier, he'd been the sole survivor of a fiery crash on Interstate 29 outside Fargo that had claimed the lives of his parents and younger sister on the eve of her graduation. One trait he shared with Guatemalans, that had made him feel so at home here, was a keen awareness that death was unavoidable. He took a sip of tea and addressed the school principal. "Tell me the gossip. The luncheon."

Don Roberto described the event that had been held in the salón, long tables hauled in, pine needles decorating the cement floor, baskets piled with Doña Rosalinda's special tamales, speeches by the regional superintendent and the mayor.

Amilcar was there, now superintendent of padrefamilias, no longer a teacher but still Don Roberto's old best friend, still scheming to become mayor. Baldomero the troublesome math teacher, his ex-wife Alma, the preacher Baudilio, Hilda Florencia, who had settled down since her marriage to the bus driver, fat Pepe whose diabetes was getting worse, Lencho and Pancho, Eva Silvia and Luz, but not Lala, and a host of others, including, of course, Amilcar's rival Cesar, who never missed a gathering where he could hold forth.

"You know that Cesar has become a Mayan priest?" Don Roberto asked.

"El Lobo goes from guerrillero to chimán. Why not? It's a sign of the times," Noah said. "An improvement, I'd say." Although he'd arrived in Guatemala after the war, he'd seen the devastation it had left behind. Noah had been a pacifist forever, even before the year he spent in the ashram in India, following his parents' and sister's deaths.

All in all, the gathering was very alegre, Don Roberto told him. They all sent Don Noé their greetings, and hoped he'd be back soon.

"Even Felipa?" Noah wanted to know. He'd never stopped carrying a torch for the Todosantera who'd turned him down, as the whole town knew, although he claimed to have moved on. *I have plenty of kids without hijos of my own,* he'd say. Now he looked tired, and a shadow passed over his face.

"I've come to bother you with something," the school principal said. He fell silent, as if unsure how to continue.

"I'm sure it won't be a bother," Noah said.

"I have to ask you a favor. There's no one else I can confide in." Roberto sighed deeply. "I have to leave Todos Santos." He bowed his head and covered his face with his hands.

Noah waited in the heavy silence for Roberto to recover. A log snapped in the fire. Finally Noah spoke in a gentle voice. "Why?"

Roberto lifted his head, but didn't meet Noah's eyes. He didn't seem to be seeing anything. "I've impregnated a señorita. A girl in segundo básico."

Noah thought that no human mishap could astonish him any longer. He was wrong. In the nineteen years he'd known Don Roberto, they'd shared confidences. He'd heard tales of Roberto's wild youth—nothing more, it seemed, than some drunken carousing in his one year of university. Roberto had been by his own admission terribly shy, and he'd been sent for his first teaching job to a village deep in a valley in the remotest part of the Cuchumatanes. The Indian children there had never seen a Ladino, a mixed breed from the department capital, and the young girls ran and hid from him in fright. He was still single at the age of thirty, when he came to Todos Santos to replace his father at Urbana Mixta, the town's main primary school, first as teacher, later as principal of both the elementary and middle schools. He remained aloof, going home every weekend (as had his father) to the house where he'd been born, now inhabited by his brothers and their children. Noah had seen Roberto's reserve breached finally in his late-blooming relationship with Samantha, when she lived in Todos Santos, an attachment that seemed destined to endure over time and distance. Roberto was not the kind of man to dally with students.

"I don't know how it happened," Roberto said. "It's been over a year since Samuela's been here. I've been lonely, depressed, beginning to think that she won't be back." In fact, he was sure of it. Although she was the love of his life, he knew he played a much smaller role in hers, far away in Nueva York. She had her two children and, now, her first grandchild. Since the birth of her daughter's baby, Samuela had been distant, distracted on the phone, forgetting her Spanish, forgetting him. Her little house on Chicken Peak was gathering dust. It was inevitable. "Magdalena offered to help in my office with the typing. You know how slow I am at typing, always behind on the paperwork."

"Magdalena Mendoza Ramirez?" Noah interrupted. "Wasn't she in segundo básico two years ago, when I was still teaching English?" His position at the middle school had always been unofficial, but by the time he left the faculty had forgotten that, so much had they taken his presence for granted.

"She failed that year. Then was out last year working at the Cooperative."

And probably, thought Noah, flirting with every tourist who came into the store to buy a pair of red and white striped pants or hand-woven huipil. He knew her as one of the more aggressive of the town's teen girls, who competed hard for the few young men who hadn't gone North.

"Now she's back at the Instituto. I thought nothing of it when she stayed late evenings. I wrote out the reports and lists of names by hand, and she typed them up, leaving me time to work on the accounts. Often we were the only two left in the school. I only worried that she wouldn't leave enough time for her schoolwork. But she reassured me. She had determined to succeed, she told me. She wanted to go on to high school and make something of herself."

"She's gotten quite pretty, hasn't she, la Magdalena?" Noah commented.

"I didn't even notice. I didn't think of her in that way. She did me small kindnesses. She would show up when I was working late, with a sandwich or a thermos of hot coffee. When arthritis pain was bothering my feet, she brought me warm socks. They helped. When I was a young man, there would be female teachers who paid this kind of attention to me, and I'd know what they wanted. But this was different, a young girl, and I'm an old man. What could she want from me?"

Noah's question exactly, but he refrained from asking it.

"On my birthday, she brought me a bunch of carnations and . . . a bottle of wine. How could she know? I always brought Samuela carnations, we always drank wine together. I suppose I told Magdalena. I talked about Samuela with her. She thought it was romantic that I was in love with a gringa.

That night, in my office, my birthday, we drank the wine, Magdalena and I. I must have had more than she. After all, she's just a young girl. That's when it happened." Roberto hung his head again and clasped his hands to his forehead. He wished he could forget. How solicitous she'd been of his loneliness, his tragic love, his needs, how she'd given herself to him, surprised him by sitting in his lap, telling him to imagine it was his gringuita in his arms. How he'd taken advantage of her youth and romantic nature, closed his eyes to the unspeakable thing he was doing, and even with eyes closed he couldn't imagine her as Samuela.

"Just that one time?" Noah asked.

"Just the once. I could barely look at her when she came back to type for me again. We never talked about it, and we carried on with our work as if it hadn't happened." Don Roberto fell silent.

"This is a big load you've been carrying. I'm glad you've told me." Don Noé stood up and took the empty mugs from the table in front of them. "Do you want more tea?" he asked.

Roberto looked up at him, suddenly aware again that he was talking to a sick, possibly a dying, man. "No. Forgive me, dear friend. I've taken too much of your time." He stood up as well.

"Sit back down," Noah said. "I have time, the doctors promise. You're not finished. You haven't gotten to the favor." He placed the mugs in the palangana in the kitchen and came back with two apples, a plate, and a knife. "The neighbors bring me more bounty from their gardens than I can eat myself. You need to help." He quartered and cored the apples as Don Roberto sat again and watched. "When did this happen?"

"Almost four months ago. Last week, Magdalena came to me in tears and told me she was pregnant. She promised to keep my secret. But . . ."

"But word will get out. This isn't a promise that can be kept, you know that." Certainly not in a town like Todos Santos, where many eyes had probably noticed the teenager working late in the principal's office and would soon be on the watch for other signs. He took a wedge of apple and chewed it slowly. "Don Roberto, how can you be sure this child is yours?"

Roberto opened his eyes wide and furrowed his brow. "She told me she was a virgin. I'm not an expert in these things."

"You could at least investigate a little. Find out if she has other . . . boyfriends."

"I could not." The principal was firm. "It would be beneath my dignity." He spread his hands. "I have obligations. I have to believe her."

Noah scratched his beard. For an educated Ladino from the department capital, Don Roberto was unworldly, even naïve, even after all his years with the Todosanteros. Noah was more skeptical. "What has she asked you for?"

"Nothing." He finally took some apple from the plate, to be polite. The two men ate in silence, each pondering the possibilities from different perspectives—American and Guatemalan. "I have some money," Roberto said. "I want to leave it with you, for the child, before I go. It's not a lot, but all I have."

"Where will you go? New York?" Noah knew that Roberto had been once to visit Samantha in the States. He hadn't liked it there, and came back after a month.

Roberto sucked in a breath. "I don't know. Someplace far away."

"You haven't told Samuela," Noah said, using the name Samantha called herself in Guatemala. He waited. Roberto took another piece of apple and didn't answer. "You should. She'll forgive you. I know her."

Roberto continued eating his apple politely. There was no way he would tell Samuela. He couldn't ask for her forgiveness when he couldn't forgive himself. These Americans with their odd notions of permissiveness between men and women, they couldn't change the way he felt about his betrayal. There was only one course left open to him.

Noah sighed. "I confess that I'm getting tired. I need to sleep. Promise me you won't do anything rash for the next couple of weeks. You have at least a month before anything starts to show."

They both stood up and shook hands. Noah clasped Roberto's shoulder. "Try to go easy on yourself. You'll do the right thing, and it will get better."

"Thank you, Don Noé, for the apple. Please take care of your health."

Noah stood in his doorway, watching Don Roberto make his way down the dirt road toward town. A tall man, he had to bend over in a somewhat courtly gesture when he stopped to greet and talk to each Todosantero whom he passed.

««« — »»»

The babble of voices and shouts, the slap of plastic sandals and hard thuds of leather boots, reverberated with the pounding of the basketball in the courtyard of the school. Magdalena and her two best friends looked down from the second floor balcony at clusters of students chatting, at the pickup game, at Enrique weaving through the players like an eel, dribbling. He dunked the ball through the hoop. The tallest boy in tercero básico, Enrique was the school star.

"Look at him," sighed Lucía. "What a novio he'd make."

"Dream on, chica," Irma said. "You'll never get him away from la Patricia, Señorita Instituto of 2011."

"Let her have him," Magdalena said. "He's going North, like all the boys. Five years from now, she'll just be another sueño americano widow."

Don Roberto came out of the principal's office and walked across the courtyard.

"Oooh," Irma giggled. "Here comes Magdalena's novio now."

"He's not my boyfriend!" Magdalena objected, feeling her face get hot. She'd made no effort to hide her relationship with the principal, but decorum demanded her denial.

"The American woman is foolish to leave him here alone," Lucía said. "What does she think—he'll be true to her forever?"

"At least Magdalena won't be a widow," Lucía taunted. "Don Roberto isn't going North."

Magdalena pulled one of her braids across her lips and wondered. Was that what attracted her to the tall, stern man? A man old enough to be her grandfather! And yet, he had a body as lean and hard and urgent as a youth. She knew; and how that special knowledge excited her. She had studied him, had penetrated behind the gentlemanly façade and discovered the shy and lonely boy. But a boy with nicer manners than any of her contemporaries. She imagined him coming home at the end of the day, carrying a bunch of carnations, entering the kitchen where she had the fire going, had hot water ready to soak his tired feet, had his supper ready, while the baby slept.

Don Roberto rang the bell hanging from the courtyard eaves, signaling the time for class. Magdalena turned away from the balcony rail. "Come on, ladies. It's time to stop your gossip."

The three girls hurried into the classroom to get their favorite row of seats, halfway back. They made a show of taking out their notebooks and ignoring the boys filing in. Magdalena placed a hand on the belly hidden beneath the folds of her thick huipil and said a silent prayer.

«« — »»

Alma hesitated at the door of a classroom that was empty of students, to address her colleague. "Cesar, do you have a minute?"

"Seño, I always have time for you. Come in." Cesar shoved papers into his moral, the bag he'd crocheted himself. The guardian of his town's traditions, he made sure that his daughters learned to weave and that his sons mastered the manly art of crocheting—a craft that was sadly dying among the younger generation—as well as planting corn with a pick and hoe. "What can I do for you? You're looking well. Sit down." He pulled up a bench for her and sat down in the chair behind his teacher's desk.

Alma brushed the bench, arranged the folds of her skirt, and sat. "The elections. I assume you'll be running." At the luncheon the day before, Don Roberto had announced his intention to retire at the end of the school year in November. The faculty and padrefamilias would elect their candidate, who would be recommended to the school board in Huehue to succeed the principal. Already the jockeying had begun.

"But I thought you'd be a candidate, Alma," Cesar said with genuine surprise. "You've been teaching as long as I have. You're a leader among women."

"I'm a woman. As you say, a strong woman. The parents don't like that. And I'm Ladina. The next principal should be a Mayan, a Todosantero." Alma had always been forthright to the point of bluntness.

"Your family has lived in Todos Santos a long time, long enough to be considered almost native." Cesar was diplomatic.

Alma snorted. "You burned my father out and threatened to kill him in '82. But bygones are bygones, Cesar. That war is over. Now we have the drug war. The school needs a firm hand and a principal who can be an example to our families. You have a son who's studying to be a doctor and a daughter who's practicing law in Guatemala, neither running off to the United States. We need our youth to stay and build the country."

"Always so passionate, Alma." Cesar smiled, showing his gold tooth, the tooth that had identified him as the guerrilla leader El Lobo in '82 through the mouth hole of his balaclava. "Why haven't you ever remarried?"

"I'm a Catholic. I'm still married, no matter what Baldomero does. I'm not here to discuss my personal life, Cesar, but to offer you my support." She turned her face away from his provocative gaze and looked out the classroom windows. Students lingering on the balcony outside peered in at them. Why did Guatemalan men, whether Ladino or Mayan, find it necessary to be womanizers, as though their virility depended on it, Alma wondered. She stood up, not wanting to fan the flames of gossip. Cesar rose as well.

"I'm flattered. I would have thought you'd support Eva Silvia or Amilcar," he said.

"Eva Silvia has the same problem I do; she's a strong woman." Perhaps for that reason, Alma couldn't stand her. "And Amilcar is washed up. It's up to you, Cesar. I have to go. See you tomorrow." Tossing her black hair that fell, thick and loose, below her waist, she swept from the room.

He watched her go, speculating. She didn't look well, despite what he'd said. She looked too thin.

Roberto left the bank, satisfied. His life savings—a stack of bills slimmer than the paperback volume of Lorca's poems that Samuela had given him—he had slipped inside a sock in his overnight case, where they were unnoticeable. Sad, but it was the lot of a schoolteacher to dedicate himself to a lifetime of great effort and poor pay. He turned methodically to the last task of his day in the department capital. He chose a hardware store near the bus terminal. It was hard to be truly anonymous anywhere he went in Huehuetenango, but at least here people came from small towns and villages all over the region to shop, with the convenience that their purchases could be easily loaded into buses and conveyed to distant homes. At least here the storekeeper wouldn't know he was a school principal, as every storekeeper in Todos Santos did, when he said he had a problem with rats, and wouldn't worry that the poison would be applied in the vicinity of children.

"This one is more modern," the man behind the counter told him, showing him a can marked in large red letters PELIGRO. "The rat, he's a very crafty animal. He takes a little nibble, and then waits to see if he gets sick before he eats any more. This poison doesn't act at once. The rat comes back to it again and again. The poison slowly builds to the point where it kills him, far away from where he ate it."

"Hmmm," said Roberto. "That requires a lot of patience. What other kinds do you have?" He kept his tone casual, as if this were a mere matter of housekeeping, not life and death.

The man searched the dusty shelves that reached into the store behind the counter and came back with a white plastic bottle. "This one is organic. Strychnine is a natural product, mixed with grain for bait. Fast-acting. Death occurs within an hour or two."

Roberto studied the label on the jar. One pound. "How much do I need?" he asked. "I have a lot of rats."

The storekeeper laughed. "One grain of this will kill a rat; a spoonful will kill a dog; two spoonfuls will kill a man. Be careful where you put it."

Roberto promised he would be careful. He wouldn't think about agony, or death throes. He had promised Don Noé to wait two weeks, but he would be prepared. He slipped the jar into his overnight case and headed for the three o'clock bus to Todos Santos, the Chicoyera.

«« — »»

Noah heard a whistle from outside and went to open his door. In his yard stood a boy carrying the firewood that Noah had ordered. The bundle must have weighed sixty pounds and was roped to José's back. "Where do you want it, Don Noé?" he asked.

"José! You carried that all the way down from La Ventosa?"

"No. I got a ride. If you like it, I can get you more. It's güito from the altiplano, burns long and won't smoke." Noah directed him to split the logs and stack them in the woodshed, and come inside when he was done. He left his door open to let in the air and sunlight, and to watch the boy while he worked. Normally Noah would split his own firewood; now he was too weak even to stand for any length of time. José was a fast, if sloppy, worker. He left a ragged stack and pile of splinters in front of the shed and approached the house shyly. "I'm all dirty, Don Noé," he said, hesitating to enter.

"Doesn't matter," Noah said. "Come in and have some tea. Cinnamon, chamomile, or Jamaican rose?" He set the boxes of tea bags out for José's selection and unwrapped a square of pan dulce, sweet yellow cake, to break onto plates. They settled on Noah's coffin-sofa, where Roberto had sat the other day. "Tell me how your studies are going. Are you keeping your grades up?"

"Not too bad. I'm passing." José dunked the pan dulce into his tea and ate it with appetite.

"This is your last year of básico, as I recall. Then what?" Noah blew across his tea before he sipped.

"I want to go to Huehue to study. If I can get a scholarship." Noah knew the boy was on scholarship now, living in a room in town and going home on weekends to his family in La Ventosa, a poor and windswept hamlet on the altiplano at the head of the valley of Todos Santos. He'd known José since he'd entered middle school, and had helped him get the scholarships that made his academic ambitions possible. "I want to be an accountant."

To work in an office, instead of the brutal physical labor of his parents. Noah could understand, although he hated to see people leaving the land of their ancestors. All the básico students aspired to become either accountants or teachers, or go North. "A good career. You can do it, if you don't get distracted by girls. Do you have a girlfriend?"

Noah detected a deeper reddening of José's brown cheeks, already flushed by the altiplano gales. "The girl I like doesn't like me," he said, looking away.

"I know that feeling," Noah sighed. "Anyone I know?"

José glanced at the door to the American's house, closed now. The room was warm, with the scent of Jamaican rose tea and cypress wood, the logs he'd brought his former English teacher burning on the hearth. The aromatic silence, the cards and flowers and candles, the illness of his teacher, gave José a sacred feeling. It seemed a place secrets could be confessed and wounds healed. "She's in segundo. Magdalena Mendoza Ramirez," he admitted.

Surprised, Noah paused to consider the chances of the coincidence, or perhaps it wasn't. He'd lived too long among the Maya to be immune to magical thinking. "She's a beauty," he said. "I don't blame you. What makes you think she doesn't like you?"

"I can't tell you." José gazed bleakly at the crumbs on his empty plate.

"More pan dulce?" Noah asked, and put another piece on the plate.

José dunked it gratefully into his mug to sop up the last remnants of hibiscus. Finally, overcome once again by the confessional urge, he said, "She rejected me."

"So you . . . spoke to her." Noah was careful to draw out the confidence. He was curious. He didn't know what José's secret would be, but he guessed that a lot was at stake.

"More than spoke! I've liked her since I was in primero, but she was ahead of me then. I never went near her; I wouldn't have had a chance. Then she was out, and back, and this year there was a Valentine's Day dance in the salón, and I don't know why, I asked her to dance." José stopped and stared into space with wide eyes.

Noah took a sip of his tea. "What happened?"

"She was with her girlfriends, Lucía and Irma. They laughed at me and pulled her away and said you can't dance with that rube, what is he thinking, and she shrugged her shoulders and went away with them without saying anything."

"Girls can be mean." Noah shook his head in sympathy. He had long experience with talking to teens. "I'm sorry. Was that your rejection?"

"No. Later that night at the dance she came up to me. The girlfriends weren't with her now. She said she was sorry for how they had treated me. She danced with me. She smiled at me." He stopped again.

"That must have been pretty exciting for you."

"Yes. We went outside. It was cold, and all the stars were out. She took my hand. She said let's go someplace where there aren't all these people around."

"Lucky you!" Noah said, although he knew this was not a tale of good luck.

"We went to my room. We made love." José couldn't believe he was telling Don Noé these things, but having started he needed to finish as expediently as possible. And really, it felt good, to get it off his chest. There was no one else he could tell.

"Wow," Noah said in English. "These things happen," he said to José. "Did you use protection?"

José looked puzzled. "What kind of protection?"

"A condom." Noah sighed, knowing the answer. "Did you have relations again?"

"Two more times. The dance was on a Saturday. She came to my room again on Sunday afternoon. She was very sweet. I felt like my heart was exploding. On Monday in school I saw her with her girlfriends and she gave me messages with her eyes. She met me between classes and whispered to keep our secret and meet her after school. She came to my room again."

"And then?"

"I thought we would be novios. She wasn't in school on Tuesday or Wednesday. By Thursday I was so eager that when I saw her I couldn't help but go up and touch her on the arm. She was with her girlfriends. What do you want, she said. Dirty peasant, she said. I thought it was because of the girlfriends. Later, I got her alone. I tried to tell her I loved her." He stopped again.

Noah could see the raw pain and humiliation on Jose's face, even before he asked the unavoidable question. "Is that when the rejection came?"

"She said I was nothing to her. An experiment. She was surprised I took it seriously. She told me not to bother her any more or she'd get me in trouble." José's eyes were moist.

"José, let this be a lesson. You must be more careful." He felt cruel instructing the heartbroken boy in the use of condoms. Especially since it was too late. Someone was already deeply in trouble.

«« — »»

A dozen old women shuffled into Eva Silvia's classroom on the first floor of the Instituto—old women with gnarled toes crammed into their plastic slippers. Magdalena watched their toes and shuddered. "Let me never end up that way!" she prayed silently, admiring her own shiny black heels. It was Sunday afternoon, a day for praying and dressing up.

Eva Silvia showed the women to desks beside the volunteers, teenage girls in básico who, for love of Eva Silvia, were spending their Sunday afternoon in school trying to teach someone's granny how to read. The old women came down from the hills wearing their worn straw hats and threadbare shawls. They could hardly speak Spanish. They had to begin at the beginning.

"Cómo se llama, señora?" Magdalena asked her student, a wizened lady with eyes bright as a sparrow's. "What's your name?" she repeated in Mam.

"María Matías," the woman whispered, and looked around as if afraid that someone would overhear.

Magdalena wrote the letters out in clear block capitals on her lined pad. "Here's your name, Doña María," she said. "Copy the letters and I'll tell you what they mean." The older woman took the pencil from Magdalena and looked at it helplessly. "I'll show you," Magdalena said. She stood behind María and leaned over her. The old woman smelled of smoke and dirt. Magdalena cupped her hand and showed her how to hold the pencil, steering it for her to form the letters, feeling the roughness of the bony hand, like a bird's skeleton, so fragile that Magdalena was afraid to hold it too tight and crush it.

Eva Silva passed down the row of desks, bending over each pair—each ancient survivor of life's pain and fresh-faced girl launching into that same struggle—to check their progress. Progress as tenuous as Guatemala's, but Eva Silvia was determined to move these women forward, if she had to carry each one on her back herself.

It was her fierce determination that inspired Magdalena and the girls of segundo básico.

«««« — »»»

"It's outrageous! Profe, the padrefamilias will never allow Cesar to run the school. How many of them lost loved ones to the guerrillas?" Eva Silvia wrung her hands in the principal's office.

"To the army, too," Don Roberto replied. In truth, the army had murdered far more citizens than the guerrillas ever did, but Don Roberto knew that truth did not govern emotions.

"Cesar causes controversy, whatever he does. Pepe wants to run, that fat moneygrubber, and Amilcar, father of an assassin, and Baudilio the evangelist, Baldomero the philanderer, Juan

214

Carlos who is lazy and stupid, the list of undesirable candidates goes on. All of them campaigning and gathering supporters to feud with the other candidates. This election is an embarrassment to the Instituto." Eva Silvia, red in the face, folded her arms across her ample chest and paused for breath.

"Don't you want to sit down, seño?" Don Roberto asked her. He was still standing behind his desk, where he had risen when Eva Silvia burst through the door. She sank obediently into the straight chair in front of his desk, allowing him to regain his seat. "It's unfortunate that there's so much squabbling going on, but Todosanteros have always been . . . argumentative," he said.

"That's why we've always had a Ladino principal. No offense, Prof."

"None taken." Roberto knew what people felt about him, a Ladino from Huehue, an outsider. He agreed that the time had come for a Todosantero to run the school.

"Don Roberto, why don't you name a successor? People respect you—the parents, the teachers, the town. If you back one candidate, you can put all this wrangling to rest."

"Who would you have me back, Eva?" No matter how he looked at it, Roberto foresaw only more troubles, more enemies. He smiled bitterly. "Yourself?"

"No . . . no. That's not what I meant." She breathed deeply and allowed herself to calm down, gazing out the window of the second floor office, seeing the mountains that rose up behind the school, pondering a calling from the heavens. "It would be a statement to the world," she mused. "A woman, and a Todosantera, the first principal of its kind at the Instituto."

Roberto sighed. "Todos Santos isn't ready for that. You do such good work, Eva Silvia, in the classroom and in your projects. It's enough for now."

The office door banged open again, as if he'd planned the ending to this conversation. In walked Magdalena. "Prof, I'm here!"

Roberto felt his face burn, and wondered if Eva Silvia saw it. "Very good. Come in," he said, as if she hadn't already. Magdalena saw the teacher sitting at his desk and stopped short.

"Magdalena, how good to see you!" Eva Silvia said smiling. "Don Roberto, Magdalena is volunteering with our literacy project. María Matías said wonderful things about you yesterday after the class, my dear. I think you're a natural teacher."

"Thank you, seño. I do my best to follow your example." She lifted her chin with an undisguised arch look at Don Roberto, which Eva Silvia couldn't fail to note. Magdalena was eager for the day when her secret would be out and for the respect her new status would command in Eva Silvia's eyes. "You donate so much time to worthy causes."

"Magdalena, here are the reports to type." Roberto held out a stack of papers and nodded at the spare desk and typewriter by the window overlooking the school courtyard, the classroom buildings, the mountaintops and clouds where, according to the Todosanteros, the ancestors sat in judgment.

<<<< — >>>>

"We're forgetting all our English, Don Noé. Profe Juan Carlos doesn't know anything. When will you be coming back?" Irma stirred spoonfuls of sugar into her chamomile tea and looked up at him from under long lashes. Noah smiled at her overt flirtation.

"Just as soon as I find a vase for these flowers. Where did you girls get such lovely roses? Are you gardeners? You must

216

have green thumbs." He left the two girls sitting side by side on his sofa while he looked in his cupboard. Containers for all the floral offerings were in short supply. All he could find was an empty can from refried beans. He filled it with water and leaned the arrangement against the wall, as the flowers were too tall for the can. Lucía, who'd presented him with the roses when he opened the door, giggled. "We bought them, Prof."

"Oh dear! You should save your money for high school. Every penny counts," he scolded.

"Don't worry," Lucía said. "I'm working and saving. I want to be a teacher, a good one who knows what she's talking about. Not like some at the Instituto."

Noah ignored the sauciness of her disrespect and addressed Irma. "And you?"

"I don't know," she said with a shrug. "Maybe I'll go to high school. Maybe I'll go North. There aren't any jobs in Guatemala."

"You think it's any better in the United States? Haven't you talked to the people who've come back?" Noah couldn't help but lecture, even though he knew that it was futile. He couldn't expect these girls to value the simple life he loved so much in Todos Santos. "Haven't you heard about all the deportations?"

"Everyone I know who's been deported can't wait to go back," Irma said. But then, as if thinking better of it, she added, "Of course you're right. Education is important. I'll go to high school." She worked the eyelashes again. "We didn't come here to talk about ourselves, Prof, but to inquire after your health. Everyone is worried."

"Thank you. I appreciate it. I'm taking care of myself. All of Todos Santos is looking after me!" These visits from his former students had become a daily event. Today it was Irma and Lucía; tomorrow it would be someone else. "Which reminds me, where is your friend Magdalena?" He knew they were usually inseparable.

"She works after school," Irma said with deliberate delicacy. Lucía giggled.

"Tell her I'd like to see her some time."

"Any reason?" Irma asked. "Is something wrong?" A signal seemed to pass between the two girls.

"Oh no," Noah dissimulated. "I'm glad she's back in school. I want to hear her plans."

««« — »»»

Rosalinda tested the water with her index finger, then lowered her tired feet into the basin. She groaned and felt the cramps releasing into the heat. Maybe she was getting too old for this job, on her feet selling all day. She stared at the dying embers in the stove and listened to voices passing in the street outside. Where was her granddaughter? It was after dark. A young girl shouldn't be out at this hour. An old woman shouldn't be alone. From the houses on either side Rosalinda could hear music playing on radios, the TVs on, babies crying, young men raising their voices. Since starting school in January, Magdalena had been coming home later all the time.

The door banged open and Magdalena walked in. "Hello, Granny."

Rosalinda tried to keep the complaint out of her voice. "Your supper is on the stove. Sit next to me, daughter."

Magdalena dropped her schoolbooks, spooned rice and beans onto a plate, and pulled a chair next to the stove.

"Do you want me to cook you an egg?" her grandmother asked.

"No, this is fine. I had a sandwich in Don Roberto's office." She said this with great contentment, as if that sandwich contained a special ingredient.

"Why does he keep you so late, Don Roberto?" Don Roberto had taught all of Rosalinda's children—six living and two dead—before they went North, leaving her with just one orphan granddaughter, child of her eldest daughter who had died in the desert crossing. Never had she known him to keep a child after school. The water in the basin was cooling off uncomfortably. She leaned over to rub her calves.

"Let me change the water, Granny." This was a nightly ritual. Magdalena put down her half-eaten supper on the edge of the stove. She fetched a towel for her grandmother's feet, and picked up the basin, carried it out of the room to dump the water in the sink, and brought it back to fill again from the kettle on the stove. Rosalinda watched with a feeling of measured gratitude. At least God had left her this one granddaughter. Kneeling down, Magdalena lifted the tired feet and placed them back in the basin. "Can I tell you a secret?" she asked, and Rosalinda could see the secret spilling out of her. "I think Don Roberto may be in love with me."

"Dios mío! That's ridiculous, Magdalena. What's going on in that office? I'll put a stop to it!" Although how she would, Rosalinda had no idea. Without a man around to beat sense into Magdalena, Rosalinda had never been able to control her granddaughter.

"No, you don't understand." Magdalena realized her confession had come out all wrong. And what had she been thinking, to tell her grandmother in the first place? Unless it was to prepare her for the inevitable revelations to come. "He's kind. He's honorable. I love him."

<<<< — >>>>

Two hours into the meeting of the faculty and school families to hear the candidates for school principal—the opening night of the campaign—people were squirming in their chairs, rows of metal folding chairs that had been set up in the salón. A hard rain beat on the tin roof. Alma, at the podium, looked out over her restless audience. Babies were fussing in their mothers' laps, children were chasing each other in the bleachers overlooking the floor. It was a school night. Alma knew she didn't have long to make her case, and she was feeling a little dizzy from nausea.

"Friends, colleagues, parents of our precious children," she kept her opening brief, "Don Roberto began this evening by saying that this is a historic night. For the first time we have the opportunity to elect a Mayan to head our school. You've heard many speeches from candidates promising to crack down on the malaise plaguing our youth. The best, the most obvious candidate, we have yet to hear. He's the man who has been a leader of this community for thirty years, a man of unwavering conscience, famous throughout Guatemala, a man who has raised his own children to be leaders in the national community. I introduce Cesar Jiménez Pablo . . . " Her next words were drowned out by the clamor rising in the room from buzz to angry roar. Alma grabbed the podium, felt a wave of abdominal pain, and slumped to the floor of the stage.

««« — »»»

Alma was up again next morning. Don Roberto stopped her crossing the schoolyard. "Are you sure you can work today? Don't you need to rest?" he asked. He placed a hand on her shoulder.

"I fainted from the heat. That's all," she said. They both knew that it had been a cold night in the salón. Only tempers had been hot. "People should have listened to Cesar. They were wrong to boo him out."

Roberto sighed. "We can't change the past, Alma."

"That's exactly what we're trying to do," she snapped. "I didn't help, by causing a scene last night. But neither did Pepe and Amilcar and Juan Carlos with all their divisive haranguing. If Todosanteros can't agree on a candidate, then they deserve what they get. Maybe you shouldn't retire, Roberto. The town isn't ready."

Roberto shook his head. "I'm an old man. I'm tired."

"Nonsense! You're sixty. I remember when you came to Todos Santos, thirty years ago." He'd been handsome, with an alluring dignity, but impossibly shy. None of the female teachers could get to him, although some tried. Not Alma; she was already unhappily married. "The school is your life. What are you going to do without it? Sit on your porch all day? You'll die of boredom."

Boredom appealed to Roberto. He'd dreamed of building a little house, planting a vegetable garden, living on his pension, Samuela at his side. A simple life, like the year they'd spent together when she lived in Todos Santos, when he was her secret lover on Chicken Peak. That dream had been snatched away by his own weakness. Now his greatest fear was the shame he would suffer if he lived long enough for his new secret to get out.

The problem of the padrefamilias nagged at him throughout the day. Teachers came and went from his office overlooking the schoolyard. They came bringing papers for him to fill out and left him with their strong opinions about who should fill his shoes, and what he should do about it. He was getting himself ready, tidying his affairs. He had promised Don Noé two weeks, then he would pick a day. It was surprising to him how easy it felt—this thought of his

221

release. He would walk up into the mountains. He had already picked a place, Puerto del Cielo. He didn't know if he would call Samuela; he didn't know if he had the strength to hear her voice. But he wanted to tell her that he loved her one last time. He didn't want to leave loose ends. He didn't want to leave the faculty at war.

A knock came at his office door and Magdalena entered, without waiting for him to speak. "I'm here, Prof," she said.

She acted as though she belonged in his office. How had he let her into his life? "Sit down, Magdalena," he said. "The reports are ready for you to type."

The stack of papers in Roberto's neat script lay beside her typewriter. How had he come to think of it as hers? She hesitated by his desk. "I brought you hot coffee. It's so cold in here. I worry about you, Profe. You work too hard. You'll wear yourself down."

She set the thermos down beside his hand, which had dropped to the desk as if steadying him against her. There was a moment when he was afraid she would touch his hand and he would have to recoil. But she moved away, patting the front of her skirt as if to smooth it, or soothe what lay inside.

"Thank you," he said and poured a cup from the thermos. He waited until she was seated, with the barrier of the large Underwood between them. Through the window behind her, the setting sun glowed orange over the school roof and mountain walls. He forced himself to look at her, to see how young and vulnerable she was, how . . . expectant. He really should have stopped her coming to his office months ago. It was his weakness, his refusal to face what he had done, that had made him passive. That would have to end. He forced himself to speak. "Magdalena, we have to talk. The child will be provided for, I want you to know."

She sucked in breath and clasped her hands together. "Oh Profe, I promise I'll be good to you. I'll make your tortillas and keep your house, if only we can raise the child together."

"No!" Roberto felt himself give a strangled bark, then tried to soften his tone. "That can't be. I'm going away."

Her eyes, staring at him, widened into hardened shields. "To New York!" She burst out in aggrieved certainty. He saw her dreams crumple, and she covered her face with her hands to catch the tears. Her shoulders shook. She spoke through sobs, "Prof, where does that leave me? With a child and no husband."

"My dear, you'll find a husband your own age. What would you want with a man old enough to be your grandfather?"

"I've never had a father, or a grandfather. Don Roberto, I love *you*." Somehow, with an insight that terrified him, he knew that she believed this to be true. He shuddered, raised himself stiffly, walked around the barricade of desks and papers and typewriter to stand behind her chair. He patted her on the back.

"Calm down," he said. Her sobs continued to rage. "Don't cry. It's not good for the baby."

<<<< — >>>>

Rosalinda picked her way down the steep cobbled street toward the town center, her heavy basket of chuchitos firmly planted on her head. The usual neighbors greeted her with the usual greetings, to which she replied automatically. She was distracted by thoughts of her granddaughter, whose behavior and recent revelation had alarmed her. The evenings in Don Roberto's office continued, although there had been no more professions of love. Rosalinda was beginning to have suspicions. If true, what a scandal! All the world knew that Don Roberto was attached to the gringa. If

Magdalena were to steal him away through some kind of brujería or trickery. . . the idea gave Rosalinda palpitations. She reached the bottom of the hill and lowered the basket onto the table that awaited her, at the corner of the main street. A woman in Ladina dress had her back to the table, her black hair flowing straight and free below her waist.

"Doña Alma!" she exclaimed. "What are you doing here on a school morning?" Rosalinda's position enabled her to keep track of every citizen's daily goings and comings.

Alma turned to her in acknowledgement and seemed to gather her thoughts. "Waiting for the bus," she replied. "I have a doctor's appointment in Huehue."

"Dear Lord!" Rosalinda pressed heartfelt palms together. "Is it serious?" She noticed how thin the teacher had become, in what seemed to be a matter of weeks, or a couple of months at most. Was it possible she was dieting?

"No, no. Just something I couldn't put off." Alma didn't expect to be believed—Rosalinda was far too sharp—but she hoped at least to set the gossip in motion with the minimal amount of fuss. She hated pity, and she'd already received more than her share.

Rosalinda picked up two chuchitos, the tasty morsels of hot corn dough wrapped in cornhusks that were her specialty, and slipped them into a plastic bag. "Here. These are for your journey."

With its horn honking the Chicoyera rumbled around the corner and pulled up to a stop at the curb. Feeling her nausea rise, Alma took the aromatic chuchitos and smiled. "Thank you, Doña Rosalinda." She entered the line of people boarding the bus.

<<<< — >>>>

Roberto had just returned from supper to his room in the back of the boarding house when his cellphone rang.

"Hola, mi amor!" It was Samuela's voice, unusually clear, from faraway Nueva York. His usual rush of pleasure came and went, aborted by his new pain. "How are you?" she asked, as if they had just talked yesterday, although it had been, what? Two weeks? Three? When they'd talked about his retirement and his plans, with no mention of her part in them.

He put the pain as far out of his mind as he could, and told her about the chaotic meeting of the school families and the problems of selecting the next principal. He had to explain the school's system for replacing him, which she didn't really understand even after he went over it several times. "So what are you going to do?" She sensed how much the situation was plaguing him, he could tell. There was still that current between them.

"I'm thinking of proposing Juanito, a young teacher, Alma's nephew. He gets along with everyone."

"A Ladino?" She used the term for his people that he found vaguely hurtful, knowing how much the Indians hated the mixed breeds who had mistreated them for five centuries.

"Pues, sí."

"All along you've told me the next principal should be a Mayan!" He heard her surprise; was it disapproval? "Pobre Roberto." Now there was sympathy. She knew how much the school meant to him; how he wanted to pass it along. "Now for my news. I'm coming down in July, for a whole month! I know it's short notice, but I wanted to wait to tell you until I was sure I could get away." There was a long pause while she waited for him to say something. July was only three weeks off. Roberto's thoughts were in turmoil. He shouldn't have been surprised. She often came in July, but he

225

had been so sure. . . Finally, as if to make certain they were still connected, she said, "I know you'll be working, but we'll have the nights and weekends."

"I'll have to get your house ready. It's been so long; there'll be a lot of dust." The adobe walls of her little house were open at the top, with no ceiling between them and the roof. They rained dirt on her furniture, covered in plastic sheets while she was away. But she refused to put in a ceiling because it would cut off light from the skylights.

"Don't worry if you don't have time. We can clean the house together, as we always do." It was true. Opening up the house had become a joyful ritual for them. Sweeping, mopping, putting out the porch furniture that was stored inside against thieves, opening up doors and windows to let in sunshine and air. "Are you happy?"

"Of course, mi amor," he said.

"I love you. Take care of yourself," she said.

"Te amo. Cuídate," he repeated. He was new to the *tú* form that had swept through Guatemala in the last ten years, and he could only bring himself to use it on the phone. In person he fell back on the more comfortable formal *you.*

They exchanged the familiar refrain several times before they finally hung up. He put down his cellphone—his little bean—on the table next to his bed. How Samuela had laughed when he told her the street name for cheap, disposable cellphones. *You Guatemalans,* she had said, *you have corn and beans for brains.* And he had laughed with her.

July. He had to hurry. He couldn't let her come.

⟪⟪⟪ — ⟫⟫⟫

Through his window Noah saw Magdalena in the distance, coming up the road. He watched her pause by the

226

ruins, saw her look up toward the mountaintops, waiting for something. He saw her toss her braids and start walking again. He thought he saw determination in the set of her shoulders. He closed the shutters of his window against the neighbors' eyes and sat and thought. After a time, he heard her voice outside. "Don Noé?"

He opened his door.

"They told me you wanted to speak to me." Unlike her girlfriends, she didn't try to flirt. Instead, she wore a kind of adult dignity like armor. He invited her to come in and sit on the couch. He pulled up his only chair and sat across from her, the table between them.

"I had a visit from José Chales, from La Ventosa," he said. He watched her face. She kept still, her head high, her eyes fixed on him. She raised her eyebrows but didn't speak.

"Magdalena, you're a strong girl, with a big heart. Seño Eva Silvia tells me how good you are with the women in her literacy class. Doña Rosalinda tells me how you look after her. You're not a selfish person. God knows that, and appreciates you." He wondered if he was confusing her, speaking like a priest, something he didn't usually do. Her gaze had dropped to her lap, where her fingers were fidgeting with her apron. She looked up again when he paused and met his eyes.

"You talk to so many people. Everyone says you're a saint."

He laughed and shook his head. "Not me. I would never want to be that good." He sighed and leaned back in his chair. His sainthood had been forced on him when Felipa turned him down and he realized that the Todosanteras would always prefer a local man. "I'm just an outsider. That makes me easy to talk to. Tell me, what do you want most in life?"

She wrinkled her forehead and looked up at the rafters, as if the answer might come from above. What she saw were the cards and drawings hanging on ribbons all about the room. "The same thing every girl wants," she said. "A family. A good man to care for me." She looked back at him and jutted out her chin. "Something I never had," she finished. She folded her arms across her chest.

"José will make a good father, Magdalena. He has a promising future. He loves you."

She took a long moment to weigh the offer against her dreams. True, Don Roberto had crushed the dreams. Tears flooded her eyes. "Maybe you're right," she whispered. But what she thought was, *Never.*

≪≪ — ≫≫

Three days later Magdalena sat down behind her typewriter in the principal's office. Stacks of attendance records in the variable handwriting of the faculty lay on the desk. But she didn't fit a blank sheet into the carriage. Instead, she stared for a long minute at Don Roberto, whose attention was riveted to his account book. "Prof," she said in a guarded tone, "when is Doña Samuela coming?"

Don Roberto looked up and swiveled his gaze to meet hers. "What do you mean?"

She couldn't read the feelings behind his startled expression. Anger at her impertinence, perhaps. Or fear at what she might tell the American woman. The thought gave her strength. "For a visit. Doesn't she come every year?"

"Hmmm. I suppose she does," he said. His voice sounded far away, as if he was drifting away from her. Hiding. "July," he said in that distant voice. "She's coming in July. Less than three weeks."

Magdalena stood up. She'd reached a decision. If she couldn't have her dreams, she'd keep her pride. "I can't stay tonight to work. I'm sorry. My grandmother needs me at home."

"Very well," he said, calling his voice back from that far-off place. "You should be home with your grandmother." He watched her walk to the door of the office. She stopped at the door.

"Don Roberto," she said. She couldn't bring herself to say his name without the title, but she could take control of her departure. "The school should get a computer."

He gave her a sad smile. "I know. Profe Juan Carlos tells me every week."

When she left the schoolyard, she didn't turn up the steep street toward home. Instead, she wound her way down the hill. It was dark. The backstreet was empty; even so, to double-check, she looked around and made sure no one saw her climb up the embankment to a small wooden shed that stood in a clearing between two houses. Light came through the cracks in its shudders. She knocked on the door. It opened. "Magdalena!" José, standing in the doorway, exclaimed.

"Ssh!" she said. "Can I come in?" She stepped in without waiting for his answer. He closed the door behind her. She looked around the small room: wooden table and chair, single bed strewn with open books. The books had been on the table when she'd come here with José the night of the dance.

"I was studying," he said, as if at a loss for something safe to say.

"I want a church wedding," she said. She watched his face. "You understand? I want us to be legally married, not just juntado. I want our baby baptized in the church." She watched comprehension spread across his features as if from a sculptor's hand.

"OK. Whatever you want." He raised his hand as if to touch her, as if he thought she wasn't real, then dropped it.

"Also, I'm not living in La Ventosa. You have to move in with me and my granny. I can't leave her alone."

"Magdalena," he repeated, and put both hands on her and she knew that in another minute he'd try to embrace her.

"Not now," she said. "I have to get home." She turned to go. "You can come by tomorrow after school and meet my granny."

<<<< — >>>>

On a cold September morning Don Roberto and Don Noé met in the town square just as pink streaks of dawn were lighting up the sky. They stood at a counter by the bus stop to drink hot coffee and eat sweet bread at a concession that opened before the first bus left. "You're looking wonderfully well, Don Noé," the stand's owner said.

"Never better, Doña Tina, gracias a Dios," he answered, willing to give God some of the credit along with the drug cocktail that had finally cleared his lungs. "Off to give my thanks under the blue dome of the sky."

"Puerto del Cielo," Roberto added, to be precise. "We're hoping to get there before the clouds come in. And please, a dozen bananas and six oranges." She counted out a dozen to break off from a stem of tiny bananas and let the two men select oranges from a basket to load into their packs.

"Better be off, then," Doña Tina said, taking their money. "Otherwise, all your struggles will be for nothing." She shook her head in wonder. "Only teachers and turistas climb mountains for pleasure."

"Guess I'll always be a turista," Noah remarked to Roberto as they left the stand and made their way through the narrow alleys of town toward the river. From the houses they passed came the sounds of morning—the slap of tortillas, the familiar DJ on the local radio station, the distant whir of a motorized corn mill.

"Samuela likes the word *gringa* better than *turista,* although it's less respectful." Roberto smiled at the thought of his gringuita, back again in far-off Nueva York. The two men crossed the river, left the road, and started on the path that led in switchbacks up the steep northern wall of the valley. Conversation flowed between them as it always had, two solitary men who liked to talk. There was never a scarcity of topics: the national news growing ever more violent, the world beyond glimpsed by Roberto on the Discovery channel, Noah's reflections from his recent meditative retreat. They climbed steadily under tall black pines and live oak, past the white-painted stones that spelled out the town's name in giant letters against the mountainside, past a high pasture and lone shepherd's shack. Roberto climbed without any awareness of strain. Noah's newly healed lungs proved equal to the challenge, although at times he gave them a rest and let Roberto do the talking. After tthree hours they reached the windswept altiplano, with its potato fields carved out of stony ground, its isolated hamlet as yet without electricity ("Next year, the mayor has promised," Roberto said). They stopped to admire the new school building, empty because it was Saturday. A dog ran out to bark at them, chased by a red-cheeked boy. "Niño!" Roberto greeted him, asked him his name and what grade he was in, and if he liked his teacher. Striding over the level plain, they turned off at a fork in the road. Cumulous clouds appeared on the horizon and started filling the sky. "Our luck may have turned," Roberto said. "I've never yet seen the view from Puerto del Cielo, all the times I've been there."

"I trust to our luck," Noah answered. "It's been good so far."

In another hour they'd left all habitations behind. The dirt road followed a spur to a place where the ridge dropped off to the west. Just below the road was a concrete platform surrounded by tall trees and mist. Here, more than thirty years before, an American had built a house at the edge of nowhere, unlike any house the locals had ever seen, with a curving staircase and grand piano, in unimaginable remoteness even with a Jeep. He'd named it Puerto del Cielo and brought his wife, an artist, and child to live here while he worked on agricultural development projects. When civil war came, the Americans left their house to the care of a couple from Todos Santos, intending to come back. But the guerillas came and burnt the house down. Nothing was left but the foundation and the stories the caretakers told.

"I heard it took ten men to carry the piano," Roberto said.

"Maybe that's what attracted the attention of the guerrillas. They should have kept it simple," Noah said.

Roberto and Noah settled down on the wall at the edge of the platform, looking out into the clouds, and pulled their lunches out of their packs. "When Samuela and I were here in July, she said that if the clouds part, it's probably a sign you're about to die. But she's not superstitious, she tells me!"

"Maybe she guessed, how death missed its shot at you and me this time." What a narrow scrape it had been, with Magdalena's surprise announcement of the church banns that released Roberto.

"This time," Roberto said, thinking that Samuela had guessed nothing. "Death always finds it mark. This time it missed us and got Alma."

Noah pursed his lips under his light beard and shook his head. "The cancer was so fast. I never guessed. Did you?"

Roberto shrugged. "It's the way she wanted it. She was a private person and suffered from gossip."

"She did so much for the women of Todos Santos. No one gave her the credit she deserved until her funeral."

"Isn't that the way it is?" Roberto asked. He hated funerals, with their hypocrisy of tears and speeches. Out of his deep respect for Alma, he'd gone to hers and joined in the chorus of accolades.

They fell silent. The mist lightened and tore into scraps of cloud that floated up the mountain walls. "Maybe our turn is coming."

They watched the clouds lift, bit by bit, revealing first the valley floor, as far below as if they were looking out of an airplane, at fields and tiny houses along the serpentine river. Then rising above the forest-clad uplands, the clouds broke and drifted into blue sky. Before the two men were row on row of ridges, reaching out as if forever, riddled with clefts and valleys and hidden streams and waterfalls, fading into Mexico.

The clearing lasted just ten minutes before the valley began filling up again with clouds that boiled up the ridge to swallow them in mist. At which point Roberto remarked that he was getting cold. They packed up, got to their feet, and began the hike back.

<<<< — >>>>

The rainy season ended just after the annual fiesta. The mud dried and projects that had been on hold for months started up. In every part of town the air buzzed and rang with the sounds of saws and hammers and earth moving machines. New houses were springing up everywhere, jostling for space on the crowded hillsides, and new roads carved their way up the mountain walls. Rosalinda, chopping onions and tomatoes for the evening meal in her smoky

233

kitchen, passed along reports of their progress to her granddaughter, as was her habit. "I heard the pavers have started down from La Ventosa." Magdalena, sitting by the wood stove, nursed her new baby girl. Rosalinda made an optimistic prediction. "Once the road is paved all the way to Todos Santos, there'll be no stopping the growth. José will have work." She sounded satisfied.

Magdalena was not. "I wanted him to be an accountant." After formalizing their union and graduating from básico, José had apprenticed himself to a local builder.

"Change your tone of voice, granddaughter. Don't let that bitterness get into your milk. You'll upset Flor de Ofelia's digestion," Rosalinda chided. The baby's name combined that of Magdalena's and José's mothers. Already the old midwives claimed the baby was a spitting image of her grandmother Ofelia, although Magdalena couldn't imagine the tired woman in La Ventosa as a baby. "How did you expect him to pay for three more years of school and support your child?" Rosalinda emphasized her words with a flicking movement of her knife. "Building is a good trade. He'll make more money than any accountant or teacher."

"Why are you starting supper, Granny? It'll be cold by the time José gets home."

Rosalinda spread tortillas on the stove to heat. "He'll be here soon. They can't work in the dark."

Sure enough, by the time she had piled the hot tortillas into a basket and scrambled the eggs, they heard footsteps on the street below, and José came in through the kitchen door. Magdalena looked up at him. Flor had fallen asleep at her breast; the satisfying tug on her nipple had released into a gentle pressure, a reassurance that this new life belonged to her, forever. For that she blessed God and, in some measure, her husband. "Well, my love," she said to José. "How was your day?"

234